OF GOOD & EVIL

Daniel G. Miller

HOUNDSTOOTH
BOOKS

Published by Houndstooth Books, Dallas, Texas
Cover design: Bailey McGinn
ISBN (paperback): 978-1-7376463-0-3
ISBN (ebook): 978-1-7376463-1-0
ISBN (hardcover): 978-1-7376463-2-7
First edition

To my wife.

My love. My joy. My support. My hope. My life.

"A mind not to be changed by place or time.
The mind is its own place, and in itself
Can make a heav'n of hell, a hell of heav'n."
— John Milton, *Paradise Lost*

Part 1
Rising

Then the LORD God said, "Behold, the man has become like one of Us, knowing good and evil;

–Genesis: 3:22

Prologue

The Cipher's fingers hovered over the keyboard for a moment. On the wall, above the computer screen, a brilliant LCD TV showed a motorcade driving through downtown Austin, Texas. The sun's beams reflected off the polished cars rolling down 6th street. Crowds of people cheered and chanted, all of them wearing red t-shirts and throwing glittering ruby confetti. A feather-haired reporter shouted into his microphone just to be heard.

The Governor of Texas sat in the center car, and beside him was a striking woman in a fiery crimson suit. She smiled out at the crowd, seeming to drink in their adoration, and graciously offered back her own. They lapped up her attention. Pair after pair of hands reached for her, hoping to touch her or to be touched by her. The camera zoomed in on a couple with tears streaming down their faces, overwhelmed by being in the presence of this titan.

The Cipher sneered in the darkness and wondered how no one else could see past the façade, past the fakery that was Cristina Culebra. The media. The politicians. The businessmen. The religious leaders. They all bowed before her or ignored her, hoping she was just a fad. How could no one else have confronted her?

Challenged her? The few people who could have fought her had fled. Only the Cipher remained.

The Cipher would make them see. Make them hear. Once the Cipher completed the work, they would have no choice. The Sword of Eden was coming for the tyrants, and there would be no escape.

The Cipher tapped the keys, and words appeared on the screen: *Find the Cipher. Follow the Cipher.*

It wasn't supposed to come to this. It shouldn't have come to this.

But this was the only option left.

Chapter 1

Albert slumped on the stained brown leather bar stool at The Duke of Cambridge pub in Cambridge, England. He held a Bishop's Finger beer in his left hand and the bar's TV remote in his right. The dim watering hole smelled of stale beer and cigarettes, which somehow matched Albert's mood. Two grizzled, hunched men chatted quietly at a booth over his shoulder. Pat, the pot-bellied, red-cheeked bartender, washed glasses behind the bar, keeping one eye on Albert.

Albert turned his focus to the news on the TV in front of him. The bright colors and shifting graphics of an evening news program zoomed across the screen, while important sounding synthesizer music hummed in the background. He lazily tapped up on the volume button and took a long pull from his amber bottle. The beer felt warm and tasted bitter.

A blonde anchor smiled into the camera. "Welcome to another edition of 'The RED Files' on REDTV, where truth is our only promise. I'm Elizabeth Galli." She radiated a confident, professional air. "On tonight's episode, we'll be diving into the meteoric rise of Cristina Culebra and her Republic of Enlightenment and Democracy. In just a few short years, The RED movement has gone from startup political party to political colossus and model of good government. Our very own Rishi Parikh has the story."

A strong jawed man with dark skin and bright, black eyes took the screen, seated in front of a rich, red backdrop with the word 'RED' layered in a wallpaper of repeating diagonal rows. He wore a dark suit buttoned just a little too snugly around his stomach.

"In just a few days, the State of Texas will formally secede from the United States and join the Republic of Enlightenment and Democracy, intensifying the brewing conflict between the Republic and the United States. The Federal Government has yet to recognize any of the independence votes as legal, despite a growing international consensus that the elections were free and fair.

"A few years ago, the Washington pundits regarded the movement's leader, Cristina Culebra, as a momentary flash in the pan. But then came Culebra's landslide victory in the campaign for Governor of California. Despite the RED movement winning over seventy percent of the vote, experts continued to dismiss Culebra and her RED Army of supporters as a West Coast anomaly, nothing more than another wacky Californian movement with little relevance to the rest of the country. Now, Texas makes the fifteenth former U.S. state to join the new movement and is arguably the jewel in the crown of the new President.

"Many experts now believe that the Federal Government in Washington D.C. will be forced to recognize the Republic. Anonymous sources within the administration have spoken of intense disagreement within the White House over how to approach this unheard-of grassroots phenomenon. The entire world, including us here at RED TV, are watching to see if the United States, itself the product of an independence movement, will accede to the wishes of its own citizens.

"One person, however, has no doubts about the future of the Republic. I was fortunate enough to sit down with Cristina Culebra herself to learn more about this incredible turn of events."

The clip cut to Cristina seated in a soft brown leather chair in her office in the California Capitol building. Behind her stood two flags. On the left, the American flag. On the right stood a red flag with a simple black tree in a white circle. The tree comprised a tall trunk, narrowing skyward, and two branches growing upward, reminiscent of a trident.

Albert finished what remained of his beer and leaned forward toward the screen. He took off his tortoise-shell glasses and rubbed his eyes to make sure what he was seeing was real. He thought back to the last time he had seen Cristina. It was in Princeton, at the funeral of his mentor and friend, Professor Angus Turner. She and her minions were responsible for Turner's death, but still had the audacity to show up at the man's funeral. Since then, Albert had seen that same audacity in the creeping advance of Cristina and her movement, everything playing out with slow precision, but that only made it more surreal, like a dream morphing into reality.

It was happening.

The news anchor looked over Cristina's shoulder and back at his notes.

"Why don't we start by talking about your new office decoration. I notice that you've replaced the flag of the State of

California with the flag of your Republic of Enlightenment and Democracy. What was behind that decision?"

Cristina smiled and tilted her head, nodding at the anchor as if he had just asked a particularly insightful question. She wore a smoke gray suit, and Albert noticed a pin shimmering on her lapel. It was the same symbol that hung on the flagpole behind her.

"I'm glad you asked that, Rishi. The reason that we replaced the flag of The State of California is that the State of California no longer exists. Neither does the State of Washington, or Oregon, or Nevada, or Utah. Those 'states' were meant to divide us. To keep us weak. Now, we are all united as brothers and sisters under the Republic. Changing the flag is just an expression of that unity."

"Feel free to ask a follow up question, Rishi!" shouted Albert, taking a long swig of his beer. The two men at the booth behind him glared in his direction. Albert noticed that they had started watching the program the second Cristina spoke. People couldn't help but watch.

"Easy, Puddles," said Pat.

"I'm fine, Pat. Just give me another beer."

Pat raised an eyebrow.

"*Please*," Albert said. He stood up and took off his brown tweed jacket, which he hung over the bar stool. Then he grabbed the beer with a nod of thanks and paced back and forth as he listened. He refused to sit still while being force-fed this propaganda. A large part of him still couldn't believe this was really happening.

"I notice you still have the American flag up behind you, though?" Rishi asked.

"Of course. That's because the United States still very much exists."

"In a slimmed down form, though," said the anchor with a chuckle.

Cristina matched his laugh. She was a master of mimicking people. It made them feel connected to her. Albert heard the gentlemen behind him laugh along with her, as well.

He had once felt that connection.

"Yes, while The United States is now smaller than it once was, we don't view ourselves as at odds with the Federal Government, but partners in making our world a better place. We believe that the former states are joining the Republic because we offer a better way of life. We are more than happy to share that with the remaining Americans."

Rishi nodded, as if what he was hearing was groundbreaking analysis instead of a reworked campaign speech.

"Let's talk about this 'better life', as you call it," he said. "Even your fiercest critics would acknowledge that your administration has made incredible progress in every measure of quality of life in just a few years' time. Children from the Republic recently came in first in reading, science, and mathematics in the Program for International Student Assessment test, the global standard in education assessment. Violent crime has dropped seventy-five percent, and the Republic is now rivaling Japan in safety. Traffic in the Republic is almost nonexistent, and average commute times have fallen by fifty percent. What's your secret?"

"It's not mine, it's *ours*, Rishi. And it's not a secret. In the Republic, we are all one team working together toward a common goal, a better society. We, the people, can accomplish incredible things when we work together. Whether it's winning World War II or the Moon landing, when all of us join forces, problems that once seemed insurmountable suddenly become quite pedestrian."

She crossed her legs and brushed the lint from her suit as she spoke.

"The old school political system prevented us from working together. It set us against each other, tearing us apart. Can you imagine if we fought World War II with half of our government pro-Hitler and the other half anti-Hitler? There's no chance we would win. Because our hatred of Hitler united us in a common cause, we extinguished a historic evil. I would argue that today's evils of ignorance, fear, and apathy are equally dangerous–just more insidious. And we should unite to root out those evils."

"She's a smart one, isn't she, Puddles?" said Pat. He shook his head. "I just wish we could get someone like that over here. Y'know... to take charge and clean things up. These wankers over in Parliament just like to hear themselves talk, but don't do a damn thing."

Albert suppressed a sneer. He shouldn't think less of Pat for being pulled in, not when the siren call was so strong. That was the genius of Cristina. She gave you everything you wanted by stealing everything you took for granted. He could envision people back home watching her and wanting to believe in her. Joining her. *When would someone else see?* He took another swig, his fingers choking the beer bottle.

"Speaking of unity," Rishi said, "one of the first initiatives you rolled out when you became Governor of California was the RED Network, which gave citizens of the Republic free internet and phone network access, as well as an ad-free search engine and social media network."

"Yes, we felt that one of the most important parts of us being united as a community was to first make sure that everyone in the Republic could communicate with each other. The world can be a very isolating place, and we wanted to make sure that everyone, regardless of income, could connect. Second, to make sure that we connected in a united way, we felt it was important to stop the hate, bullying and incessant bombardment of ads that come with current search and social media and make it a place where people can share and connect in a safe space all in favor of a common cause."

The anchor crinkled his brow and put on his best probing anchor face.

"This all sounds great, but what do you say to those who say that you're a tyrant and that all of this is a means of control? After all, the Republic has suspended elections, and you do have full control over all the branches of government."

Albert took the last drink of his bitter and nearly spit it out. With a swallow of beer in his mouth, he half-gargled, half-shouted, "Finally! An actual question!"

The other patrons of the pub stopped and stared at Albert. "Hey, pipe down, you. I'm trying to listen to the lady speak," said one of the old men behind him.

Albert glanced back at them and shook his head. Even across the Atlantic Ocean, Cristina was winning converts. He returned his gaze to the screen.

For a moment, it seemed Cristina might lose her composure. She was grinning, giving a low chuckle as if she could hear Albert's yells through the television screen. But when she looked up, and Albert saw the determination in those wolf eyes, he knew that whatever question the media threw at her, Cristina would make it hers.

"Rishi, I actually laugh when those in the remaining United States call me a tyrant, because it's as absurd as the abuser blaming the abused for the fact that they hit them. The people of California *voted* to elect me their Governor–by a historic margin–and *voted* to suspend the state legislature so that I could do my job. The people of the states that have joined our Republic have, likewise, *voted* to join, and the people who use the RED Network *choose* to do so.

"This is, of course, threatening to some politicians. Politicians don't want people to have choices. Real choices. That's why, traditionally, the people who lived in the United States have had very little choice over the laws that governed them. They've had to live under a government that neglects them, squabbles amongst itself, and takes their tax dollars and sets them on fire. *That* is tyranny!"

"Hear, hear!" shouted Pat and the rest of the bar.

She pivoted and looked directly into the camera. Albert felt her eyes penetrate him.

"But it is not the only choice anymore. To those of you who are tired of being alone, tired of poor schools, bad roads, and dangerous neighborhoods, you have a *choice*: join us. Join the Republic, and see what's possible when we all come together to do something great!"

Rishi nodded and shuffled his papers, barely able to stifle his enthusiasm.

"Thank you so much for taking the time from your busy schedule to be with us, today. One last question. What do we call you now? Governor Culebra? President Culebra?"

Cristina pivoted back to the anchor and issued a warm smile. "My formal title is President of the Republic of Enlightenment and Democracy." She winked. "But you can just call me Cristina."

Albert slammed the TV remote down on the bar and hurled his bottle against the wall. Glass smashed and a small stream of beer crept through the cracks between the wood floor planks.

"Alright, that's it, Puddles." Pat pointed at the door. "You're cut off. Get out, go on home, sleep it off."

"Ahh, fuck you, Pat." Albert grabbed his suit coat and threw it over his shoulder. "See you tomorrow?"

Pat shook his head. He knew a lost cause when he saw it. "Yeah, see you tomorrow."

Chapter 2

Albert stumbled out of the pub onto the cobblestone of Hills Road. He glared at the uneven stones, leaning and twisting in every direction. Cobblestone always looked charming, but it was a menace to walk on, far too easy to twist an ankle with one wrong step.

Even when he was sober.

He tiptoed along the road, using corner stores and brownstones to steady himself. His head felt heavy, and his feet seemed to strike the ground at random. He kept meaning to check his watch and kept forgetting. It was sometime in the indeterminate black past midnight when he looked up to realize that he was lost.

He missed the streets back in Minnesota: straight lines running north, south, east, and west in a numbered grid. Instead, here he was stuck in Cambridge, an illogical mishmash of former horse paths crisscrossing each other like a maze.

He continued down the crooked lanes, trying to wind his way home through the drunken haze, his frustration growing by the minute. The roads seemed to weave back and forth, doubling back on themselves. He missed home. Cambridge in the darkness could be an eerie place, full of shadows–made paradoxically more prominent by the streetlights.

Jack the Ripper would have loved it here.

The thought of the Ripper mixed poorly with the alcohol in Albert's stomach. He bent over at the waist and braced himself against the corner of a building to steady his gut. His face flushed, and a hot sweat broke out on his forehead.

"Look at what we have here, boys." The voice, thick with a rough accent, bounced off the sidewalk. "It appears one of the toffs has lost his way."

Laughs echoed through the narrow lane.

Albert looked up. A tall, young man in a gray hoodie stared down at him, a forty-ounce beer in a paper bag clutched in one hand. Behind him stood a gang of four other young men in hoodies, each with their own bottle.

Or was it eight young men? Albert was having trouble counting them.

Nausea spread from his belly to his mind. He was sick of this. Sick of insufferable people. Sick of living in Cambridge. Sick of hiding from Cristina. Sick of missing Angus. Sick of knowing the future. Sick of knowing no one would listen to him. Sick of drinking too much. Sick of being lost.

He swallowed hard to keep the vomit from escaping and used the building as a crutch to push himself upright. He inhaled deeply through his nose, hoping the crisp winter air would bring a bit of clarity to his mind.

"Guys, I don't want any trouble." He swallowed hard when some bile rose in his throat. "And I'm *this* close to vomiting, right now, so can you just leave me alone?"

"Ohhh, an American toff. Even better." The gang's leader took a long pull of his beer and let out an exaggerated burp. He placed his beer bottle down on the curb and motioned his followers closer. Steam from their hot breath poured into the air as they approached.

So, this is how it was going to be? Albert recalled everything that Angus had taught him. About the Tree of Knowledge and the use of mathematical decision trees in everyday life. How just as grandmasters could see several moves ahead in chess, he, and other mathematical savants like him, could anticipate the moves of people in the real world by picturing every move and countermove in a branching tree of possibilities. How the Tree could be used for peace or for violence and held nearly limitless power once fully mastered. How he had so much more to learn.

Albert closed his eyes and let the decision tree unfold before him. *How could he deal with these thugs? Could he flatter them? No. Could he bribe them? No. Could he convince them? No.* Every branch led to one inevitable conclusion. Violence.

He gave a sardonic laugh. When Albert had first encountered the Tree of Knowledge, he was fascinated by the idea of predicting people's actions through mathematical probability, and using that knowledge to steer the world around him to a better place. But as he immersed himself in the Tree, he realized that seeing the future was a curse. The future was shaped by people, and people seemed hell bent on destroying themselves.

Rather than steering the future, Albert was merely defending himself from it like a sailor battening down the hatches in a storm.

It reminded him of the Shakespeare quote that his mentor, Angus Turner, used to always tell him "The fool doth think he is wise, but the wise man knows himself to be a fool."

Seeing the future was a curse he would not wish on his worst enemy... the irony was she shared that same curse.

The thought of Cristina galvanized him. He straightened up and stared silently at the gang leader and shook his head.

"Toff!" The gang leader waved his hands in exaggerated gestures. "I'm talking to you!"

Yelling and puffing himself up like an animal trying to look bigger: classic signs of insecurity.

Albert squinted to tighten his field of vision and focused his mind on the thugs in front of him, starting with their hands. The boy in the black hoodie held a knife. A hint of light glinted off the blade.

Their first mistake. They had just given him a weapon that he could use.

He assessed their clothing. They wore sweatshirts and jeans that hid their underdeveloped frames.

Their second mistake. No padding, no protection. A knife would slice clean through.

Another set of people bent on self-destruction.

In a fight, the temptation was always to go for the leader, and then take the rest as they came, but what really mattered was the threat level. As his friend Brick had liked to say, *if a bear and a puppy are coming toward you, Puddles, you don't start with the puppy just because he's closer.*

Albert looked around the lane. So many weapons, so little time. The brick walls of the buildings. The metal wire trash can on the corner. A beer bottle resting on the curb. A loose pipe on the corner of the building to his right. All were at his disposal. Using the Tree for violence had become second nature to him. It was familiar...

... and infuriating.

The gang's leader took a step closer to him, and his companions followed. As the boy came into the light, Albert made out the face under the hood, and held back a wince. The leader was too young for this, no more than eighteen. His face was marked with the remnants of acne and the beginnings of a beard, still not full enough to take shape.

"Guys, I get it," Albert said, his voice rising. He held up his hands and hoped he wasn't swaying too obviously. He continued to run scenarios through his mind to see if he could find any way to escape this mess that didn't end in someone getting hurt, but his mind stumbled. "I remember being your age. You're pissed off. You're angry and you want somebody to take it out on. And I'm the perfect target. I'm an American toff wandering around by myself. I would probably want to fight me, too."

They laughed but kept coming.

Fools.

Go home to your mothers, Albert wanted to say, but he knew it wouldn't work. There was no way for them to back down now.

He assessed the other gang members. Some of them were even younger, with scrawny physiques, affected poses, and unsure steps. Albert knew that these youth gangs were common in the UK, but seeing their faces, now, it was difficult to accept. Instead, he thought back to when he was that age. He had only been a *kid*–and he'd been in chess club, and bullies just like this used to go after him. Anger welled up inside him.

"But here's the thing," Albert said, and he could hear the anger in his voice now. "You don't know me, and so you don't know that

I've been trained by the guy who literally wrote the manual on hand-to-hand combat. This will not end well for you."

More laughter.

The gang leader took another step closer. He was now just five feet away. "You? *You've* been trained in hand-to-hand combat? You're going to have to do better than that, mate."

Rage burst through Albert's body. He had been suppressing this for far too long, and tonight, he was too tired to fight it. He was tired of the bullies. Of the ignorance. Tired of the people who wouldn't listen. Tired of the world throwing punch after punch at him. It was time to punch back.

The gang leader's hands hung at his sides.

An opening.

Albert had found that the best way to win a fight was to start it before his opponent even knew the fight had begun.

He took one step forward and jabbed the gang leader in the bridge of his nose with his right hand. The leader's head snapped back, and Albert heard the crack of breaking bone followed by a high-pitched shriek. The leader fell to his knees and raised both hands to his nose. Blood poured through his fingers.

"No," Albert said. "Actually, *you're* going to have to do better than that."

He hated himself for the words, but they felt good to say. He crouched down and snatched the oversized beer bottle from the curb, the green glass thick and heavy in his hand. He whipped it at the teenager holding the knife, and the bottle thunked off his head, sending him staggering backwards. *An opportunity.* In his surprise, the boy's grip on the knife had weakened. Albert took two long strides toward him. He pivoted on his left foot and with his right, he kicked the knife from the boy's hands.

The knife tumbled against the wall to Albert's left.

The boy in the orange hoodie scurried to the wall to grab the knife...

... just as Albert had envisioned it.

This boy had been hanging back. Albert could see he was anxious. Albert had surprised him, and the boy wasn't sure of how to regain his footing. Now, he was brandishing a knife to intimidate Albert.

Or, possibly, attack. That would establish his place at the top of the pecking order.

Albert couldn't take that chance. He reached for the loose pipe on the wall and hauled at it, but it wasn't as loose as it seemed. He hadn't anticipated that.

The boy fumbled for the knife, but then finally got a grip and turned toward Albert.

Albert pulled on the pipe with everything he had. It broke loose.

The boy thrust the knife toward Albert's chest. Albert danced out of the way, but the knife sliced through his shoulder muscle. He winced in pain, his anger turning to fury, and he slammed the pipe down on the boy's head. There was the sickening sound of bone cracking against metal and the boy fell to the ground. He attempted to get back up, more on instinct than out of any rational plan, but Albert struck him again in the back, and then again.

Again. His rage was taking over. After the seventh blow, the boy stayed down.

Albert picked up the knife and prepared to take on the other two thugs. He smiled. Turner had taught him that a fight was nothing more than your opponent's assessment of strength. You could manipulate that assessment by projecting confidence. Albert grabbed the pipe with his left hand and twirled it in his fingers for effect. He stepped toward them, maintaining his wild-eyed grin.

The boys looked at Albert, then looked at each other. Then they turned and ran, sprinting in the other direction as fast as they could.

Their assessment had been corrected.

Albert looked behind him to survey the damage. Three boys rolled on the ground, groaning and nursing their injuries.

Albert shook his head. *What a waste.*

He grabbed his arm and grimaced at the pain. Blood oozed through a small tear in his suit coat and shirt. He inspected it with his hand. It was a flesh wound, not as deep as he had originally thought. The wound was minor, but the burning was fierce.

The fight had grounded him, and he now recognized where he was. Albert pivoted and began walking down the block toward home. He took out his pocket square and put pressure on the wound before wedging it between his skin and sleeve. He paused and bent down to grab one of the unopened beer bottles a gang member had left behind. He twisted off the cap and took a long sip.

It tasted awful.

He kept drinking and headed home.

Chapter 3

Ying Koh sighed. It was stuffy. She and Michael Weatherspoon had been sitting inside the detective's navy-blue cop car for two hours. The car sat halfway down the block from an Upper East Side brownstone where Cristina Culebra's top security advisor, General Isaac Moloch, was scheduled to meet with senior leadership of the armed forces. The two had been surveilling Moloch for months and had little to show for it.

She reached out to poke him in the arm. "What are we even doing here, Mike?"

"It's Michael. Don't call me Mike, you know better." He spared her a brief glance. "And what do you mean, what are we doing here? We're doing surveillance. This is what surveillance looks like. It's not always glamorous like what you see in the movies. Here, have some jerky." He threw a bag of beef jerky at her and returned to snapping pictures as cars arrived outside the residence.

Ying caught the jerky and sighed. "I *know*, but this is *so boring*. And all we *ever* do is take pictures. At some point, we do actually have to *stop* the criminals, don't we?"

Weatherspoon put down his phone and pivoted his ample frame toward her. "Look. You're lucky I even let you sit here. You're a civilian with no police training. And I'm not supposed to be doing stakeouts with civilians or anyone else, for that matter."

"Hey, I'm all for calling quits on the stakeouts whenever you're ready–"

"And do you think I want to be here?" He sounded annoyed now. "I'd much rather be home watching the game with Cheryl and Buster. I'm not getting paid for this. My captain doesn't want me anywhere near it. I'm doing this because you and Puddles begged me to, remember? Because we all thought Moloch would slip up and we might get some justice for what he did. But he hasn't, and I feel more stupid every day for doing this. Does *any* of that ring a bell?"

"Yes." Ying tried to keep her tone from becoming sulky. He *had* gone beyond the call of duty. As weeks turned to months, and months turned to years, she knew Weatherspoon had been tempted to give up. She had, as well. But he was treating this as if Moloch would follow some predictable pattern, and she *knew* he wouldn't. Moloch made moves with restraint and cunning.

Weatherspoon continued. "This is called building a case. When we build a case, we have to show *evidence*. You know we don't have enough evidence to get Moloch for shooting your man, Turner, so we have to find something else. This is called collecting evidence."

Turner.

It didn't matter how long it had been. Just hearing his name again and the memories from that rooftop in L.A. came roaring through Ying's mind. She could envision the old man's kind blue eyes, see the way he looked at her. The way no one in her family ever had: with belief.

Angus Turner had believed in her.

Then she remembered the gunshot. She heard it rip through the sky from Moloch's gun and then watched Turner tilting back over the building's edge, falling. She had wanted to reach out with her hand and grab him as he fell, but fear and panic had kept her rooted to the spot, scared she would fall herself... or that Moloch would shoot her, too. Now, she could not stop reliving it. *Could she have caught him?*

She pushed the dark thoughts from her mind and forced a smile. "I understand we need to have evidence, but you know Moloch's planning something. And you know what I can do, what *I'm* capable of. Let me help you."

Weatherspoon *had* seen what she was capable of. At first, he had laughed when this tiny, little Asian girl and the skinny white professor had told him about the Tree of Knowledge and what it could do. But after each of them had dropped him to the ground three times in a field on their road back to Jersey, he became a believer.

Still, he raised his eyebrow. "What do you want to do, knock down the door and go all Bruce Lee on everybody? What's that going to accomplish? We still have these things like the Constitution. The Bill of Rights. Trial by jury. Due process. You know, things like that."

Ying snorted. "You think Moloch cares about due process?"

"No, but I do. And that's what separates us from him."

A black Suburban with bulletproof windows pulled up in front of the brownstone, and a man Ying recognized stepped out.

"Look. It's Moloch." She grabbed Weatherspoon's arm, seething as she watched the General's smug smile.

Weatherspoon took more pictures as another man emerged from the vehicle. "And, *boom*! That's David Sicario, Chief of the National Guard."

Moloch placed his long bony hand on Sicario's shoulder and ushered him toward the townhome, while another black Suburban pulled up in front of the residence.

"We've got to do something," said Ying, tossing the beef jerky onto the vinyl seats behind her.

Weatherspoon rolled his eyes heavenward, praying for patience. "We *are* doing something, remember? We literally *just* spoke about this. We're gathering evidence." He continued to take pictures.

She slapped his shoulder. "I mean, we've got to get *in* there, see what they're meeting about, something. We don't have time to wait. At the rate we're going, he'll be running the country, and you'll still be building your photo album." Ying's head nodded furiously as she agreed with herself.

Weatherspoon sighed. "No, we're not doing that. It's illegal, for one thing, and for another, they have security at both entrances. Let's just get these pictures. Then I can get this and our other evidence to the FBI. *Then* maybe we can get a–what are you *doing*?"

Ying had opened the car door, and now, she hopped out. "*I'm* a private citizen, and *I'm* going to take a nighttime stroll." She threw him a mischievous smile. "*You* can stay in the car and 'gather evidence'."

"Do not do that." Weatherspoon jumped forward to grab her, but his seatbelt restrained him. "Ying!" His voice was a furious whisper. He fumbled to unbuckle his seatbelt. "Do *not* go near that house. *Ying!*"

She heard his door open and turned her head to call back over her shoulder, first checking that she was downwind of the townhome, and then keeping her voice pitched a hint above a whisper.

"Better stay back, Spoon. I'd keep clear of any loose cannons like me. I wouldn't want you to get in trouble with your supervisor, right?"

She winked and ignored Weatherspoon's hissed pleas from behind her as she strolled down the block. Fortunately for Ying, East 68th Street was relatively busy this evening, so a random woman walking up the block attracted little attention. She crossed the street and slid in behind an elderly couple walking their bulldog—or, rather, the bulldog walking an elderly couple.

"Easy Nelson. Slow down," cautioned the old man to the bulldog as he scampered in front of them. Nelson was either oblivious to his owner's commands, or unconcerned about them. He leaned hard against the leash and pitter-pattered along with a giant, inflatable donut covered in drool dangling from his mouth.

In the distance, Ying heard the hustle and bustle of Park Avenue: horns honking, people laughing. But this block was entirely too quiet. There was no way she was going to get near the house without the security guard out front noticing. She thought of using her understanding of the Tree of Knowledge to overpower the guard, but then if he failed to check in with the rest of the security detail, Moloch would know something was afoot.

Watch and wait. The Tree and surveillance are all about patience. That would be her friend Gabe's advice. She loitered by a car and pretended to check her phone. Eventually, something would come up that would allow her to sneak in.

It didn't take long. Nelson the dog decided that the security guard was badly in need of a toy and dropped his inflatable donut at the guard's feet. As the guard bent down, Nelson lunged forward for a lick, and Ying darted down the alley just to the right of the townhome's black iron gate. The building was three stories high, and through the open window on the second floor, Ying could overhear the self-satisfied hum of powerful men talking. She strained to listen, but the street din muddled the conversation.

She scoured the side of the building for a fire escape, but the builders must have installed it on the back side. With the security guard in back, that would not be an option. She inspected the brick wall. Ivy covered every inch, and Ying ran her hands through the leaves. The vine was thick in parts, but was it thick enough?

Only one way to know. She grabbed the highest, thickest part of the vine and steeled herself.

"Onward and upward," she whispered.

She hoisted herself up on the ivy and propelled upward with her feet driving against the brick. She looked for the next highest piece of vine to grab and lunged for it just as her upward momentum stalled. The vine gave a bit but didn't rip from the façade, and she now hung ten feet off the ground.

The voices sounded clearer, now. That was good. She would need to climb another five feet to reach eye level with the window, though. Ying pushed herself up further with her sneakers until her chin was resting on the vine, on the same plane as her hands. She could hear everything, now.

Moloch was speaking in his raspy, growling whisper. "Gentleman, I'll cut to the chase. I need your help. As you can see, our RED movement is sweeping the country. A new state joins our Republic every week. It won't be long until people are going to have to pick sides on whether they're going to be part of the Old Republic or the New Republic."

Silence followed. The unique silence that follows an uncomfortable truth. Ying knew it well, having spoken many of them herself.

Moloch leaned in to the quiet. "I'm asking you to be a part of this New Republic."

"What you're asking is close to treason," responded a deep baritone voice.

"The difference between treason and patriotism is only a matter of time, David." Moloch had not missed a beat.

A higher, whinier voice chimed in. "I actually don't think it's close to treason at all. We are supposed to be 'The United States'. If all the states choose to join this New Republic of Enlightenment and Democracy, then wouldn't it be our duty to serve *that* Republic?"

Ying needed to see more. She scanned the outer wall. Another hearty piece of vine protruded from the right of the window opening. If she jumped, she could grab it and swing to the side of the window, out of eyesight. *Would they see her?* She had to chance it.

She closed her eyes and tried to remember swinging from the rings at the playground at her elementary school in Singapore when she was a child. Her Dad used to tease her and call her "Xiǎo hóuzi", which meant "little monkey" in Chinese.

Ying forced the soles of her shoes against the wall below and rocked her hips back and forth for momentum. On the third sway, she launched herself to the right toward the vine. She grabbed it with her right hand. It held, but her feet didn't. The ivy beneath her toes gave way, creating a loud rustling noise as she tried to gain traction on the wall. Finally, her feet found resistance. She pressed herself flush against the wall. *Did they hear her?*

The conversation fell silent. Footsteps from inside. The sound of wood soled shoes on the townhome's hardwood floors. Someone was coming. She glanced and saw a well-built young man dressed in a black suit walking toward the window. He walked with stiff, robotic movements. Ying turned her face away from the window and placed it gently against the ivy, hoping the alley's darkness would shield her. She heard the creak of the old walnut framed window opening, and a man's hands leaning on the cracked sill to look outside. She held her breath for what seemed like an hour. The sill creaked as he shifted his weight from one side to the other, looking up and down the alley.

"It's nothing, General. Must have been from neighbors."

He closed the window back down and exited the dining room, shutting the door behind him.

Ying exhaled.

The men resumed their discussion. The voices were muffled, but she could still make out the conversation through the poorly sealed window frame. She leaned to the left and peered through the window to evaluate the scene. Three men sat around a long rectangular mahogany table in the townhome's dining room. A large silver ice bucket surrounded by glasses of scotch was the lone table decoration. Ying recognized two of the men. Moloch sat at the head of the table. General David Sicario, Chief of the National Guard, sat to his right. That would make the third man General Ponti, Chief of the Army, sitting to Moloch's left.

Sicario leaned back against his chair with his arms crossed, frowning. "I swore an oath to the United States of America. I didn't swear any oath to this New Republic of yours, Moloch. Besides, I don't think it's at all clear that states will continue to join. Uncle Sam still has a lot of appeal for most of the people in this country, myself included."

Moloch nodded and pulled his thin lips back against his crooked, stained teeth.

"David, I can assure you the states will all join. And when they do, it is just a question of whether you want to be on the train or get run over by it."

The threat rang naked in his voice, but Sicario didn't take the bait. He sat up straight and cleared his throat. Broken blood vessels in his cheeks came to life. "Look, *Isaac*, your little 'RED Army' is cute. But, let's be honest, it's no match for the full power of the United States military."

"I wouldn't be so sure about that." Moloch turned his head toward the closed dining room door. "Jack!" When his aide-de-camp walked in, the General said, "Will you bring General Sicario's security detail in as well as our special guest?"

Jack nodded and left the room.

Minutes later Jack returned with Sicario's bodyguard and a skinny girl with red hair. The bodyguard wore a form-fitting black suit on his six-foot frame. He was well-built with a crew cut and sharp chin, while the girl beside him couldn't have been over fourteen. She wore the uniform of the RED Army and a determined expression, but looked more like a girl scout than a soldier. Sleek, frameless wrap-around glasses rested on her nose. Ying had seen those glasses before. She owned a pair. Her brow furrowed at the thought of what would come next.

"What's your name, soldier?" said the General to Sicario's guard.

"Lang, sir. Patrick Lang."

"Lang. I'd like you to meet Cynthia. Cynthia is one of our top students at our RED military academies. I'd like you to fight her."

Sicario stood from his seat and put his hands on his hips. "What is this, Moloch? A joke? I don't have time for this."

Moloch motioned both hands downward to calm him. "Please, David, indulge me."

Sicario huffed but resumed his seat. He nodded to Sergeant Lang to proceed.

Ying's arms ached, but she couldn't look away. The bodyguard considered the ethics of what the general had ordered, but then shrugged and faced the girl.

An order was an order.

He sized her up for a moment and then fired a half-hearted right hook at her head. Cynthia ducked–almost *too* fast, thought Ying–and grabbed Lang's groin with all her might, dropping him to eye level. He squirmed backwards. She released her grip. She took one long step forward with her left foot and with her right unleashed a powerful sidekick to Lang's jaw, knocking him to the floor. He cradled his groin and rocked back and forth on the ground, dazed.

Cynthia looked down in disdain and put her hands on her hips. She turned to Moloch and said, "Well, whad'ya think?"

Ying couldn't help but laugh to herself watching this girl overcome such a powerful man.

"Fantastic!" shouted Ponti, clapping at Cynthia's performance. "You're welcome to join my army when you turn eighteen, young lady."

Sicario adjusted the collar of his well-starched shirt and wiggled in his chair. He stared at Moloch, chastened. "She's very impressive, Isaac."

Moloch finished his Scotch and slammed it down on the table. "Good, because on January 20th, we'll be marching on Washington with ten thousand more just like her."

Chapter 4

Albert leaned on the rounded corner of the polished wood bar of The Henry and observed the scene before him. He sipped his beer and played with the label on the bottle. He used to hate bars like this. Every aspect of the place seemed designed to stimulate and dull the senses simultaneously. The pulsing music. The mysterious lighting. The glamorous people. The overwhelming scent of cologne and perfume.

He understood it, now, though. It was an escape. Here, Albert's past receded into the background like a barely remembered dream. Nobody knew him. Nobody cared about him. He was just another decoration in the elaborate spectacle that was this place. He finished his beer. A warm glow rushed through his cheeks, and he smiled as the familiar wave of undeserved confidence and temporary amnesia overtook his mind.

Albert spotted a stunning woman standing at the bar. She had straight, sandy hair the color of stone, and her eyes crinkled into dark brown slits when she laughed. She glanced at Albert, and her unburdened smile made him forget his pain, if only for a moment.

He wished he could just talk to her without pretense. Listen to her and let the conversation wander and drift to those new, exciting places that emerge in that first human connection. But he knew too much, now. The Tree was inside him. He couldn't turn it off. He walked toward her. As he approached, he couldn't help envisioning how their conversation would unfold, just as Ariel had taught him years ago in that bar back in Vermont. It was a play in three parts.

In Act One, he would sidle up next to her close, but not too close. He knew that if he approached her head-on, it would be threatening, and she'd have an innate desire to backpedal. But if he simply stood next to her and ordered a drink, his physical presence would build intimacy, but in a non-threatening way.

If she was interested, she would turn his direction. When she did, he would simply introduce himself. "Hi, I'm Albert," he would say and shake her hand. He had experimented with many other lines at this very bar, but the straightforward method was the most predictable, and thus, the easiest for him to control.

"Hi, I'm Olivia," she would say–she looked like an Olivia, and it was the most common name in the UK for a woman her age–and the two would shake hands. He would hold the shake a little longer than normal to continue to build the connection. She might comment on his soft hands, a benefit of a lifetime of avoiding manual labor.

Then Albert would say, "It's very nice to meet you, Olivia." He would be sure to repeat her name because, as Ariel would say, "there's no sweeter sound than the sound of your own name."

She would show surprise and say, "Oh, you're American."

He would nod and joke, "No, I'm actually British, but I just thought the American accent gave me an edge."

They would both laugh politely, the end of Act One.

At the beginning of Act Two, he would say, "So, what about you? What's your life story?"

She would then step back, a little shocked by the enormity of the question, and repeat what he said, "My life story?"

He would insist. "Yep, start to finish."

She would then tell her life story. Where she was born, her family, job, etc.

Albert would listen to that life story. Really listen–most men never listened. This was his favorite part. He found people endlessly fascinating. He would ask more about certain topics. Find commonalities where they existed. Make light jokes as they presented themselves. At a moment of genuine laughter, he would move to the last act.

"I'm so excited for our first date," he would say with a smile.

"First date? That seems a little presumptuous."

"Is it?" he would say with a twinkle in his eye, and the steady confidence of a man whose seen this play unfold too many times.

And the play would be over.

Albert returned to reality as he reached the spot next to the woman at the bar.

"What can I get you?" asked the bartender.

Albert should have been excited, or at least nervous. He was about to speak with a beautiful woman. A beautiful woman with kind eyes. But when he looked inside himself, there was nothing. He had read life's script, and it held no surprises anymore, just disappointment and grief.

"I'll have a beer, any beer," said Albert. As he spoke, the girl turned and looked at him. Albert smiled and stuck out his hand. "Hi, I'm Albert."

She smiled back. "Hi, I'm Olivia."

***

Albert awoke later that night to the gentle purr of Olivia's snoring. His bedroom was dark, but in the moonlight easing through the blinds, he could see the freckles on her shoulders rocking up and down as she breathed. He felt sick. As it turned out, Olivia was a wonderful woman. Funny. Smart. She worked as a chemist and told more bad 'chemistry jokes' than Albert thought possible. But something wasn't right, and Albert knew it. Still, he went home with her, hoping he was wrong. He wasn't. And now, in a few hours this wonderful woman was about to realize that she had gone home with a miserable man.

Albert slid out of bed, grabbed his white, stretched-out V-neck t-shirt off the floor and crept out to the living room. He tiptoed toward the fireplace on the hardwood floors, trying not to wake up Olivia. The floorboards moaned with each step despite his best efforts. He bent over and removed one of the bricks at the base of the fireplace. He fished his hand inside and pulled out a leather journal with the words "A.T." on it. Albert dusted off the cover and blew on it. The pages were yellowed, and the book swelled with earmarks.

Albert tucked the journal under his armpit and made his way to the large oval window that overlooked the river Cam. He drew back the curtain and looked outside. The black river ambled along in silence, oblivious to the concerns of the world going on around it. He took a few steps back and eased himself into his reading chair. He ran his eyes along up and down the window glass. Chalk scribblings covered every inch. The scribblings of a madman. Symbols, numbers, notes, ideas. All leading to the same place. Nowhere.

His scribblings.

He opened the journal and looked inside. In blue pen, written in a cursive that had long been forgotten, lay a brief note.

Albert,

The future is written, but yet to be revealed.

-Angus

Albert's hands quivered as he flipped the page. The first page teased a series of symbols printed in perfect rows. He flipped the page. More symbols. He flipped again. Now, symbols arranged in decision trees. He continued to flip faster and faster. Page after page of undecipherable code stared back at him. Finally, he slammed the book shut. He looked back at the window, at his failure, and in silence, he fought back tears.

Chapter 5

President Culebra stood on stage and surveyed the crowd. Floodlights illuminated the red granite of the Texas State Capitol behind her. The sound of brass and drums from the "Marine's Hymn" chimed through the crisp January air. Thousands of supporters waved home-made signs in red and white with messages like "We ♥ Cristina" and "Viva La Presidenta".

She was as mindful of her posture and her expression as always: never stiff, always elegant and self-assured. Unlike many other female politicians, she did not scrabble and push to be part of the Boys' Club of politics. She was not 'one of the boys', and she never had been. She was a woman with a mind like a steel trap and ambitions greater than they could imagine.

She was not simply going to rule the world. She was going to make the world beg her to rule it. And they would be thankful they did.

As so many already were. Spectators roared their approval as the RED Army marched and stomped through the grounds clad in crimson fatigues and shimmering medals. Systematically, they worked their way through the sections of onlookers to form three columns connected by a bottom row. Once in place, they gave a shout and snapped to attention, forming the same symbol that stood out crisply on the blood red flags fluttering on the TV screens: the black, three-pronged tree symbol of the new Republic at the center.

The Governor of Texas stepped up to the podium and smiled out at the cheering crowd. After a promise that he would keep his remarks short so that they could hear from the woman they were *really* here to see–a statement greeted by raucous laughter, whistles, and applause–he launched into an introductory speech, linking his state's fierce, historic independence with Cristina's values of hard work and achievement.

Cristina kept her smile fixed firmly on her face despite the flutter of disquiet in her chest. This moment was supposed to be a celebration. Texas, the second most populous state in the Union, had voted to secede from the United States and join Cristina's Republic. The Republic of Enlightenment and Democracy now represented almost half of the United States population. It should be her day of triumph, but she felt no such sensation. *This was too easy.* A chill ran up her back. Her eyes watered, and her nose threatened to run from the cold. She wanted to pull at the collar of her shirt where the starch chafed.

Those were the thoughts of a woman less disciplined than she was. *What was happening to her?*

She thought back to the all-encompassing plan she had used to plot her rise to this very moment. She had learned long ago not to ignore the feelings that told her something was out of place; It had been part of her for so long that it had sunk into her core, and it often spoke through her instincts.

Picturing the Tree brought a vivid memory of the white board in her office, the one she had shown Puddles so long ago. She had found her way to where she wished to be, so what was the problem?

This was too easy, her mind insisted again. There had been missing steps. Intrinsic to all her calculations was the reliance on Newton's Third Law of Motion: *for every action, there is an equal and opposite reaction.* Cristina had found that this was not merely a law of motion, but a law of power. If one person took power from another, there would be a reaction.

Yet, thus far, Cristina had not seen a reaction. There had been no pushback, no bang–only a whimper. States fell into the Republic like so many dominoes, and the only visible reaction had been impotent whining from Congressmen, newspaper editorials, and some trolls on social media.

Hardly equal and opposite. There should have been something... more. A general or an admiral speaking up, perhaps. Something–"Please give a warm Texas welcome to our new President, Cristina Culebra," bellowed the now former Governor of Texas.

There was no time to think about it, now. Cristina strode to the lectern, waving to her supporters and letting her look of polite interest grow into the one hundred-watt smile she used for speeches.

"Thank you so much for welcoming me to your state," she called. The cheers rose, flags were waving wildly, and she knew just what to say next to send the audience over the top. "And let me be the first to welcome all of *you* to the New Republic."

At the thunder of screams and whistles, she spread her arms and gave a delighted laugh, sharing a glance with the governor. He was soaking in as much of the attention as he could. He had no inkling that anything about this was off. He was just another one of the rubes that surrounded her. Even now, she would bet he was composing his own speech for the day *he* would be President.

Dream on, she thought.

Cristina did not need to focus as she began her stump speech. She had given it a hundred times, and every breath and smile was rote memory, by now. She leaned in at the correct moments, urging the crowd into cheers and chants of her campaign slogans– and, meanwhile, she searched the crowd for her next opponent.

Opposition could come from only two places. External or internal. Her external foes could be an organization or an individual. No individual was strong enough to stop her, now. It would have to be an organization. The Federal government? A student protest group? A terrorist group? None of those entities had shown the coordination or determination to pose a threat.

What about internally? General Moloch? He was a true believer in the movement, a rabid dog on a leash. He had no power base without her. He might come for her someday, but not now. He needed her. The Governor of Texas? He undoubtedly *wanted* her place, but he was a moron and a coward. He had neither the intelligence nor guts to plan an assassination. Even if he did, she would see it coming long before he had time to act. Her daughter, Eva? Never. *So, who would challenge her? Who would come for her?*

A flash from above interrupted her thoughts. Cristina looked skyward to see a drone flying above her taking video and pictures of the rally. She resumed her speech. It was time to close strong. There would be time for the competition later.

"I'm so proud to have the support of the wonderful people of Texas in our movement to make the world a better place. With your help, we can create a world in which our children can thrive, in which our grandparents can be cared for, in which our parents can be proud. Above all, we can build a world in which we can..."

An object fell from the sky and bounced along the stage in front of her.

Time slowed to an interminable, almost liquid drip. A small spherical device rolled back and forth in a semi-circle. As she peered closer, she noticed the device held a screen with white numbers. The numbers counted down. 13... 12... 11.... Caught in the eternity of each second, Cristina could not move quickly enough to flick her eyes up at the drone–but she didn't need to.

Everything fell into place with a click: *Newton's Law isn't dead.*

She looked at her security detail, but they hadn't noticed the small noise amidst the scream of the crowd. Adrenaline surged through her body, jolting her back into the normal flow of time. For Cristina, who had lived her life on the high-wire, the chemical had a strangely calm and clarifying effect. She leaned into the microphone and spoke with steadiness and authority.

"Ladies and gentleman, we have a minor security situation. I need everyone to leave the area around the stage immediately."

Someone shouted, "Bomb". Screams rang out from the audience. Spectators ran in every direction, colliding in the turmoil, and Cristina looked back down at the device. It had rolled to an eerie stop, and the numbers were flashing on its face: 7... 6....5...

There was no time for her to leave the stage. Eva was screaming, trying to reach her, as part of the security team dragged her away. Cristina nodded to them once and then shook her head at the agents who were running for her.

A child stood alone, staring at her, curious and confused.

High risk, high reward. She was in motion, but she hardly felt it. The lectern was steel, intended to serve as a bulletproof refuge if necessary, and she put her back into hauling it around on one corner. Then, with the hollow side facing the device, she shoved with all her might, and threw herself across the lectern to hold it down.

Either she died now, a hero who had laid the groundwork for Eva's rise, or she survived–a hero who had sacrificed herself while everyone else had run. Was Eva ready for this? No time to wonder. No time for regrets.

She heard the final countdown chirps of the device, and then a deafening bang burst forth. The lectern vibrated as if it were a giant gong. There was smoke, and there were screams.

Cristina waited.

There was no pain. She hadn't looked forward to the pain, but there was none. Just silence, followed by a rising murmur.

She lifted her head and felt her midsection. No blood. She looked to make sure. No injuries. She pushed herself off the lectern and peered under it. Black smoke billowed out, but no sound.

"Mama!" Eva's voice.

"Keep her back," Cristina called over her shoulder. It was the voice that said to her security detail, 'keep my daughter safe, or you will pray for death long before I grant it to you'.

She looked again to the crowd and saw that, instead of staring at her, they were looking *past* her, over her shoulder.

Newton's Third Law. Whatever was waiting behind her...

She closed her eyes for a moment and then turned to look. The LED screen that had once shown the RED logo now displayed something entirely different. A bright, white flaming sword against a pure black background. Above it was a mysterious sentence:

SOLVE THE CIPHER.

FOLLOW THE CIPHER.

Blood filled Cristina's cheeks–and rage boiled in her chest. She turned to Moloch and pointed toward the exits.

"Find out who did this." Mindful of the cameras still rolling, she kept a measured expression on her face and gritted the words out, but he could not miss the fury in her eyes. "*Now.*"

Chapter 6

A riel! You gotta see this."

Ariel finished slicing down the length of the habanero and lifted her knife away before looking over her shoulder. Getting habanero juice in a finger cut was the sort of mistake one only needed to make once in life.

"What is it?" she called after a moment. She raised a hand to wipe a stray blonde hair from her forehead, then remembered the other mistake she had once made with peppers.

Grabbing the damp towel next to the cutting board, she headed into the living room to see her husband Chris on the edge of the sofa, leaning on the coffee table. His eyes were glued to the screen.

Ariel frowned and came a little closer. "Chris? I thought we were done watching Cristina Culebra."

"Check this out." He pointed to the screen.

"I told you, it's just propaganda. Also, I think the taco meat is about to burn–"

"I'll take care of the tacos." He stood up and guided her over to the couch. "You need to see this."

"Chris—"

"Look at the damned television screen, light of my life." His voice floated back over his shoulder.

Ariel smiled after him and then looked unwillingly at the Texas rally, her jaw dropping open as she watched the chaos unfold: the projectile landing on the stage; Cristina Culebra saying something calmly into the microphone; taking a few precious moments to make sure that her daughter was safe and then wrestling the podium over what looked like a bomb.

The video looped over and over, sometimes zooming in on different angles, while the commentary reached such heights of uselessness that Ariel set the TV to mute with a wince.

She shook her head slightly and refocused on the screen. At first, Ariel wondered if Cristina had staged the attack, intending to rob any resistance movements of power. Cristina Culebra had behaved like a hero, at once a decisive leader and a caring mother. Arguably, she had not had *time* to run, but that wouldn't have stopped most people from trying. But by the third watch-through, Ariel was fairly certain that Culebra had not been involved in this scheme, and by the fifth, she would have bet money on it.

The key was the woman's utter fury—and not at the bomb. Culebra had expected either to die, or to be grievously wounded, and she was now ashamed that she had been made to look a fool. When she spoke to Moloch, she had pointed not at the bomb, which she could later have explained away as a question about how a drone had gotten through, but she instead pointed at the backdrop. It was the message on the screen that shook her, not the bomb.

At the message about the mysterious cipher. Or was it Cipher, as in a person? Organization?

Mulling this over, she headed back to the kitchen to find Chris speaking in hushed tones with Shawn. Shawn was growing by the minute, getting big and tall just like his mother. When he saw her, Chris perked up.

"Well, little buddy. Should we ask Mommy what she thinks of the lady on the television?"

Shawn slurped on his milk, leaving a perfectly groomed milk mustache. "Yeah, Mommy, what do you think of the lady on the television?"

"So?" Chris asked.

"*Very* interesting," Ariel said. Her mind was still humming along in the background as she took over at the chopping board again.

"What do they think happened?"

"Nobody knows, yet." Ariel kept chopping; the motion helped her think. "I was able to see video from a few different angles and I'm thinking, now. But I'm sure the internet is going crazy investigating it. I'll look into it after you know who's in bed. Until then..."

Her husband tilted his head to the side. Sandy-haired and lanky, Chris's effortless athlete's body had put on a bit of padding around the middle, and there was some gray at his temples. Ariel smiled when she looked over at him, now, and counted her blessings that she had married him so young. Youthful infatuation had deepened to something better–or, at least, been joined by it. He still made her go weak at the knees.

"What?" he asked her, and he was grinning. "Right now? I could throw on some cartoons for the little man here, but we should take the taco meat off the stove if–"

Ariel laughed and kissed him, holding her hands carefully away. "Trust me, after I've been chopping peppers, you do *not* want me to touch anything delicate."

"Mmm." He rummaged in the silverware drawer. "And you're sure you don't need to keep watching the news? I can bring you a plate."

"That's very sweet, but I think it would hurt more than help, right now." She handed him the bowl of taco meat.

"Your call." Chris carried over the bowl of cheese and the plate of tortillas to the kitchen table. He leaned over to Shawn. "Are we ready for some tacos?"

"Yeah!" Shawn said.

The family sat down for dinner. Conversation was fragmented over the next few minutes, between assurances to Shawn that he *had* enjoyed peppers before, reminders that he *did* have to try a bite, and much more emphatic reminders that there would be no dessert if he didn't have any dinner. Since she knew it would take time for the facts of the Culebra rally to come out, Ariel did not mind.

It was only later, after she and Chris had wrestled Shawn to bed and were discussing the day over a glass of wine, that Ariel allowed herself to analyze the event.

"It's interesting. She's been almost entirely unopposed. I think, if I were her, I'd be nervous."

Chris raised an eyebrow. "Well, if this is the opposition, I don't think she has much to worry about. They couldn't even get the bomb to go off."

"I don't think it was supposed to." Ariel took a sip of her wine. "Right now, I'd say it was intended to make her fear for her life, however briefly, and then make sure *every* news channel in the world showed what was on that screen."

"Why not kill her, though?" When Ariel's eyebrows shot up, Chris shook his head. "Not–I didn't mean it like that. What I *meant* was, if someone is opposing her, why not just kill *her*? She's the driving force behind this movement. If they could get an explosive onto that stage, they *could* have killed her... so why not just do it?"

That was a good point. Ariel nodded as her mind sorted through possibilities. She needed more information. She needed to know who the person or people were who did this to replicate their motivations.

"I don't know. Maybe they're worried that if they killed her, they would make her a martyr. Or that someone even worse, like Moloch, would replace her. Or they were only using this as a vector for promoting something else," she said finally. "It could be a one-off, some artist looking to make a statement, do a Banksy thing?" Her mouth twisted. She wasn't very sure of that theory.

"Hmm." Chris finished his wine. "You want some more?"

"Nah, I have to be thinking." She held her glass out to him. "You finish mine."

"You don't have to ask me twice." He came to get her glass and dropped a kiss on her cheek. "And try to come to bed tonight, would you?"

"What?" She was laughing.

"I know that face. That's the 'I will not sleep until I've figured this out' face." He was smiling fondly as he disappeared back into the house. "You have to get sleep, too, you know."

"I don't need sleep," she called after him. "I need *answers*."

A few hours later, she sat at the white wood desk in the center of her cozily lit basement home office. She had covered the rich green walls with printouts of the anonymous online newsletter she had started called *The Voice*. She was now using it to chronicle, and criticize, the rise of the RED movement in Texas, using subtle principles from the Tree of Knowledge that Turner had taught her to make her articles more engaging... and more likely to leave people with uncomfortable questions. She had a small group of subscribers, and they were growing rapidly.

Now, she smiled as her TV screen flashed images of the chaos that unfolded at the Culebra rally that evening. Culebra looked genuinely rattled, a sight that was both rare and welcome. By now, just as Ariel had predicted, her message board had not only pieced together a continuous stream of video from each angle available, they had also identified the make and model of the drone and some factors about the construction of the incendiary device.

So far, there had been only one statement from Culebra's camp, downplaying the events instead of publicizing them. Though they condemned violence in the strongest possible terms, their spokesperson said, there was no way to know yet who had disrupted the rally or why, and they were pleased to announce that no one in the crowd or on Cristina's team had been injured.

Other than her pride, Ariel thought, with a small smile. She was even more sure, now, that Culebra was not behind this. The statement revealed a staff who wanted everyone to forget what they had just seen: Cristina Culebra facing something beyond her control.

Meanwhile, there had been no mention in the RED statement about the mysterious Cipher... which was shaping up to be a writer's dream.

Ariel settled her noise-canceling headphones over her ears and called up her playlist of Louis Armstrong songs, starting with

"Wonderful World". She wasn't above a bit of petty celebration at Cristina's expense, and she loved listening to jazz while she wrote. As Louis Armstrong's vocals purred through the headphone's speakers, Ariel's deep voice hummed along, and she composed her headline:

A Puzzling Conclusion to Culebra Rally in Austin

She chuckled at her bad pun and continued typing, quickly settling into a writer's trance. She had been on the debate team in high school and had taken several political science classes in college before joining Army PsyOp. The challenge of how to present information to sway an audience was one she wholeheartedly enjoyed. Sometimes Ariel hesitated to use her skills, but she had no problem using it against the woman who would be queen.

A soft vibration from above interrupted her trance. She flipped the headphone off her right ear and listened.

"Chris?" she called softly.

No response.

Ariel listened for a beat longer, shook her head, and moved her right headphone back to her ear in time to catch the opening strains of "La Vie en Rose". She closed her eyes and attempted to regain her lost momentum.

Where was she? Ahh, the Cipher.

She looked back at her computer screen to a picture an attendee at the rally had taken. The photo showed a large black screen sitting on a stage. The screen was slightly obscured by smoke, but an image in white stood out clearly. At first glance, it looked like a large, medieval sword with fire surrounding it and an elaborate design on the blade and hilt. It was not easily visible in this image, but Ariel had seen the deconstruction online: the shape of the blade and hilt was, in fact, composed of a series of symbols not unlike some codes she had seen during her time in the military, including a skull where the pommel should be.

Members of the message board were currently working to figure out the symbols, while Ariel privately wondered if this person just had a flair for the dramatic. After all–

Another creak from above.

Now, she knew what was going on. Ariel took off her headphones and stood up, trying to get her frustration under control.

"Shawn Thomas Kelly," she said, in her most commanding 'Mom voice', "You get your buns back to bed, right now, young man!"

Normally, she would have heard Shawn take off and scamper up the stairs, his tactical retreat being the second movement of what could easily turn into an hour-long process of getting him back to bed. Shawn might be standing his ground this time… or he was getting sneakier, and hoping she would assume she had been wrong about hearing him awake.

She climbed the stairs. It was strange that the living room light was off. Shawn was scared of the dark.

She frowned and quieted her tone so as not to wake Chris as she reached the top step. "Shawn, honey? It is *way* past your bed–"

A gloved hand covered her mouth, and she was yanked off her feet to dangle in the air. Her legs thrashed, before another hand clamped across her windpipe and a man's voice whispered in her ear:

"Make a sound and your son dies."

Ariel froze. She could smell the plastics and stale sweat from the glove and the rough edges of both weapons and armor pressed against her on multiple sides; one man holding her, she calculated, and two more with him. She scanned their fatigues to see if she could see any insignia on their armor, but the room was too dark.

She peered down the hall until she was able to pick out one thing: another figure dressed in all black armor, facing the door with a rifle raised.

Waiting for the order to kill her son.

This was real. Ariel could tell from any of a number of details. These weren't failed SWAT recruits, hired to rough her up and scare her. They were professional killers who had absolutely no qualms about inflicting pain or death to further their employer's ends.

Their employer? Ideas sprinted through her mind. Ariel had covered her tracks well when she set up the newsletter, but she knew better than to think she could hide all her digital tracks from a sophisticated organization such as RED. It would simply be a waste of time. Over the passage of the months, she had assumed Cristina Culebra had long since stopped caring about the activities of her and her colleagues. Ariel's articles might be well-written, but they had so far had all the effect of throwing toothpicks at a tsunami.

Tonight, that had changed. They had come for her.

She hung her head with acceptance and then gave a single nod.

In a dizzying whirl of motion, her mouth was duct-taped, zip ties were put around her ankles and wrists, and she was carried down the long hallway out into the back alley of her home. They had done this before, she thought, a part of her mind entirely detached. No one fumbled in the dark for the zip ties or the duct tape.

As if expecting her every means of escape, the two would-be assassins exited first, within her line of sight, while the other men carried her down the long hallway and out to the alley behind her home. The single light above her garage illuminated two nondescript work vans, quietly steaming in the winter air.

Past midnight. A good neighborhood. No one was around to witness this.

The man carrying her swung her off his shoulders easily and manhandled her into the van. Her head slammed against the metal interior wall as they forced her onto a bench. Her ears rang. She slid herself on the bench seat and evaluated her surroundings. She wasn't alone. To her left sat three others. Across from her, four more. All of them hogtied, faces covered in shrouds. As she leaned forward to get a better look at her passengers, the masked man opened the front-passenger side door and entered the van. He sized her up and with one swift move swiveled in his seat and yanked a shroud over her head.

All was black.

***

In a quiet room in California, Eva Fix leaned back from her computer screen and refrained from rubbing at her forehead. General Moloch was sitting with her, the two of them overseeing the evening's mission, and Eva did not want him to see the emotions running through her head.

The sleepy suburban neighborhood on the screen was almost entirely silent. There was the shuffle of boots, a thud that was likely a skull against metal, and the sound of the van doors closing.

This is a mistake. The thought pulsed through Eva's head and she struggled to keep it from showing on her face.

Of everyone in her mother's organization, she was beginning to despise the General the most. Everything annoyed her, from his contempt to his ever-present cigarettes, and the fact that her annoyance was mostly born of jealousy made it even worse. She should be above that.

Instead, she wanted to spit curses at him. *This is wrong. Abducting people to find out who attacked the rally. This isn't what RED is about. This isn't who we are.*

The General took one long, last drag of his cigarette and snuffed it out in a grungy ashtray as the two of them watched the vans creep out of the alley. Then Moloch stood. His rough, almost purple fingers closed the buttons on his uniform.

"And that's how it's done, Fix. In and out with barely a whisper." He stared down at her, and she knew that, whatever she had done to hide her expression, it was not enough. "Something troubling you?"

She knew the real question: *Are you loyal to me? To your mother? To RED?*

She looked up and assessed the General's gaze, searching for even the smallest sign of doubt about what they were doing. That would tell her she was wrong about him, and she wanted to be wrong.

But there was nothing. His were the eyes of a fanatic. No doubt. No hesitation. Only blind belief.

She sighed. "No. Well done, General. I will see you back in New York for the interrogations."

He smiled his lizard smile. "Yes, the interrogations. See you back in New York."

Chapter 7

The J. Edgar Hoover Building stood on Pennsylvania Avenue just a few blocks from the White House. The concrete frame, peppered with window after window of offices and conference rooms, reminded Ying of a cheese grater laid flat on its side. This nondescript building housed the Federal Bureau of Investigation, tasked with finding and eliminating domestic threats to the United States.

Such as, for instance, an impending coup.

Weatherspoon's friend at the Bureau had reluctantly agreed to hear the evidence they had collected on Moloch. As he presented their case, Ying assessed the four FBI agents in the oversized, overheated conference room.

The two agents closest to her were obviously junior. They both had full heads of closely cropped hair and carried the smug, intimidating stares that mask the underlying insecurity of youth. They pretended to take notes, but Ying guessed their thoughts lay elsewhere. Two other agents sat at the end of the conference table.

The two were a study in contrasts. Taylor was all soft and squishy, with a rotund body, soft cheeks, and a soft white broom mustache. Moini was all hard lines and sharp edges. A razor-sharp jaw, a thin, hooked nose, and crisp, springy curls in her black hair. Taylor asked most of the questions, while Moini observed, brown eyes loaded with intelligence, and took detailed notes. *Typical. The man does most of the talking, and the woman does most of the work,* thought Ying.

Weatherspoon finished his PowerPoint presentation and looked at Taylor. "So, what do you think, Sam?"

Taylor cleared his throat and shifted in his seat. He ran his hand back and forth along the gray hair atop his head.

"Spoon, this was certainly a thorough presentation, and I appreciate you bringing this to my attention, but you know we can't pursue this. The evidence you have here is circumstantial at best. And even if I believed that there was some magical tree of knowledge that gave people superpowers, which I don't, I can't devote limited resources to investigating a four-star general because he had some meetings. I certainly cannot pursue sedition charges based on the evidence of a non-citizen who was admittedly trespassing when she overheard it."

Weatherspoon dropped his head and took two deep breaths. He opened his mouth to say something but thought better of it. He gathered his photos and presentation notes into a manila folder. "I understand," he muttered.

Ying saw, now, that Weatherspoon had never believed that this would work. That was why he had deflated so quickly when Taylor said he did not believe in the Tree of Knowledge. But Ying had fought bullies like Taylor in grade school. She stood up from her chair and leaned on the conference table.

"Wait! That's it? We have evidence that Moloch is staging a coup in less than two weeks, that he has the power to do it, and is actively courting connections within the military, and you're not going to do anything?"

Taylor rose from his seat and tucked his portfolio under his arm. He motioned to the two junior agents. "Alright, we're done, here. Tony, Fred, will you please escort our guests out?"

Weatherspoon shot a glare at Ying and, through a forced calm, said, "Let's go."

But Ying had come too far to turn away. She had spent night after night sitting in that stinking police car 'collecting evidence'. She had scaled buildings and risked her life to procure this particular piece of evidence.

And now that they finally presented their case, it was tossed aside like trash?

"No, I'm not going. Agent Taylor, The Tree of Knowledge is real. Can't you see that?"

Taylor kept walking toward the door. One of the younger agents grabbed Ying's shoulder, "Alright, let's go, lady."

"Don't touch me!" snapped Ying. She slapped his hand off her shoulder.

The other junior agent approached her. "Ma'am, let's not make a scene." He grabbed Ying's bicep.

Ying slapped the other agent's hand away, stepped back, and looked at Taylor. She reached in her shoulder bag and pulled out her sleek combat glasses. The ones Turner had given her. The ones that enabled her to see a punch before it was thrown.

"You don't believe The Tree of Knowledge is real?"

Taylor stopped and stared at Ying with an amused look on his face. "No." He pointed to the door. "It's time for you to go."

Weatherspoon stepped forward, arms out. "OK. Everyone, just calm down. Ying, don't do anything rash."

But the junior agents weren't listening. Simultaneously, they lunged at Ying.

Ying side-stepped as both agents went crashing into the conference room wall opposite Taylor. She assumed a fighting position.

"Ying, no!" Weatherspoon shouted.

The agents recovered and crouched in a defensive posture. Through her combat glasses, Ying could see their fists glowing red, poised to throw a punch. The first one swung at her. Ying tilted her head a few inches to the left as the punch flew by. He swung again. She tilted her head two inches to the right this time. She smiled, mocking him.

Enraged, the agent ran at her and crouched over to tackle her. Ying danced out of the way and used his forward momentum to slam him into the laminate conference room wall a few feet from Taylor. He collapsed to the ground stunned, nose bleeding. Taylor looked down at the agent in disgust.

The second agent pulled his gun.

"OK. That's enough!" shouted Taylor. "Tony, put the gun down."

Ying grinned. "Oh, don't worry, Agent Taylor. That's not a problem."

She assessed Tony through the glasses. His groin glowed green. She braced her left leg and launched her right foot in between the agent's legs. He dropped his left arm to block the kick, but he was too late. The kick landed and he crumpled over. Ying grabbed the slide of the gun with her left hand and twisted his wrist with her right until he released it. She turned back to Taylor. Maintaining eye contact with him, she removed the magazine from the agent's gun and gently placed them both on the conference room table.

"Now, do you believe us?"

There was a pause while Taylor looked her over.

"No," he said finally. "No, I do not."

"But the Tree," Ying argued. "Moloch is trained in it; his soldiers are trained in it."

"Miss..." He shook his head, unable to remember her name and not even respectful enough to ask for it again. "There is absolutely no evidence that the RED movement intends to use means other than democratic votes to achieve their ends, and that is a matter for courts, not for the FBI."

"There *is* evidence," Ying gritted out. "We *gave* it to you."

"Ying," said Weatherspoon.

"No! He doesn't get it. He doesn't see that Moloch rose with Cristina Culebra, and now, he's going to use *her* power to stage a coup. He's dangerous, we know how dangerous he is. We saw him—" Her voice trembled and she broke off.

She gathered her composure and looked back at Agent Taylor. "This rally is not just a rally. I saw Moloch say so. I heard it plain as day. I showed you the training his soldiers have. If you are not willing to believe me, then I have to wonder—"

His face darkened. "I think you had best shut your mouth, Miss Koh. You have already attacked two agents on federal territory, and now, you are alleging professional misconduct because we don't believe a crackpot theory that has come without a single shred of actual evidence. You have successfully proven to me that General Moloch went into a house. Congratulations. Now, get out of this building before I have you arrested."

The door slammed behind him, and Weatherspoon looked at Ying, his face a mix of pity and resentment. He had wanted her to give up immediately.

She barely saw him, however. Her mind was circling on one very important point:

The Tree had pointed her here. She had chosen the best path to persuasion.

Why hadn't it worked?

Chapter 8

Five minutes later, FBI security ushered Ying and Weatherspoon out of the building. The fading sun reflected off the glass structure across the street, a metaphor for their hopes of catching Moloch. Steam wriggled from the manhole covers in the street. Ying's skin instantly transitioned from sweat to goose bumps. Tour buses roared past them spewing welcome hot air from their vents. Ying assessed Weatherspoon as the bear of a man paced back and forth, avoiding eye contact. *Best not to say anything,* she thought.

"Your presentation was shit," said a voice from behind her.

Ying turned to see who was speaking. Agent Moini stood leaned up against one of the leafless maple trees dotting the sidewalk in front of the complex. She chewed a massive wad of bright pink bubble gum and blew a giant bubble.

"Thanks," said Weatherspoon. "And thanks for your help in there."

Ying had never seen the cop so glum.

Moini popped the bubble with her teeth and continued gnawing on her gum.

"Yeah. Well, Taylor's a fucking idiot, so I didn't want to waste my time. But I did enjoy watching this girl kick some ass in there. Very cool stuff–plus, it's always good for the junior agents to remember that an unlikely-looking person can be a threat."

Ying looked at Weatherspoon who shrugged and turned to Moini.

"OK. Well, as fun as standing out in this cold with you is, we're going to head back to Princeton, now. C'mon Ying, let's get out of here."

Ying hesitated, and eyed Moini, but the agent just looked off in the distance, chewing her gum. Ying turned and jogged behind Weatherspoon.

"I think you might be on to something," shouted Moini.

The pair stopped and turned.

Moini popped another bubble and smiled. "C'mon let's go for a walk. You never know when some asshole is listening to you around this building."

Minutes later, the three of them strolled along the Capitol mall. The setting sun spilled against the water of the Lincoln Memorial Reflecting Pool. Moini offered each of them some Big League Chew. They both declined.

"I used to smoke, but now that we're not allowed to have any fun, anymore, this is the best I've got. Anyway, we've... I should say, I've because I've being doing this by myself because the damn Bureau won't give me any resources... I've had my eye on the RED movement for a while, now. Culebra has never sat right with me. From Day One she's been up to something."

Ying interrupted, "Agent Moini. This isn't about Cristina Culebra. This about General Moloch. He's behind all of this. We don't even know if Culebra knows anything about it."

Moini snorted and snapped another bubble.

"I thought you were the smart one in the group. I promise you that Culebra is involved on some level."

Weatherspoon chimed in. "She's right, Ying. I sincerely doubt that Moloch's gone rogue on this whole thing."

"I... I..." Ying stammered. She refused to believe that Culebra was behind this. The woman had done so much good in the Republic. "It doesn't matter. We can agree to disagree. Are you going to help us take down Moloch or not?"

Moini stopped and bent down to grab a pebble off the gravel sidewalk next to the reflecting pool. She reached back and with the grace of an athlete effortlessly skipped it across the water.

"Yeah, I'll help you."

"Good," said Weatherspoon. He paused. "I don't mean to look a gift horse in the mouth, Agent Moini, but what exactly can you do for us? It's pretty clear Taylor's not on board with our program."

"Fuck Taylor. That guy hasn't left his desk in 20 years. How do you know him, anyway?"

"We played football together back in the day."

"Taylor played football? *Those* days are long gone, huh?"

Weatherspoon nodded wistfully and rubbed his belly. "Yeah, for both of us. Long, long gone."

"The good news is Taylor pretty much lets me run my own show, so while I can't do a lot for you, I can do a few things. I've got clearance to create a task force, and I can get you on the task force so that you can take temporary leave from Princeton PD for the next couple of weeks. Ying, I don't even know what you do during the day, but I'm sure I can get you out of it. I've also got a safe house we can use to run the operation."

Ying ignored the slight. "That would be amazing. Thank you."

"Weatherspoon, what else do we need?"

"Just the basic surveillance gear. And we may need a warrant at some point."

"No problem. But I'm going to need one thing from you."

"What's that?"

"Albert Puddles."

Chapter 9

Ariel felt the rumble of the plane's engines in her chest. The shroud blocked her vision, but she could tell from the hard steel seat beneath her and the faint metallic scent that she was on a military transport plane. She had ridden on planes like this before during her time in the service. The plane had been in air for what seemed like a couple of hours, now, so they could be anywhere. The question was, where was she being transported? The man beside her shook quietly and sniffled. He clearly wasn't optimistic about their destination, either.

She thought of Shawn and Chris back home and fought back her own tears. How could she be so stupid? She had put her family at risk. And for what? To make herself feel better? She knew Cristina Culebra and her people played hardball, but it never occurred to her they would go this far. Until now, Culebra had relied on her charisma and her knowledge of the Tree to talk circles around journalists, making those who opposed her look like fools.

Abducting journalists, however? That was new, and it was reckless.

Not to mention, Ariel was barely even a journalist. She wrote a crappy little newsletter.

This had to have something do with the rally. The Cipher maybe? But she knew even less about the Cipher than they did...

A cruel hand yanked the shroud off her head and ripped the tape from her mouth, revealing a bullet-headed, older man with deep creases running in all directions across his face. Tobacco smell emanated from his being, and his sadistic eyes ran up and down her body. He leaned in close to her, daring her to lean away. Ariel held firm. He nodded as if she had passed a test, pulled back, and resumed an officer's posture. He held a file folder in his hand.

Ariel used the opportunity to evaluate her surroundings. She was right. She was sitting in a small military cargo plane. The plane was totally unfinished and held nothing, save twenty red grated metal seats partially filled with other terrified passengers gagged and bound like herself.

Soldiers guarded both the front and rear of the plane, and the cockpit was sealed and locked. The parachute hooks clinked and clanked empty against the cabin's walls. She wasn't escaping this plane until they landed.

"Mrs. Kelly." The man put faint emphasis on the *Mrs*, to remind her of her family. "I am General Isaac Moloch."

Ariel nodded. "I know who you are, General."

"Good." The General strode back and forth on the plane like the head of a marching band. He was making a show of looking at her file. "You're probably wondering why you're here."

"Yes," she said, with as much as deference as she could muster. This was almost certainly going to be unpleasant for her. She ran the potential actions and reactions in her mind, finally settling on what Sun Tzu would have called a strategic retreat. She must stall as long as she could without giving the General an excuse for violence.

"As I'm sure you know, there was an incident at a rally in Austin last night."

"Yes."

"We would like to know what you know about that incident." The General continued to pace, looking down at the file.

This was what Ariel was afraid of. They thought she had something to do with the Cipher at the rally. The problem was, she didn't–and, not only that, she didn't know *anything*.

In her experience, interrogation without information did not end well.

She gathered herself. "General, with all due respect, I would love to help you, but I honestly don't know what happened last night." She *wouldn't* love to help him, but she couldn't say that, could she? "The first I heard about the incident was when I saw it on the news last night. I was researching it when I was–when your agents collected me from my house."

The General nodded with faux empathy and turned away from Ariel.

Then, like a viper, he sprung back around and cracked Ariel across the face with the back of his hand. For a moment it felt as though he had knocked her eye loose from the socket. She blinked to make sure it was still there and then looked back at him with her good eye. Rage exploded through his face.

"You'd love to help me, would you? Love to? Your shitty little newsletter has done nothing but try to tear down our movement with lies. And now, you say you want to help me? I find that hard to believe. I might almost think you were lying to me, Mrs. Kelly."

Ariel took deep, steady breaths and tried to slow her heart rate. She could feel each beat in her eye socket. She was on dangerous ground. "You're right, General. I am an opponent of your movement. My newsletter has asked questions I believe need to be asked–and are not being asked. But right now, I'm tied up in an airplane and you hold all the cards, so believe me when I say that I want nothing more than to give you what you want."

There was a pause while she held her breath. She had chosen her words carefully, and if she had miscalculated…

The General's face softened. "Good. Why don't you tell me everything you know about this 'Cipher'?"

Ariel looked at the floor to buy time. The truth was she knew nothing about the Cipher, and she needed him to believe that.

"All I know is what I *don't* know, General. I don't know who or what the Cipher is. The language suggests that it is a code of some sort, but I also checked extensively for the name in various places online. I did not find it mentioned as a group of its own, or a subset of any known resistance movement. Of the people who have been covering your rallies, General, I saw almost all weighing in online, suggesting that they were searching for answers just like I was. Nobody seems to know anything."

The General's face didn't so much as flicker. Instead, he cleared his throat and nodded toward the two men standing at the front of the plane. One man opened the jump door. The other grabbed Ariel and pulled her to her feet.

Her right eye was swelling shut, but from the cold wind whipping through the cabin and the distance of the lights in her left eye, she knew the plane hovered thousands of feet above ground. Her mind raced back to Shawn and Chris.

She couldn't leave them.

She summoned all her strength and threw her shoulder into the soldier behind her, slamming him against the fuselage. She leaped forward as far as her bound legs would allow her until the General's clammy hand grabbed her neck and thrust her against the wall of the plane. She stood inches from the jump door, now, his hand still clasped around her throat.

Ariel searched the plane for help. But all the other captives just sat with their heads bowed, hoping for a better fate. Violence was not an option. She had to rely either on mercy, or on changing the General's calculus. Mercy on its own would not be enough.

"General, I have a husband. I have a son. I promise you. I will do anything you ask. I will hunt down this Cipher, myself, if I have to, and trust me when I say that I am one of your best chances to do so–I have contacts who are also critical of your movement, I can save you a great deal of time and effort. Please."

The General eased his grip. "I believe you, Mrs. Kelly... I believe you." He stepped back and ushered her away from the wall of the plane.

As she stepped forward, however, crossing in front of the open door, he slid one foot behind her and slammed his palm into her chest. Pain burst through her torso and, before she could stop herself, she shuffled backwards stumbling over his leg.

Off the edge of the plane. She reached for the door's edge. Her bound hands held the frame, but her momentum pulled her outward. Her hands slid from the frame's edge, but there was nothing beneath her. She plunged, screaming, into the unforgiving Appalachian wilderness.

Chapter 10

Albert awoke to the sound of knocking on his door. He rolled over and surveyed the room. At first, he assumed a delivery person was delivering a package. He ignored it. The knocks continued and as they grew in volume, he noticed they emitted a musical quality. Dun Dun Da Dun Dun, Dun Dun. Dun Dun Da Dun, Dun Dun. The melody sounded familiar.

He heaved himself out of bed–he noticed it had been getting harder every day–and slid on his leather slippers. His temples throbbed and his mouth stuck together. He slalomed his way through the organized stacks of cryptography books to the door and peered through the peephole. His eyes sprung open. Weatherspoon stared back at him through the fisheye with Ying by his elbow.

Albert opened the door a crack but kept the chain lock secured.

"What are you doing here?"

"We're here to see you," replied Weatherspoon.

Albert leaned his head against the wall and rubbed the sleep from his eyes. He was not in the mood for this.

"Michael, Ying, it's very nice to see you, but can we connect later. This isn't a good time. I just woke up."

"No, we cannot 'connect' later. Ying and I had to haul our asses out here to England to see you because you won't return our calls or texts." His eyebrows snapped together in a frown. "And what do you mean, you just woke up? It's noon."

Albert started to close the door, but Weatherspoon stopped him by slamming his palm against the wood. Albert pushed harder, but the cop leveraged his full three hundred pounds into the return force. Weatherspoon shoved his shoe into the door crack. Albert stepped back, evaluating whether Weatherspoon had the nerve to break down his door. He did.

Ying stepped up to the door. Their eyes connected. It was good to see her face, thought Albert. Those big brown almond eyes. He softened.

"Albert, we need your help. Michael and I have been tailing Moloch. Everything you said would happen is happening. Now, will you just let us in?" Her mild expression shifted to one of conspiratorial humor. "You and I both know that I can use the Tree to get in if I want to, and I'd rather not. I've climbed enough walls lately."

Despite himself, he smiled... and then sighed. Ghosts from the past were knocking at his door. He wanted to turn them away, but he knew they would keep coming back.

He pulled down the chain from the lock and let them in.

Ying and Weatherspoon crossed the threshold of his apartment and looked around. He noted the surprised look on their faces and waited for the inevitable question.

"What happened here?" said Ying.

Albert put his hands in his flannel pajama suit pockets.

"I've been doing some reading."

"Some reading? It looks like your apartment was in a head-on collision with a library."

"Yeah, well, I've been working on figuring out a way to stop Cristina."

While they talked, Weatherspoon began lifting books off the couch and stacking them on the coffee table. Albert couldn't tell if he was attempting to create a sliver of couch on which to sit, or whether the mess was offending him on a personal level.

"And how's that going?" said Ying.

Albert put his hands up and turned in both directions. "How does it *look* like it's going?"

"Not well," said Weatherspoon, paging through one of the cryptography books and barely looking up. "Which makes sense, because you're doing it all by yourself."

"What's that supposed to mean?" said Albert.

Weatherspoon gestured to Albert to sit down. He complied, depositing himself in the studded club chair across from the cop.

"Look, I know nothing about cryptography besides what you all have taught me. But I do know *people*. And this?" He gestured around him. "This ain't healthy."

"What isn't healthy?"

"You. Holed up in here with enough stacks of books to be running a Goodwill surplus store. Sleeping 'til noon. Trying to solve a cipher by yourself that Moloch and his team had thirty code breakers on. Wearing that God forsaken pajama suit that looks like something Bill Cosby would have worn in the 80s. *That's* not healthy." He raised an eyebrow. "And don't think I can't smell the booze on you."

Albert crossed his legs. Crossed his arms. A human 'X'. He knew where this conversation was leading and had no interest in the destination.

"Is this why you guys came here? To take shots at me, my apartment, my life?"

Ying grabbed some more books from off the couch and placed them on the coffee table. She sat down next to Weatherspoon and leaned forward toward Albert. Her face was so kind. He smelled the light fruity fragrance of her hair. It reminded him of better days.

"We didn't come here to take shots at you, Albert. We came here because we want you to come *home*. We can help you with this, and... we need you. Moloch is planning a coup on January 20th. Michael convinced the FBI to set up a task force, but we don't have a lot of resources or time. We need your help."

Albert stood up from his chair and walked into the kitchen nook next to the living room. He grabbed one of his morning breakfast bars, unwrapped the wrapper and nibbled on it. The oats and blueberries settled his stomach. He took out his glass coffee pot and began filling it with water.

"Ying, I wish I could help you, but it's too late."

He placed the coffee pot onto the heating plate and started the coffee maker.

"What do you mean, it's too late?" said Ying.

"Ever since that day in Cristina's office when she told us about her plans, I've been running scenarios of how this plays out. There isn't one where we stop her from taking over. I'm afraid our democracy isn't long for this world."

The coffee maker gurgled in the background, and the smell of ground beans filled the air.

"That's impossible," said Weatherspoon. "Now, I admit we got a little bit of a late start on this, but we've still got over a week."

"Yeah, I thought that at first, too. But then I thought back to something Cristina said to us back in L.A. She mentioned how this whole game of hers was just like chess and that she played the game at a much higher level. She was right. This is just like chess. In chess there's an opening, middlegame, and endgame. But in many games the winner is decided in the middlegame, long before the full game is technically over. The actual details of the ending may vary, but the winner will always be the same. As the old chess saying goes, 'Before the endgame, the gods have placed the middlegame'."

Albert took a triumphant bite of his breakfast bar.

Weatherspoon shifted in his seat and raised an eyebrow. "But in the words of Yogi Berra, 'It ain't over 'til it's over'."

"Michael's right," said Ying. "It's true that the odds are against us, but there's still time. Plus, we don't even know how involved Cristina is in Moloch's plans."

Albert poured out three cups of coffee and laughed. "Ying, if you don't think Cristina is involved with this, then you have even less of a chance than you think."

He handed each of them a cup and started drinking. The coffee stiffened his resolve.

"Look. I appreciate you guys coming out here. And it really is great to see you. But I just can't help you. The RED movement has come too far. We just can't stop it. You should talk to the rest of the people Turner trained in how to use the Tree. The 'Book Club' as he called us. Maybe Brick, Gabe, Salazar, and Ariel can help you."

Weatherspoon and Ying exchanged glances and turned back to Albert.

"What?" said Albert looking at Ying.

She swallowed hard and in a soft tone said, "Albert, Ariel's missing."

Chapter 11

Agent Moini collected Albert, Ying, and Weatherspoon at Dulles Airport that afternoon, driving a nondescript gray sedan with a rideshare sticker in the rear window and wearing a t-shirt and baseball cap. Albert had been on high alert for one of Cristina's goons ever since they had landed, but as the car twisted and turned south along the George Washington Parkway, he relaxed.

Weatherspoon chatted with Moini in the front seat while Ying dozed in the back of the car, leaving Albert with nothing to do except look out the window. The Potomac rumbled along to his left. Foam tumbling off the rocks. His eyes wandered over the rich, robust trees hulking above the river, but all he could see was Ariel Kelly.

She was dead.

In truth, Albert had known she was gone as soon as Ying and Weatherspoon told him she was missing, but he had gotten on the plane back to the States in a vain hope that he could recover her. He owed her that much.

He had spent the flight trying to find any way to avert the middlegame, but by the time they got off the plane, a park ranger in West Virginia had found her: bound, dead of impact injuries. Thankfully, those were her only major injuries. It had been a swift death.

Albert's own relief at that last detail sickened him. He would not wish torture on anyone, least of all a friend, but his calculation–*at least it was quick, at least they didn't question her for long*– had happened instinctively and immediately. It was not a thought he would have had several months ago, and it seemed dangerously detached.

Nor did any of it seem real. How could she be *dead*? When he and Ying had trained with Turner and the Book Club at Brick's farm, Ariel had been all intelligence and control. If you spoke to Ariel, you spoke on her terms. No part of her displayed weakness. Imagining her as a victim–a victim of *anything*–was incongruous. Not to mention, of the Book Club members, she had been the one with the most normal life: a spouse, a child, a home.

His heart ached at the thought, and, despite himself, he craved a drink. He had woken up, now, had come out of his daze, and the shame of his actions was enough to make him want to escape once more.

He knew he couldn't, though. Ying and Weatherspoon had reminded him of what mattered. It wasn't his job to keep everyone else out of danger. It was his job to stop Cristina Culebra and her RED Army, no matter what it took, and that meant harnessing every resource at his disposal. Turner had chosen him to carry on the fight. He couldn't let him down.

Moini turned the car left onto a side road and then right into a secluded driveway. The drive sloped downhill to reveal a peaceful colonial home overlooking a wooded lake. Ducks waddled and quacked along the heather lawn. Moini pulled the car around the circle and stopped at the navy-blue, paneled front door.

Weatherspoon gave a whistle as he exited the front seat and began unpacking the trunk. "You folks at the FBI really know how to host someone."

"Seriously," Ying agreed. "I need to join task forces more often."

"Yeah, OK, take it easy." Moini blew another bubble. "And don't get too comfortable. I had to move heaven and earth just to reserve this through the end of January. After that, they boot our asses out of here."

"We only need until the 20th," Albert murmured.

The others exchanged glances, but no one wanted to tackle that particularly depressing statement.

The group wheeled their suitcases and a few bags of groceries through the front door. Albert paused in the entryway. The house was immaculate. Beautiful dark hardwood floors. Delicate, pastel-colored wallpaper and precisely upholstered couches. Tables so polished he'd be scared to put his drink down. And straight ahead, a pearl kitchen that looked out onto a sanguine gray-blue lake.

"This is beautiful, Agent Moini," said Albert. "But what do you expect us to do here? We have so little time to–"

If he had only woken up sooner, if he had stayed in the states....

She held up her pointer finger. "First, we eat. Then, we talk."

"But–"

"Dr. Puddles, I've run many time-sensitive missions, and I can *assure* you that launching into work on an empty stomach after a long flight, is both miserable *and* counterproductive. I recommend you get your ass upstairs, put your bag away, take a quick shower, and then come back down and have a glass of wine."

Albert was not sure he believed her, but he knew better than to argue. He put his bag upstairs, washed his face, and changed his clothes. He wasn't going to take the time for a full shower, but he *did* feel refreshed and settled by the time he arrived back in the kitchen.

Agent Moini had cracked open a bottle of red wine and poured a glass for each of them and was now moving with single-minded speed. Albert had been gone for a scant couple of minutes, but the grocery bags were unpacked, the stove was on, and she was chopping vegetables like a short-order cook.

Mana was a joy to watch. She placed the meat in a pan, and while that cooked, she mixed some type of sauce that Albert had never seen: rice here, yogurt there, spices both in careful spoonfuls and in generous dashes. A blur of cooking expertise. When Ying and Weatherspoon arrived, the three of them sipped their wine while they observed.

Mana dipped her fingers in the sauce. She licked them and nodded, pleased with herself.

"Can I help you?" Albert asked.

"No, you'll just fuck it up." Her distraction and ready grin took the sting from the words. "Nobody messes with Mana in the kitchen. Sit. Enjoy your wine."

Albert sat and raised his glass to toast the others. "To another adventure."

"To another adventure," they replied in unison, though Albert noticed their smiles carried the same uncertainty as his own.

When he saw Ying's eyes go down, a branching pathway appeared in his mind. She wanted to say something, but she was nervous to do so. He could let her sit with it, or he could open up the conversation, which might derail them...

Or provide a clean slate.

"Ying?" he asked. He waited for her to look up. "What is it?

Ying swirled her wine and took a sip while she thought. "So, what happened to you out there in Cambridge?" she asked at last. "When you left, I thought you were going to take on Cristina, but when we found you..."

"I know. I thought that, too." Albert closed his eyes. The smell of onions, saffron and simmering chicken filled the air. Already, his time in Cambridge seemed like a bad dream. "When I first got to Cambridge, all I *did* was think about how we could stop Cristina, how we could stop the General.... How we could avenge Angus.

"But the more I mapped it out, the more I used the Tree, and the more I watched as state after state after state fell... the more I realized I was too late."

"So, you just gave up?" said Weatherspoon. "That doesn't seem like you."

"No. I definitely thought about it. But no, I didn't give up." Albert reached in his coat pocket and pulled out a leather journal.

Ying perked up in her seat. "The journal!?"

"Yes." Albert turned to Weatherspoon. "Before Angus died, he gave me his journal. The actual Tree of Knowledge. All his notes, his predictions." Albert let his fingers rest lightly on the cover. "Everything."

"Dinner is served," Moini announced. She stepped away from the stove, pans in each hand. "Get yourselves silverware and plates and go sit at the table."

The other three grabbed silverware and their wine glasses and went to sit in the dining room, where the lake shone red from the fading sun.

"So, what does Turner's journal say?" Ying asked.

"I have no idea. I can't break the code." Albert resisted the urge to drink his wine in one gulp.

"What?"

"Yeah. After I realized we were too late to stop Cristina, I felt like my last shot was Angus's journal. Cristina and Moloch obviously wanted the journal, so if they wanted it, I thought there might be something in it that could give us a chance. The only problem was when I tried to crack it, I realized it's uncrackable."

"No code is uncrackable," called Moini as she came into the room. She placed the serving dish on the table and raised her eyebrows at Albert.

Albert prayed for patience. "Yes, *technically*, that's true. But, let me put it this way: whatever key Turner used to create that code would take years to crack. By then, Cristina will be too powerful to stop. She knows that. That, right there, is the only reason we're still alive."

There was a long silence at the table. Ying looked at Weatherspoon, as if hopeful that the policeman had heard something different. Albert drained his glass and reached over for a second bottle of wine.

"And that's when I started drinking," he said, as he opened it.

Mana snorted. If she was discouraged by his assessment, she didn't show it. "Well, you're here, now. And here, we eat and drink."

Ying, Weatherspoon, and Moini dove headfirst into their meals. Even Albert had to admit the smell was intoxicating. Still, he unwrapped one of the nutrition bars he had packed and started eating. He needed *some* form of normalcy after his time in Cambridge.

"This tastes fantastic," said Ying, her words muffled.

"It does!" Weatherspoon shook his head. "What is it exactly, and how have I not known about it, all these years?"

Moini smiled. "It's called 'Tacheen-e-morg', and it's a traditional Persian dish. Persian food isn't very popular in the United States. To get this near Princeton, you would likely have had to be friends with some of the Iranian students. My sisters and I used to cook it together while my mom hovered and told us what we were doing wrong. Good times."

She went to take another bite and then paused. Her gaze fixed on Albert, chewing on his nutrition bar.

"What are you doing, Puddles?"

"Oh, don't mind him." Ying rolled her eyes. "He doesn't eat regular food. He prefers regulating his calories with bars."

Mana raised a peaked eyebrow, sharp enough to cut glass. "Puddles. Don't insult me. Put down the nutrition bar and eat the rice."

"No thanks, Mana. It's nothing personal, just how I prefer to eat."

In response, Mana slapped the bar out of Albert's hand so hard it hit the window. In the shocked silence, she spooned up a plate of food and handed it over to him.

"It's rude to refuse hospitality," she said. "Eat the rice, or you'll find out what my grandmother would do when someone was rude in *her* house. You're on a team, now, Puddles. Act like it."

Albert dutifully took a spoonful of rice and let out an appreciative sound. With his sole link to normalcy lying on the floor next to the window, he expected to be upset... but he couldn't really manage it when the food was so delicious.

Weatherspoon and Ying stifled grins.

"Okay." Moini sat back in her chair and cradled her wine glass. "Now that Puddles is eating like an actual human being, let's talk shop." She rapped on the tabletop with her knuckles. "The first thing I want to know is, what changed, on that rooftop in L.A.? I know that prior to L.A. Cristina Culebra and her people seemed awfully interested in you and your crew. Then Turner gets popped on that rooftop, and *whoosh*–they just let you go. Why? What changed?"

"I've been wondering the same thing," said Weatherspoon. He nodded to Albert and Ying. "When I took you two back to Jersey, I kept eyes on your place and Ying's for months. Nothing."

"It was way too easy to stay hidden," Ying agreed.

"That's what I've been trying to tell you guys." Albert stood up from the table and grabbed a yellow legal pad from his leather satchel. He sat back down at the table and began scribbling.

He wrote the words ABSOLUTE POWER on the left side of the sheet and then began drawing the branches of the decision tree out from the words. His fingers turned deep red as he clenched the pen.

"What do we know is Cristina's end goal?" he asked them rhetorically. "Absolute Power."

"Well, we don't know that," Ying argued.

Weatherspoon sighed. From the look on his face, this was an argument he'd had many times.

"Of course, we do," Albert said bluntly. "She said it herself."

"She didn't *say* it," Ying insisted. "It was on the board in her office. Maybe she just wants power so that she can fix some of this country's problems. God knows we have enough of them. Look at what she's done already."

"Yes, she's been a very effective tyrant, Ying. If she'd wanted to solve problems, *that* would have been the stated goal."

"But–"

"Okay." Albert put out a hand to stop her. Ying was determined to think well of Cristina, and he knew he would get nowhere in a head-to-head argument with her. "Just humor me, for now, and we can go over your theories soon, okay?"

Ying didn't look happy, but she nodded.

"Okay. So, for the purposes of this analysis, our assumption is that Cristina wrote 'Absolute Power' at the center of her diagram because that is what she wants."

"I think that's safe to say," said Moini.

Ying held her tongue, but her face was mutinous.

Albert settled for that, with the guess that it was the best he was going to get. "With that assumption, if we want to know what Cristina is going to do, we have to look at the components of power. What are the ingredients of power? What makes it complete–and, therefore, absolute?"

He drew two branches.

"At the most basic level, power is the ability to make others do what you want them to do. You can do that in one of two ways."

"Through force or through persuasion," said Ying softly. She gave Albert a small smile, and he saw that this was a peace offering of sorts.

He smiled back. "That's right."

Now he sketched lines firing forward from left to right.

"Force can be harnessed through weapons or soldiers. Those weapons and soldiers can be professional or they can be civilian."

More lines.

"They also need to be armed. I'm going to posit that it's no coincidence that Cristina happens to run a defense company that manufactures and stores weapons."

"She also runs military schools that crank out thousands of soldiers every year," said Weatherspoon.

"That would set her up for a war," Ying argued, "and I know you think I'm giving her too much credit, but, seriously, think this through. She's not stupid, you all know that. And you'd have to be stupid to take on the U.S. military."

"True," Albert acknowledged. "In a *war*. But how else can military victory be achieved? By the surrender of the other side. And, as you found out, Moloch's meeting with generals. He wants to scare them into *capitulating*. That would give her a near monopoly on force."

"What about civilian arms?" Moini pointed out. "We've still got three hundred million civilian weapons in this country. Not normally something the FBI considers a positive, by the way. Ah, how, times change." She took a sip of wine.

Albert shook his head grimly. "We used to have that many, but not anymore. Cristina made it a condition of joining the Republic that citizens had to surrender all weaponry 'for public safety', so, if you live in a RED state, the only weapons are held by the government."

"The Governor of Texas was in negotiations with her about that," Moini pointed out. "It didn't sound like it was an absolute thing."

"Yeah, but how are we going to know if it is? News is now passing largely through her networks." Albert sighed. "And, almost every day, a new state joins the Republic."

"And that's why you think we're fucked." Moini considered.

"Yes–and, more to the point, so does Cristina... which is why she stopped caring about us. Turner saw this coming. But once he was dead, and we were scattered, she knew that even if we did anticipate her next moves, we would be too late to stop her." He gave a humorless laugh. "Oh, and I haven't even gotten to the worst part, believe it or not. The *persuasion* part of the equation is the real kicker."

Weatherspoon considered this, then took another, heaping serving of food. His expression said that, if they were completely screwed, he was going to go out with a full belly.

Albert swiped his pen on the legal pad seven times and wrote seven words before tapping his pen on each in turn. "Reciprocity, commitment, social proof, authority, liking, scarcity, unity. She can pull every one of these levers because she's got nearly everyone in the Republic watching RED TV, surfing the RED Network, and posting pictures on RED Social."

"She won't even need the weapons and the soldiers," said Weatherspoon.

"Probably not."

Ying stood up from the table and began pacing. "But what about Moloch? He's the one who killed Turner, and who *probably* killed Ariel. *He's* the one who's meeting with generals to overthrow the government."

Albert put his pencil down and took another long sip of wine. He thought for a moment.

"Maybe you're right, Ying. Maybe Moloch is worse than Cristina. But regardless of who's pulling the strings, the path they're taking is very clear, and right now, we're too far behind to catch them."

"Then why are you here?" Ying's composure was breaking down. "Why come with us at all?"

Albert stood up from the table and grabbed the remote to the TV. He flipped channels until he hit a news station. The headlines showed scenes from the Culebra rally alongside a graphic of the spinning sword. He changed to another news channel. Again, the Cipher image and an expert talking about cryptography. He switched to the local news. The Cipher led the top stories.

"*That's* why I'm here," said Albert.

"The Cipher." Weatherspoon chuckled. "I've gotta be honest, I'm not even sure she didn't plant it herself."

"She didn't," Albert said, with absolute certainty. "Someone else did, and that someone understands that they can't fight her on her terms. Cristina Culebra's rise to power was built on a very delicate equation. And right now, The Cipher is the one variable that she didn't count on."

Ying nodded. "So, what do you want to do?"

Albert paused the television.

"I want to do what it says: 'Solve the cipher. Follow the Cipher'."
"

Ying rubbed her hands together. "Sounds like we got work to do."

Albert only smiled.

Chapter 12

Albert sat at the kitchen table engrossed in one of the two computer screens he had set up in their temporary war room. The clock showed it was just after 4 AM, but he was barely aware of the passage of time. He frantically tapped the cursor keys up and down, searching. Weatherspoon had gone to bed, and Moini had returned to her family. Ying sat at the kitchen island, slumped over with her head pillowed on her arms, trying to catch some much-needed sleep.

"Ying, I think I've got something," shouted Albert.

"No more gummy worms!" shouted Ying, awoken from her dream. Her head snapped up from the kitchen island. She wiped drool from her face.

"Sounds like you were having quite the dream over there."

"Oh, man. I dreamed gummy worms were chasing me in a cartoon field. Very disturbing."

Albert shook his head and turned back to his screen.

Ying tiptoed over, pulled a chair next to him and sat down. She leaned forward and stared at the monitor. "This spreadsheet is just delightful," she announced after a moment. She pressed her hand to her lips in a dramatic chef's kiss. "What am I looking at?"

Albert waved his hand along the two screens. The left screen displayed a zoomed-in image of the flaming sword, and the coded symbols that ran across the blade. The right screen showed an interminable spreadsheet with those same symbols in the first column and a different set of letters in the neighboring column.

"You know how you told me that since we weren't having any luck with the Vigenère, Bellaso, or other traditional cipher methods, I should write a simple program to convert symbols into letters at random and then flag the conversions that had more than one known word?"

"Yeah?"

"Ta Da!" He splayed out his hands toward the two screens on his desk.

"And my friends said you were no fun," said Ying as she kissed his cheek, knocking his glasses askew.

"Your friends told you I was no fun?" He adjusted his glasses back on his face with a wounded expression.

Ying didn't respond. She wasn't prepared to answer questions from Albert on why she was talking to her friends about him. Instead, she gestured at the screen. "So, did we hit the jackpot?"

Albert pulled up a table with row after row of jumbled letters. He scrolled through the spreadsheet. Occasionally, a word would pop up, but the rest would be gibberish. When he reached line two thousand five hundred and seven, he stopped and pointed to the cell. It read:

You will find the Cipher here:

https://
www.cipherwkhpilnemxj7asaniu7vnjjbiltxjqhye3mhbshg7k
x5tfyd.onion/

Albert watched as Ying leaned her face inches away from the screen, mouth agape. From the glow, he could see her nostrils flaring, a funny habit of hers he had noticed when she was concentrating.

"Whaaaaaat." She drew the word out in a long breath and then turned to him, wide-eyed. "This is a Tor address." She started shaking his shoulders while she talked. "Do you know what that means? Looks like we're about to take a river boat ride into the dark web. This is amazing."

Albert stood up from his chair and paced the cold wood floors.

"I don't know. Should we even go to the site?" He spoke quickly and as he got excited the words fired out of his mouth at an increasing rate. "Most people use .onion domains because they don't want to be tracked because they're doing something illegal. I'm not enthusiastic about being part of the underground drug trade or a child sex ring."

Ying grabbed a gummy worm out of the bag she had left on the table and started gnawing on it.

Albert looked askance, but decided not to mention her nightmare.

"Oh, we're definitely going to the site. We didn't spend the night on this just to turn back, now. And I'm pretty confident that underground child sex rings don't go around hacking presidents. Not exactly good for business. Besides, we can definitely sell *you* for good money on the black market if worse comes to worse."

"*Me?*"

"You're very smart, in good health—you could be a household bookkeeper for some rich person somewhere." She smiled and grabbed the mouse.

Albert took a long look at Ying, the bun on her head bobbing up and down as she clicked. *This* was why he enjoyed her company so much, and why he had missed her: She took him to places he would never go...

... for better or worse. He sighed and sat back down next to her. "I guess you're right."

"Awesome." She opened her Tor browser and looked over at him. "You ready to light this rocket?"

"Commence launch." He grinned back. He couldn't help but wonder. If Ying had gone with him to Cambridge would things have been different? Would they have been able to crack the code to Turner's journal? Would he have stopped drinking? Would he be happier?

The thought made him flush.

Luckily, she didn't seem to notice. Her eyes darted between the two windows as she typed in the URL.

"That's a terrible rocket joke by the way, but I'll lean into it. 3... 2...1..." She pressed the Enter key. "And liftoff."

The familiar flaming sword stood guard over the website in the center of the screen.

Albert searched the screen for a menu.

Nothing.

He hunted for an 'Enter' button.

Nothing.

He clicked the top of the page. The bottom. Left and right.

Nothing.

"What the hell? There's nothing here."

Ying scratched her head and leaned in closer to the screen. She hummed as she searched for an answer. Another endearing habit of hers.

"Check the source code."

Albert pulled up the source code that powered the mysterious website. He scrolled through the lines of code and stopped. Amidst row after row of code stood another flaming sword. This time letters, dashes, and spaces combined to form the swords outline.

Ying smiled. "Stick with me, kid."

Beneath the sword ran five hundred rows of numbers.

Albert ran his finger down the screen along the rows. "Are these...?"

"GPS coordinates!" Ying finished excitedly.

Albert opened Google and searched the first set of coordinates. The first was in London. The others returned a location in Johannesburg, one in Tokyo, and the fourth:

42.347153, -71.145578

"That would be..." He hit Enter and nodded. "Boston."

Ying jumped up from her chair.

"Boston! We can get *there*. I'll get my coat!"

"*What*? Ying, it's five in the morning!"

"Perfect! No traffic." Her voice echoed back into the room as she ran across the hall. A few moments later she was back wearing a giant vintage sweater with a cartoon Alice from Alice in Wonderland at its center.

Albert looked her up and down and laughed. "Is that what you're wearing?"

Ying shrugged. "It's sort of appropriate, don't you think? I mean, we are headed down the rabbit hole... aren't we?"

Chapter 13

Eva sat on a cushioned wicker chair on the stone balcony of the Mandarin Oriental Hotel, overlooking the magnificent expanse of Central Park. A beige row of buildings served as a backdrop to the winding rows of snow-covered trees. Bundled couples strolled the sidewalk holding hands. Cyclists swayed back and forth along the trails. It was Sunday morning. Time for her weekly breakfast with her mother, a tradition the two had observed since she was a child.

Eva used to love these meals. She would talk to her mother about the perils of childhood, the gossip at school, the boys, the cliques. Her mother would teach her about the world, reminding Eva that the world was larger than the problems that seemed so pressing to her at the time.

Eva welcomed these lessons on what to look out for, *who* to look out for. She could not stop caring about the events of her own life, but it was comforting to remember that there was more beyond them. She listened as her mother taught her how to succeed, and about what gave life meaning. She especially welcomed her mother's reminders of what she could become.

On a good day, her mother would give her riddles. Eva saw a man in hospital scrubs trundling along the sidewalk below and thought of one of her favorites: The Surgeon and the Son. In the riddle, a father, and son drive along a narrow, winding country road when an oncoming vehicle strikes their car, causing a horrific accident. The son suffers grave injuries, and the paramedics transport the father and son to the hospital, where they wheel the boy into the operating room for emergency surgery. But, just before the surgery begins, the surgeon stops and says, "I can't operate on this boy. He's my son."

Eva recalled struggling with the riddle, asking the inevitable questions. Was the father mistaken? Was the surgeon mistaken? Is he a stepson? Does he have a doppelgänger? She labored for several minutes. How could this be possible? Then it hit her. "The surgeon is a woman!"

Her mother had smiled with pride. "That's right, my Evalita. Now, let that be a reminder to you. The world tells you that a surgeon must be a man. And if you're not careful, soon you'll think that, too–as you did when I first asked you the question. But the world is wrong." She ended that lesson the same way she ended all the others:

"You can be...?"

"...whatever I want, Mama," Eva would say.

Eva could not remember when, exactly, she had come to dread these breakfasts, but she knew it was after her mother had introduced her to the Tree of Knowledge. Once she had learned the principles of it, the two could rehearse their conversations in their minds without saying a word. *If I say this, she will say that. Then, I'll say this. Then, she'll say that.* And so on. Now, too much of their time at breakfast consisted of alternately smiling at each other and looking out at the view. Occasionally, they would ask each other for a piece of information that they couldn't map out, but the mother-daughter connection was lost.

Today, however, Eva had come to breakfast with purpose. To find the truth.

"My Evalita," Cristina said as she threw open both patio doors and swept out onto the balcony. She wore a black mink coat and giant sunglasses that looked like they had been placed on her face by Audrey Hepburn herself.

Eva shook her head and smiled. It was always a grand entrance with her mother, and she had noticed that her mother's breakfast entrances had become even more dramatic and luxurious since her political career had taken root. Now, Cristina was almost always wearing her red suit in public, so she used her rare private moments to show a different side of herself.

"Hi, Mom." Eva stood to give her mother a hug, and she held on for an extra beat.

"Uh-oh." Her mother pulled away and tapped Eva on the nose. "What's wrong? That was a serious hug, not a happy hug."

Moms know all, Eva thought. *Even when they* don't *have the Tree of Knowledge.* That made her mother a double threat.

For now, she managed a smile. "I'll talk while we eat."

The two women sat down at the table. A smorgasbord of food was laid out: eggs, French toast, pancakes, bacon, fruit, juice, coffee. Cristina always over-ordered for these meals, a remnant of her days in Chile when food was scarce. Eva poured herself a coffee to ward off the chill. She didn't feel much like eating. The familiar smell of French vanilla calmed her.

"I need to talk to you about something," Eva said finally. She had envisioned this conversation in her mind a thousand times. She had kept her wording vague to see how her mother responded.

"I'm pretty sure I know what this is about," said Cristina as she filled her plate with eggs, bacon, and French toast. Eva could never understand how her mother could eat so much and stay so thin.

"Do you?" said Eva, raising an eyebrow.

"Yes. Your mission the other night." Cristina took a large bite of eggs and chewed neatly.

And that's why we don't talk anymore, thought Eva. She and her mother could both anticipate everything the other was going to say, so what was the point of having the conversation?

Or... they could when they had the same information. And so, she had to know what her mother knew.

"Yes," she said, now, as neutrally as she could. "After we detained those journalists, the Gen–"

"You mean terrorists?" Cristina placed her fork down on her plate with a clink and turned her undivided attention on Eva. The smile was still on her face, and Eva could almost swear that her mother hadn't moved a single muscle, but there was no warmth in the smile any longer.

Eva looked inside herself at the reactions her mother's expression evoked. She had the sense of having breached a social norm and recognized her own urge to apologize. Cristina was a master of this game, and her reaction had been both deliberate and unusual. She was not reminding Eva of the party line, as she normally would. That reminder would be a sign of treating Eva as a colleague.

Cristina was, instead, treating her as an inferior, her expression conveying both the logic and the disappointment that she needed to remind Eva of it at all: *They're not journalists, they're terrorists. Because if they're journalists and we abduct them, that's bad. But if they're terrorists and we detain them, that's good.*

But the Tree split off into a branch she would not have expected, and Eva followed it. Cristina might not simply be treating her as an inferior. Perhaps the woman no longer saw the distinction. The thought was unsettling, and she had to test the branch at once.

"No," she said, in the light, impersonal tone her mother had taught her. "I've seen no evidence that they were terrorists, nor did I notice from their dossiers that any of them were influential."

"Please, Eva. Don't be so naïve."

Eva took a deep breath and sipped her coffee. She had expected her mother's defense: distraction. What she had *not* expected was the unusual undercurrent of emotion in her mother's voice.

When Cristina was certain of herself, pushback was greeted with smiles, and so, she was out of her element, now. The knowledge was cold, and almost unwelcome, but Eva had been trained too thoroughly in the Tree to stop just because she had worries about what she might learn.

She disregarded her mother's insult. "After all of them had been detained, Moloch and I agreed to meet at a secure location outside the city for the interrogation. Neither he nor the detainees showed up."

A flash of worry passed across Cristina's face and vanished just as quickly. She picked up her fork and resumed eating her French toast. "And?" Her voice was calm again; whatever worry she had felt, she had masked it.

"What I'm saying is that I don't think those journalists ever made it to New York." Eva used the same tone and expression her mother had used a few moments before: *I'm going to spell this out for you, but I should not have to.*

"Please, Eva." Cristina gave an artful sigh and dabbed at her mouth with her napkin. "Let us not descend into dramatics. I'm sure Isaac just diverted them to another location. Have you spoken with him about it?"

Isaac, Eva noted, detached. *Isaac instead of the General. So smooth. A General could do unspeakable things, but not Isaac. Isaac is your friend.*

"I haven't," she heard herself say. "I wanted to talk with you, first."

Her mom painted on her best smile and sat back in her chair.

"Well, I appreciate you coming to me with this, and I will look into it first thing when I get into the office. I'll let you know what I find out."

Eva put down her coffee cup. She was genuinely unsettled, now. Her mother did not know what was going on, that much was clear, and she had been worried by the information Eva brought. At the same time, she was continuing to shield Moloch and erect roadblocks between Eva and the truth.

That was not good. It was not normal.

To her surprise, it made her angry, and so she chose a path of the Tree that she would not normally use. Her voice was cold as she asked,

"Why *are* we abducting journalists? This isn't who we are. This isn't what RED's about."

Cristina stood up from her chair so fast that Eva wondered if her mother was going to strike her. The older woman's finger came up to point at Eva's face.

"Those were not *journalists,*" she said. Her voice was not as crisp as it should have been. "I have now told you that twice, and I

OF GOOD & EVIL

should not have had to say it at all. I will not say it again, Eva. Those were terrorists who were hellbent on stopping our movement."

There was a pause. Eva knew exactly what was expected of her, and she also knew that she was going to do none of it.

"Were?" she asked softly, echoing the verb tense. *You think they're dead. You didn't know what he had done, but you assume they're dead.*

Fury flashed in Cristina's face, and again, it was mixed with panic.

Again, she deflected. "Think of what we've done in such a short time," she said, and stood up straight. "Children are actually *learning* in our schools. Neighborhoods are safe." She took a long breath through her nose and brought her hands to her chest. "The *air* is cleaner, for God's sake. Do you want to go back to the way things were?"

I see what you're doing. "You know my answer to that. You know how strongly I believe in our new world." Eva knew that her voice was trembling with emotion. She meant this with every fiber of her being. She waited for her mother to relax slightly before finishing her statement: "And I want it to be better for *everyone*. I don't want to terrorize innocent people."

"Innocent? You call people who are plotting an insurrection against us *innocent*?" Cristina began to pace.

Debating with her mother was like resisting the tide. Cristina's arguments always drew her opponents toward the rocks with false choices. *Are you on the side of terrorists? Are you against clean air? Don't you want the kids to learn? Aren't you against insurrection?*

Eva had to stay focused on what mattered. "What about Albert? What about Angus?"

Cristina stopped pacing. She looked out over the park. She said nothing. Eva wondered what thoughts danced through the queen's mind. After a minute Cristina walked over to Eva and sat in the chair next to her, pulling it close. She grabbed Eva's hands.

"Evalita, there isn't a moment that goes by that I don't think about that day. I loved Angus. I really did. He was a good man, and he taught me so much. More than that, he gave me you. And I should not have hidden the truth from you. That was wrong. But you know that I never intended for him to die. If I could go back and change it, I would. But I can't."

Eva searched her mother's eyes. She saw genuine contrition, the same regret Eva held for that security guard back in Princeton. But beneath, in the depths of her mother's eyes, she saw something else. Something familiar. Something she had seen in Moloch's eyes a few nights ago. The spark of fanaticism.

Eva pulled her hands away and stood up. She placed her napkin on the table. Her mother watched her every movement. Eva needed to know one more thing before she left.

"And what about Albert? You ran him out of the country, for God's sake." Her voice shook, and it surprised her.

Cristina stood up as well. She was graceful, now; her own moment of weakness had passed. "I didn't run him out of the country. He left because he's a coward. He doesn't want to be a part of what we're doing for this country, but he doesn't want to fight it, either. The only thing I can say for him is that he's smart enough to know when he's been beaten."

Eva gathered her purse, slung it over her shoulder and opened one of the patio doors to head inside. Just before she closed it behind her, she turned back to her mother. "That's the point mom. It's not always about beating people."

"Where do you think you're going?"
Eva called over her shoulder and didn't look back.
"A place I should have gone a long time ago."

Part 2
Ethereal

He drove the man out; and at the east of the Garden of Eden He assigned the cherubim and the flaming sword which turned every direction to guard the way to the tree of life.

–Genesis: 3:24

Chapter 14

The Shrine of Fatima rested atop a gentle hill in a tidy, Catholic neighborhood in Boston. Albert and Ying exited the car and took in the setting. The January wind bit into Albert's cheeks. He raised the collar of his camel overcoat to shield himself. The surrounding neighborhood was quiet. Pine trees a hundred feet high, dusted with snow encased the large, rectangular plot. The shrine stood still and empty.

Hundreds of years ago, a small group of monks had constructed a monastery on this site. As the two wound their way up the footpath toward the shrine, Albert noticed a graveyard resting steps away from the entrance. Albert swore he could hear the monks' voices echoing in the winter wind.

"Well, this is the creepiest place I've been to in a while," said Albert, looking over both shoulders.

Ying grabbed his hand. The tall lights of the neighboring houses reflected off her face, giving it a pale hew. Graveyards, dead monks, howling wind, the chill in the air. The whole scene reminded him of a horror movie. He remembered, now, why he never liked horror movies.

"Yeah, it's definitely creepy," said Ying. "Hopefully, this Cipher has something good for us." She rubbed her hands to fend off the frost.

The pair reached the front doors of the shrine. It was a futuristic hexagonal building with large glass panes separated by occasional rows of light brick. In the center of the shrine stood a statue of the Virgin Mary bent slightly at the waist praying. Mary wore intricately embroidered cream robes and a brilliant, blue crown that luminesced in the evening light.

"Why do they call it the shrine of Fatima? They didn't teach me a lot about this in Buddhism, but I'm pretty sure that's the Virgin Mary," said Ying.

Albert laughed. "They taught me too much about this at my mom's Catholic Church, so I can tell you that is definitely the Virgin Mary."

Ying pulled out her phone and searched: *Shrine of Fatima.*

"It says here that Fatima is the town in Portugal where in 1917 the Virgin Mary appeared. Three little peasant children, Francisco, Jacinta, and Lucia were tending their family's sheep when a brilliant lady in white appeared, floating above a bush."

Albert reached for the door handle. "That would certainly get your attention."

Ying laughed. "I don't think that door's going to be op–"

The door opened.

"What were you saying?"

"It's 9 PM on a Saturday. I assumed it would be closed."

"Yeah, you definitely didn't go to Catholic church. A lot of churches and sites leave their doors open as a sign of openness and welcoming."

Albert followed Ying inside. The wind slammed the door shut behind him.

His heart jumped through his chest.

"Jesus, you scared the shit out of me," whispered Ying.

"I scared the shit out of myself."

Albert squinted his eyes and scanned the surroundings. The shrine was remarkably simple. A stained-glass mural of Jesus watched over the room. On the rear wall hung three panels with a variety of pictures posted by parishioners and a sign that said, "The Three Secrets of Fatima". The Virgin Mary stood at the center of the room surrounded by smaller statues, two lambs and three women in sky blue dresses with white aprons, not unlike the Alice on Ying's sweatshirt. The coincidence unnerved him.

"I think this Cipher guy is toying with us," said Albert. "What do you say we go someplace warm that doesn't remind me of the Exorcist and sort this out?"

"Absolutely not. Not until we find out why the Cipher sent us here."

"We don't even know what we're looking for, Ying."

Ying tapped on her phone and resumed reading.

"Well let's learn a little more about Fatima, and maybe that will point us in the right direction. It says that from May through October of 1917, on the 13th day of the month, the Virgin Mary would appear before little Francisco, Jacinta, and Lucia and speak to them. Being nice responsible children, they told their parents about what was happening, and their parents soon told other villagers." Ying continued to run her finger over her phone, scanning the text. "Pretty soon people were coming from all over to see what the fuss was about. In September, Mary told Lucia, the oldest child, that she would make one more appearance and deliver her final message. Seventy thousand people came to Fatima that day to witness the miracle. On the 13th, as she had before, Mary appeared, but was only visible to the children. She shared three secrets with the children and then pointed to the sky. Lucia told everyone to look to the sun where there was a so-called 'sun miracle'.

Albert rolled his eyes and wandered around the shrine, inspecting the decorations scattered throughout.

"And what were these three secrets?"

"I'm glad you asked, Albert. The first secret says, 'The light seemed to penetrate the earth, and we saw, as it were, a sea of fire.' Does that mean anything to you?

"A sea of fire?" He looked around the shrine for something that would resonate. "Nope, nothing."

Albert continued to walk toward the back of the shrine. He looked at the boards with pictures that visitors had pinned to them. Each board was labeled Secret One, Secret Two, and Secret Three. He made his way from left to right. The pictures varied. Pictures of Jesus. Pictures of Mary. Pictures of smiling families. Pictures of lost soldiers. He thought of Angus. *What would he do?*

"OK. Secret number two has something to do with the consecration of Russia. Does that mean anything to you?"

"Nope. I haven't been boning up on my Russian history lately."

Albert made his way to the third board.

"Me, neither. I guess we'll dive into that later. Secret number three. 'At the left of Our Lady and a little above, we saw an Angel with a flaming sword in his left hand; flashing, it gave out flames that looked as though they would set the world on fire'. "

Albert spun around.

"Wait! Did you just say flaming sword?"

Ying smiled back. "I sure did."

He spun back to the third board of pictures. Ying sprinted over to him. The two scanned the photos looking for anything that could be from The Cipher. Nothing stood out. A picture of someone's dog. Mary in the manger. Jesus haloed in gold light.

"Here!"

Ying ripped a picture off the board and shoved it two inches from Albert's face.

A gold flaming sword hovering in a bright blue sky stared back at him.

Ying flipped the picture over to reveal a message written in simple block letters.

"SPEAK OF THINGS PUBLIC TO THE PUBLIC, BUT OF THINGS LOFTY AND SECRET ONLY TO THE LOFTIEST AND MOST PRIVATE OF YOUR FRIENDS. HAY TO THE OX AND SUGAR TO THE PARROT."

Chapter 15

Albert's bare-bones Corolla rental car sputtered through the snow and slush of I-90. The flakes fell faster, now. His wipers fought a vain battle to keep up. The wind howled through the poorly sealed windows, and the bald tires shimmied and danced on the concrete below. Drivers in other cars rubbernecked as they passed, trying to gain a glimpse at who could possibly be driving a car so slowly.

"Uh, Ying. I'm not sure we should be driving in this weather," said Albert.

"I have total confidence in you, Albert. Especially since you're practically moving backwards, you're driving so slowly. It's like you're trying to sneak up on the highway." She paused and giggled to herself. "Can you believe we were the first ones to solve the Cipher?"

"How do you know we're the first ones?"

"Unless whoever did this is going back to the shrine every day and putting up a new picture of a flaming sword, I'm pretty sure we're the first ones. At least in Boston. Now, let's see what we can find out about this picture. Have you ever heard this quote before? 'Speak of things public to the public, but of things lofty and secret only to the loftiest and most private of your friends. Hay to the ox and sugar to the parrot'."

Albert leaned forward and willed his eyes to see through the blur in front of him. The road was more of a rumor at this point than an actual object in his field of vision.

"Yeah, it's a quote from Johannes Trithemius in *Steganographia*. But right now, I'm just trying to make sure I don't kill us both."

"OK. That gives us something. I mean, Trithemius invented steganography, or it was named after him or something. Did you know, in ancient times they used to do crazy things to hide messages. They would shave a guy's head bald, then write a message and then let his hair grow out to cover it. Or they would put a message they wanted to hide in wax and then stick that side to a backing, and then put a harmless message on the front side, so nobody would think to look on the back side."

"Ahh, those were the days. Yeah, there must be something encoded in this card."

"I hope so, or this weekend's been a real bust."

Albert looked over to Ying and smiled. Out of the corner of his eye, red lights burst through the storm. He slammed the breaks and felt the car fishtail on the ice. He released his foot from the brake and spun the wheel back to center. The car was sliding, now. The brakes were useless. He reached his right arm out in front of Ying and braced for impact.

The nose of their sedan missed the rear of the car in front of him by inches. Albert looked into the rearview mirror. The car behind him hurtled toward them. The horn pounding in his ears.

The driver swerved around them. Albert's Toyota slid onto the shoulder to a stop.

"Are you OK?" he asked Ying. His arm still draped across her chest.

"Yeah, you?" She blushed and removed his hand.

"Yeah, sorry." His cheeks ran red, as well.

"How about we sit here for a moment while we figure out this Cipher thing?"

Albert calculated the probabilities: the likelihood of a stopped car being hit, of them being buried in snow–he was getting loopy. Albert rubbed the prominent bridge of his nose and took a deep breath. "I think that's a good idea."

"OK. What were we talking about?"

Ying took off her pompom hat and dusted the snow off it.

"We were talking about the fact that this picture and message probably has some type of cipher going on. We just don't know what kind. I know in *Steganographia*, Trithemius frequently used the Ave Maria cipher, where words are replaced by Latin expressions about Jesus, which would certainly fit this card, but I'm looking at the message on the back and there's nothing particularly unique about it. No unique letter styles, no Latin phrases."

"Yeah, but Trithemius didn't just use ciphers. He also used covertext. It's got to be hidden in the picture, then. Try this. Try flashing your camera light on it. Can you see anything underneath the picture? Any other tones?"

Ying turned on the light of her phone's camera. The beam lit up their car as vehicles tore by on the snowy highway. She leaned in closer.

"No, nothing."

"Yeah, I figured. We're going to need a black light. Do you have one?"

"Yeah, I carry one around for special emergencies like this."

She dug into the pocket of her jeans.

"You do?"

"No, of course, I don't have a black light with me." She rolled her eyes at Albert's gullibility.

"Good one," said Albert. "Very helpful."

"You know where there are black lights a plenty?" said Ying. She smiled and raised a mischievous brow.

Albert scrunched his forehead. "No, but I don't think I'm going to like this."

She pointed out the window. "The comic convention."

Albert looked out the window. Above them, beside the highway stood an illuminated, parking lot hotel sign that read "Super Megafest Comic Con. Welcome!"

"No... way... They won't even let me in wearing this." He pointed to his sweater and slacks.

"Don't worry. I've got an idea. Just drive. It's only two minutes away from here."

"I do not like the sound of this."

Albert shook his head and placed the gear shift into drive. He turned on his right blinker and puttered down the shoulder, steadily gaining speed as they merged onto the slush drenched highway.

After two harrowing minutes Albert turned the car into the entrance of the New England Super Megafest Comic Convention at the Sheraton Hotel. Even in the inhospitable weather the parking lot was packed. Avengers, Batmans, Stormtroopers, Jedis all slid their way through the snow and ice to enter the hotel lobby.

"OK, what's your plan?" asked Albert.

"Take your sweater off."

"What?"

"Take your sweater off."

"Why?"

"Just do it."

He took off his sweater so that he was wearing only a button down and slacks.

Ying removed her keys from her bag and stabbed them through the shirt. She began ripping his shirt sleeve off along the seam line.

"What? Why?

"You're going to be the hulk after he shrinks back down to size. Bruce Banner, post-hulk."

Albert wriggled as Ying ripped the sleeves of his shirt and bottom half of his pants. The frigidity of the evening ran across his skin. Goosebumps broke out across his arms and legs. Ying rubbed her hands back and forth along his arms to warm him up.

She noticed the wound from back in Cambridge on Albert's shoulder. "What happened to your arm?"

"Oh, that? It's nothing. I… I ran into a coat hook."

Ying frowned and leaned closer to inspect the wound.

Albert pulled back and tried to change the subject. "I look ridiculous."

"Yes, you do. But it will be good enough to get us in the door and get us a black light."

Albert nodded and untucked his shirt.

Ying took some lotion out of her purse and squirted it on her hands. She rubbed it in her fingers and then teased Albert's hair higher and higher into the air to mimic Bruce Banner's disheveled style. She grabbed green eye shadow from her bag and slapped it on his face and chest.

Ying leaned back to admire her handiwork.

"It's not good. But it's not the worst thing I've ever seen at a Comic-Con."

"And what, may I ask, are you going to be? Wonder Woman?"

Ying threw her hair into pigtails and, to Albert's shock, shimmied off her sweater and jeans, down to her underwear and bra.

Albert gaped at her, then looked away with his cheeks flaming. "Uh, Ying..."

"Albert, I'm an Asian woman at a comic convention," Ying said, with a businesslike tone that would not have been out of place in a boardroom. It was so convincing that Albert turned back to make sure she was still in her underwear.

She was. He looked away again.

"Uh... yeah?"

"Do you seriously not get it? The depictions of women in these things are so sexist I could be just about any female anime character you can think of. Now, let's go!"

**

Bruce Banner and Generic Anime Girl entered the crowded lobby of the Sheraton. Characters from all different dimensions mingled amongst each other and drank mysterious cocktails out of undersized plastic cups. Ying swiped a couple of guest badges previous guests had left on a side table. Albert made eye contact with the hotel manager who appeared to be questioning why he ever agreed to host this convention in the first place. Ying's anime costume drew appreciative nods, while Albert's Hulk garnered looks of bemused disapproval.

OF GOOD & EVIL

"This is humiliating," said Albert as they blew past the meet and greet and ambled toward the main convention hall.

"It's exciting! We're about to see the mystery behind this pic."

In the commotion of near-death experiences and rapid costume changes, Albert had almost forgotten why they were there.

The couple turned the corner and entered a convention hall draped in spectacle. A large black dais with microphones and glasses of water anchored the back of the room. In front and in all directions around the dais stood booths of all sorts and shapes. Captain America and the Iron Man snapped photos with onlookers at the Marvel booth, while Wonder Woman and Batman posed by the DC comics station. Aliens roamed the floors and dwarves mingled with giants. Albert couldn't stop himself from staring.

"Jackpot!" said Ying pointing to a dark booth covered in neon graffiti writing. "I guarantee you those guys are using a black light."

Albert and Ying walked toward the booth. In front stood a tattooed man with spiky hair and eyeliner. Behind him Albert could see a black light glowing purple. The two walked past the tattooed man around the side of the steampunk graphic novel booth. Ying pulled back the rear curtain and snuck inside. Albert peeked his head outside. Most of the costume-clad conventioneers were distracted by the various goings on, but Albert noticed something amiss out of the corner of his eye. In the right corner of the hall stood a man in black. He stared at Albert, watching, but did not move.

Albert ducked his head back into the booth.

"Ying, we need to hurry."

"OK, OK."

Ying removed the picture from her purse. Albert noticed that her hands shook. As she slid the picture under the black light, the image of Jesus faded to the background, replaced by a mysterious message in haunting neon handwriting.

"A MAN WHO TRIES TO ACT VIRTUOUSLY WILL SOON COME TO GRIEF AT THE HANDS OF THE UNSCRUPULOUS PEOPLE SURROUNDING HIM."

There was a pause.

Ying looked at Albert. "This doesn't bode well for us."

Chapter 16

Cristina Culebra's black, bulletproof SUV navigated the crowd of reporters and onlookers. The vehicle stopped outside the RED Network's new headquarters in the old Port Authority building in Chelsea, Manhattan.

The new President issued an obligatory smile and wave to the assembled crowd as she exited the vehicle and entered the coffee-colored brick structure. Cristina strode through the gold polished doors and marveled at how her architects had transformed this staid former government building into a bustling hive of innovation. Bright colors and murals burst from every angle. Snack jars lined the walls, and ping-pong tables stood ready to host a game. Young employees huddled over laptops at common room tables and typed frantically at standing desks. The aura of the place infused her with energy. She would have loved nothing more than to roll up her sleeves and dive into a problem with one of them, but she was here on more important business.

Cristina and her entourage marched through the echoey workspace. The clomp of heels clicking against the tile floor reverberated through the high ceilings. General Moloch marched in step beside her, trailed by security personnel and hangers-on.

"Did you get anything from those reporters you picked up the other night?" she asked without preamble.

Moloch looked straight ahead as the two walked down the corridor.

"No, Madame President. There appears to be no connection between the Cipher and any known agitators."

"What did you do after you interrogated them?"

"Madame President, these details are the things it would be better for you not to know. It is important for you to keep your hands clean, and... well, it is unpleasant. I think it would be better for me not to say any more."

Cristina stopped short just before they entered the elevator, nearly causing an entourage pileup. She looked back with one eyebrow raised and everyone besides Moloch backpedaled to give them space.

Cristina grabbed Moloch by the collar and pulled him into the elevator. She hit the button to the top floor and waited for the doors to close. The second they shut, she spun and pointed at Moloch.

"You're right, Isaac. I *don't* want to know. But, from here on out, I don't want you pulling any of that third world dictator shit again, are we clear?"

"Yes, Madame President." He kept his face serene, but she thought he looked hurt.

"Remember, we're here to serve people, not terrorize them."

"Yes, Madame President."

"I expect you, of all people, to remember that dead bodies spark questions."

"Yes, Madame President."

Somehow, his agreement made her anger flare out of control, and she felt her lip curl as she looked over at him. "Eva is *this* close to leaving me because of that stunt you pulled, and I'm *not* losing my daughter because of you. Got it?"

Now, the hurt was clear, but he nodded once more. "Yes, Madame President."

The elevator pinged and the doors opened. Cristina fired her best smile and walked off the elevator.

"Good, now, let's see what the kids have been up to."

She swung open both doors of the fishbowl conference room on the top floor and with a booming voice shouted, "Alright, what've we got?"

A crowd of nervous developers in joggers and sweatshirts gathered in a semi-circle staring slack-jawed in awe at the great woman. The walls of the room were all glass, hence the name, except for a fifteen-foot-wide presentation screen on one side. The screen showed the feed of a sample RED Social user, updating every few seconds. The space held no chairs, only a glass, standing height conference table.

Cristina liked to keep her meetings brief, and she had learned that people got more verbose the more comfortable they were. Standing kept people comfortably uncomfortable.

At the center of the group of developers stood Chibuike Abdullah, lead developer of the burgeoning RED network.

Chibuike carried a large oval head atop a skinny body. It reminded Cristina of Humpty Dumpty, if Humpty could write code. She had discovered Chibuike herself when she was setting up cybersecurity for one of her companies on a trip to Nigeria and had offered him a job on the spot. It was a decision she had never regretted, and she was pleased to see that, today, Chibuike was beaming with confidence.

"We've got mostly good news, ma'am."

He had a soft accent, and his manners were impeccable, the sort Cristina's mother and grandmother would have approved of. He turned to the screen at the front of the room and tapped twice on the tablet in his hand. The screen lit up with a series of charts all trending upward.

"We've reached seventy percent penetration across all levels of the RED Network. Ninety percent of the Republic's users are using the RED Internet and RED Browser for internet access. Seventy-seven percent of the population are using RED Social. And we just reached Seventy percent of users on our search engine."

Cristina nodded but gave no words of affirmation. "What else?"

Chibuike cleared his throat and swiped up on his tablet looking for more good news to give the boss.

"Ah. We've made real strides on your Artificial Intelligence initiative. We can now adapt our advertisements and even news articles regarding you and the RED movement to each individual user to match the user's preferences. For example, if the user is an environmentalist, we focus the news on all the environmental progress we've made in the Republic and all the environmental degradation outside of the Republic."

Cristina smiled. "Good. But is the message dynamic?"

"I'm sorry, what do you mean exactly?"

"I mean it's good that we're targeting an environmental message to an environmentalist. But what I *really* want is for us to steadily adjust and tweak until it isn't just a *good* message, it's the *perfect* message. I want to be sharing news with people that isn't just good news, it is exactly the news they want to hear. And I don't want it to be the news they want to hear in general, I want it to be the news they want to hear at that very moment on that very day. If they're sad, I want them to know I can make them happy. If they're scared, I want them to know I can make them safe. You follow?"

"Yes, ma'am. We will get to work on that right away." Chibuike tapped a few buttons and the screen returned to the main feed of RED Social. He did not mention that this was a multifaceted problem with multiple hurdles standing between it and completion, and she liked that; even more, she liked the fact that she could be certain he was already cataloging those hurdles in his head.

"Good," she said crisply. "Now, what have you found out about this Cipher?"

The room fell silent.

The developers looked down at their tablets.

Chibuike, to his credit, met her eyes. "Very little, ma'am. I apologize. Whoever is doing this is very good. He or they use multiple VPNs and several layers of encryption so there is no way to determine who he is or even where he is."

"And what about the code buried in that image of the sword? Anything on that?" Cristina scanned the rows of developers and then turned to Moloch. "You? Your people were also working on it."

Moloch shook his head. "No, but the good news is that there have been no more messages. There's a significant chance it's just a prank intended to divert our intelligence res–"

Before he could finish his sentence, the sound of static ripped through the fishbowl followed by a grinding, repetitive beeping sound like an Amber alert. All eyes darted around the room before finally settling on the screen. A familiar white image burned against a black background.

A sword and the same six words.

"Solve the cipher. Follow the Cipher."

Cristina gazed at the screen in astonishment, but the beeping sound continued. It echoed around her.

Beeeeeeep.

Beeeeeeep.

Beeeeeeep.

She pulled out her phone and unlocked it. Her screen flashed the same image.

"SOLVE THE CIPHER. FOLLOW THE CIPHER."

She felt the tap of Moloch's hand on her shoulder. The phone in his palm cast the glowing sword, as well. She looked around. Every person in the room held their phones in their hand, each one screaming with the same grating beep and pulsing the same message.

"SOLVE THE CIPHER. FOLLOW THE CIPHER."

Cristina placed her phone back in her pocket and tried to modulate her voice. "Find out who this is," she said crisply, "and bring them to me. *Now.*"

Chapter 17

T he message glowed in the black light.
A MAN WHO TRIES TO ACT VIRTUOUSLY
WILL SOON COME TO GRIEF
AT THE HANDS OF THE UNSCRUPULOUS
PEOPLE SURROUNDING HIM

"We gotta get out of here." Albert grabbed Ying's arm and yanked her away from the steampunk booth and toward the convention exit. He scanned the room to make sure no one was following them.

"Where are you going?" Ying wasn't keen on following, but she seemed to have decided that standing her ground wouldn't work very well. She trailed after him, sighing occasionally.

Once they were free of the worst of the crush, Albert slowed down and walked beside her so he could speak quietly. He spared a thought about what people might think if they were watching and decided that they appeared to be having a lover's quarrel. He felt a desperate urge to say that it wasn't like that; that they were work friends.

Only they weren't, anymore, and things between them had shifted, somehow.

Even before she stripped down to her underwear in front of him.

He kept his eyes focused away from her as they walked. "This whole thing is all wrong. We're picking up messages in graveyards, reading creepy quotes in black lights. None of this seems like it is going to end well. I thought the Cipher might lead us to something that can help us stop Cristina, but the more I get to know this guy, the less I like him."

He threw open the lobby doors of the Sheraton Framingham and took a long breath of the crisp, cool air. It braced him after the claustrophobic chaos of the convention floor. He and Ying jogged past a group dressed as Alvin and the Chipmunks.

"For all we know," Albert said bitterly, "Moini was right, and this guy is just bonkers."

"Oh, come on." Ying was shivering, but she was so engrossed in her argument that she didn't seem to realize she was walking in her underwear, outside, in the winter. She strode after him. "Albert. Albert. We can't stop, now. We're on the verge of discovering who the Cipher is. Don't you want to find out?" When he said nothing, she added, "And I don't know about you, but this is by far the most interesting thing that has ever happened to me. And given what we've been through, that's saying something."

Albert refused to respond to that line of reasoning, no matter how persuasive it was actually proving to be. "Can we just get in the car and get moving, and then discuss this?"

"Fine."

Ying was full-body shivering by the time they reached the car, and her teeth were chattering while she pulled her clothes back on.

Albert fired the car's ignition and screamed out of the parking lot as soon as Ying was dressed and buckled back in, while she sat silent beside him.

To his surprise, she did not press her point. Instead, she sat quietly in the passenger seat and let him mull over what she had said. He peered through the blinding fog of streetlights ahead. The skyline of downtown Boston shined like a beacon. Calling him. His hands tremored, but he realized he hadn't felt this way since Angus died. Like he mattered. He realized that as much as he wanted to, he couldn't stop, now. Not until he knew who the Cipher was. And if he could help them.

"Can you read that message to me again?" he asked Ying.

"Really?" He didn't have to be looking directly at her to sense her smile. Her joy lit up the air inside the car. "We're doing this?"

He sighed. "Yes, we're really doing this."

"I knew it. I knew you couldn't resist."

"No, I just couldn't handle the awkward silence, anymore."

"Sure, sure, whatever you say. She put on her bright red reading glasses. Here's what it says: 'A man who tries to act virtuously will soon come to grief at the hands of unscrupulous people surrounding him.' I'm pretty sure that's from Machiavelli's *The Prince*."

"I'll take your word for it. Political philosophy isn't my thing. I guess the first thing we could do is search for any statues of Machiavelli in Boston. You know, like the shrine of Fatima?"

"Makes sense. Let's see what the Google machine has for us."

Ying pulled out her phone and tapped away. After a few seconds she wagged her head.

"I got nothing. There's a statue in Florence, Italy. How's your Italian?"

Albert laughed. "Nonexistent."

"Let me just try 'Machiavelli Boston' and see what I get."

Albert kept both hands on the wheel but watched out of the corner of his eye while she scrolled through the search results. Watching Ying read was always entertaining. Her facial expressions–the nose squinches, the eyebrow raises, the eye rolls– told the story for you. Judging from the clown-like frown currently on her face, the research was not going well.

"Ugh. I'm not seeing anything. There are some courses on Machiavelli. Some library resources, but nothing that seems relevant."

"What book did you say it was from?"

"The Prince."

"Maybe try Prince Boston?"

Albert tried to focus on the slush soup that was I-90 while Ying searched on her phone. Every few seconds he checked her facial expressions out of his peripheral vision.

Finally, he saw a bug-eyed expression that seemed to show she was onto something. "Ying?"

"What about Prince Street?" She was almost vibrating with excitement.

"What about it?"

"Maybe the Cipher is telling us to go to Prince Street."

Albert considered it for a moment. "That's not much to go on. It's a big street. *Where* on Prince Street?"

"That's it!" Ying slapped her head. "It's a book cipher. The address! It's the chapter and line. Hold please." She did her best impression of a computerized voice and put one finger up in the air as her other hand typed furiously.

"This quote is from Chapter fifteen, line sixteen of Machiavelli's *The Prince*. Set your navigation to 1516 Prince Street."

"This car isn't even close to having navigation."

"Fine, I'll look for it in Maps."

"I'm pretty sure that's the North End. Just out of curiosity, what's at that address?"

Ying crinkled her brow. "Hmmm... nothing, right now. It looks like it's for lease."

"That's promising." Albert couldn't decide if he was being sarcastic or not. "Well, we've come this far..."

"Whoa," Albert murmured as they turned onto Prince Street.

"Whoa, what?"

"I need to come to the North End more often."

Even in the depths of winter, the old Italian neighborhood displayed a winsome charm. The narrow streets zigged and zagged in random directions, almost daring him to follow them. The old brick buildings hovered over romantic cafes in unique shapes and sizes. Striped awnings, hand-carved wood, and twinkling lights all intermingled to make him feel like he had escaped to some place out of time... and where Cristina Culebra didn't exist.

What was also strange was that, as the car puttered down the ragged blacktop of Prince Street, Albert *knew* they were in the right place. He knew almost nothing of the Cipher, but the one thing he did know was that the man had style. Everything was planned to perfection, but also with a certain mystery, a certain secretiveness–and the North End was a place that kept its secrets.

"Up here on the right," said Ying, pointing to a building a hundred feet ahead of them.

1516 Prince was a light brick structure with a dark gray ornamental façade. The building sat wedged between two nondescript red brick buildings, making the decorated metal stand out. Three swords stamped in the metal stood guard over a dark blue door.

Albert pulled the car over to the curb, and the pair stepped out to inspect the site. The building's awning held no signage, just a fire escape to the apartments above. Meanwhile, the street was silent and dark. Only one of the three streetlights worked, giving an eerie glow to the block. The slam of their car doors echoed through the silence.

Albert's certainty wavered as he took in the spooky setting.

"I think we might have misfired on this one," he murmured to Ying, his breath clouding the air. *Please agree,* he thought. *Then we can go home.* Everything about this reeked of a trap.

Ying bounced on the balls of her feet and rubbed her arms to stay warm. "Give it a minute. Let's see what we can find." She headed toward the building, shoes crunching on snow and ice. She shot him an annoyed look when he hung back. "Come on."

Albert reluctantly followed. The building was divided into two sections. They peeked through the tiny, framed windows of the first unit. The glass revealed nothing but an empty room with weathered hardwood floors and a battered paint job. Albert squinted into the darkness, trying to make out the details in the shadows.

A clang burst from behind him. Albert jumped, but it was just the wind knocking over a road sign down the street. Albert steadied his breathing, trying to stay calm.

"Let's try the other unit," Ying whispered.

They crunched their way through the snow, Albert looking around to make sure no one had noticed the intruders in the neighborhood. The last thing they needed was a visit from the cops, asking questions they couldn't answer. They peered in the other set of windows. Again, there was nothing. Just a beautiful, dusty, old bar standing empty.

"I think we need to go back to the drawing board." Albert took his hand away from the window and sighed.

"No. Not yet."

"Ying..." He gave a helpless gesture at the window. "Do *you* see anything in there? Plus, it's late, I haven't slept in twenty-four hours, and I'm freezing my ass off out here."

"Yeah, I guess you're right." She headed back to the car. "God, I just don't get it. It seemed so perfect. Prince Street."

"I thought so, too." He stifled a yawn. "I supposed we had to get one wrong at some point, though."

"Sure, but... the swords on the façade. Flaming swords. I mean... c'mon. I just th–wait!" She grabbed his arm.

"What?"

"Look!" Ying pointed at the door of the second unit. A QR code sticker hung to the mail slot at the bottom of the entry to the suite. She turned on her phone's flashlight and crouched down. The sticker showed nothing but the QR code. No label, no heading.

She looked up at Albert, who nodded. His exhaustion was still present, but he couldn't walk away, now.

She scanned the QR code and took an unsteady breath as it directed her to a website.

WHO LED YOU HERE? The black letters stood out on a plain white background.

"The Cipher," Albert whispered.

Ying nodded. She was already typing it in. A moment later, she swore in Chinese and showed him the screen.

INCORRECT. YOU HAVE ONE MORE ANSWER REMAINING.

"What?" Albert ran his hands through his hair. *Who else could have led them here?*

"Machiavelli?" Ying suggested. When he nodded, she typed it in, blew out a breath, and crossed the fingers of her other hand briefly before pressing the enter key.

The screen went blank.

"Did I–did it send?" Ying banged the side of her phone. "Dammit. If I lost connectivity, right now, the phone company is going to get one hell of a–"

A grinding sound vibrated through the door followed by a clunk. The deadbolt retracted, and the door swung open with a macabre whine.

"... Uh." Ying stared into the darkness.

"Hmm," Albert replied.

"Do we... go in?"

"Do we have a choice?"

Ying nodded, and they stepped into the abandoned pub.

Albert smelled dust, mold, and a hint of stale beer. Through the dim light, he could see two rats scurry along the far wall. A couple of old tables and chairs stood empty in the corner, strung together with cobwebs, one chair on its side. Dust covered the grand, hand-carved mahogany bar and the few remaining bottles stacked on the shelves. The silence was punctured only by the occasional scurry and squeak of the rats in the walls.

He took another step toward the bar, and the floorboards moaned as if warning him. Goosebumps crept over Albert's body, and he moved back instinctively, looking around.

He saw a hunched figure creeping in the darkness.

"Ying," he hissed as he ducked behind the bar and pulled her down with him.

He listened, but the room returned only silence. He searched the darkness. Something touched his hand on the floor. He flinched, but then heard a squeak. He shuttered. Another rat.

He braced himself and put his finger in the air to signal to Ying that he was going to stand up. Whoever this was, whatever this was, that he had seen. He must face them.

He rose from beneath the bar. His eyes crept over the edge and peered to the rear of the room. Another pair of eyes stared back at him. Albert's heart leaped, but then dropped back to earth. It was his reflection.

Albert released a heavy sigh and tapped Ying to stand up. A large mirror hung in the middle of the bar amidst the bottles. But unlike the bottles, it was perfectly clean, not a speck of dust on its surface. Albert walked behind the bar and examined the mirror, but didn't touch it.

"Does the website say anything new?" he asked Ying.

"Oh, let me check. Yes. It's another question: *where were you last?* I'm going to say 'The Shrine of Fatima'. Sound good?" She waited for Albert's nod. "Okay, it's–"

"Look." Albert pointed at the mirror. Sparks were swirling behind the surface. They converged, then burst to life to reveal a black screen with a flaming white sword spinning on its axis. The sword dissolved a moment later to reveal a message:

CONGRATULATIONS. YOU ARE AMONG THE PRECIOUS FEW WHO HAVE FOUND THE CIPHER.

The words faded, and new words appeared.

AS A REWARD FOR YOUR INTELLIGENCE AND DARING, I WILL TELL YOU WHO I AM.

Albert held his breath. Whose face would he see?

No face, it turned out. There were only more words. He swallowed his disappointment and read on.

I AM THE LEADER OF A SELECT GROUP OF INDIVIDUALS WHO BELIEVE THAT OUR WORLD HAS BEEN CORRUPTED BY LIES, IGNORANCE, TYRANNY, AND GREED.

WE BELIEVE THAT THE BRIGHTEST AMONG US HAVE A RESPONSIBILITY TO HUMANKIND TO CREATE A BETTER WORLD.

THE QUESTION IS...

DO YOU?

Albert and Ying looked at each other.

"Can it hear us?" Ying whispered. "There's nothing on the website."

Albert shrugged. He cleared his throat and said awkwardly, "I'd like to make the world a better place."

"Me, too," Ying said softly.

They nodded to one another and both turned to the mirror screen.

"Yes," they said in unison.

The screen dissolved and posed a new question.

DO YOU BELIEVE WE SHOULD RID THE WORLD OF TYRANNY IN ALL ITS FORMS?

Albert pictured the waving flags of dictators the world over and felt not a single speck of doubt. "Yes."

DO YOU BELIEVE WE SHOULD DO THIS BY ANY MEANS NECESSARY?

Now he hesitated, but he knew the answer he was supposed to give–and he had come too far not to solve this puzzle. "Yes."

ARE YOU WILLING TO HELP?

"Yes."

THEN YOU MUST PASS ONE FINAL TEST...

AT THE BACK OF THIS BAR ARE TWO TELEPHONE BOOTHS. ONE IN THE LEFT CORNER, ONE IN THE RIGHT CORNER. ONE OF YOU MUST ENTER ONE OF THEM. THE OTHER MUST ENTER THE OTHER.

Albert swallowed and looked at Ying. She nodded. They walked in the darkness past the dust covered tables to the back of the bar. Cobwebs tickled Albert's cheek. He brushed them aside, but the feeling stayed with him.

In both corners about thirty feet apart stood two, modern soundproof phone booths, a strange juxtaposition against the dusty, historic bar. Each phone booth faced the wall. Albert, realized that once he was inside, it would be blackness he wouldn't be able to see out. He had never liked tight spaces. Once again, he asked himself how much he trusted the Cipher.

Ying's courage bolstered him. She strode to her phone booth and glanced back at him, waiting for Albert to enter his. He tiptoed to his phone booth and cracked open the door. It was dark but appeared empty. A rotary phone hung from the wall. He took one last look at Ying who nodded one more time. Albert entered the booth and closed the door behind him.

It was a shade lighter than pitch black in the booth, with a hint of light creeping into the window that faced the wall. The window was covered in black and white stickers depicting grotesque demons. Each with a name beneath them. Beelzebub, Osiris, Belial. In all, twelve demons stared back at him. Albert's first thought was to get the hell out of this bizarre confinement, but he knew that this was a test. He wondered what to do next. *Was there something hidden in the booth? Something on the other side of the glass behind the demons?* He could still make out the outline of the phone, so he did the most logical thing he could think of and picked up the receiver.

A grainy computerized voice began speaking on the other end.

"Hello and welcome to your final test. A test to see if you are truly worthy of joining the Cipher."

The voice paused. Albert stayed silent.

"I am Lucifer. You and your friend now find yourself in the center of Hell, held captive by me and my demons." Albert wondered if this was more than just a metaphor. "If you look ahead, you will see twelve demons. Your friend sees an unknown number of demons, but all of them differ from the ones that you see. Being a lover of tricks, I will give you the chance to flee from Hell if you can answer one question: How many demons in total are guarding you and your friend? eighteen or twenty?

"You may not leave your position or communicate with your friend. However, I will give you the option either to guess the number of demons or to pass. If you guess correctly, you will be released and join the worthy. If you guess incorrectly, the game is over and you are unworthy. If you choose to pass, I will call again in one minute and ask again. Your friend will be subject to the same rules. I will call in one minute."

The line went dead.

This was insanity, Albert thought. He was on no sleep, standing in a dark phone booth in an abandoned bar in Boston. And now he was expected to guess how many 'demons' Ying had in front of her. It was impossible. The Cipher must be insane. He thought about walking out of the booth, and just going home. What would happen if he did? Would the Cipher let him? Or was he in too deep, now? Regardless, he had come too far. He had to know.

The phone rang.

He picked up the receiver.

"How many demons are there?" asked the metallic voice.

Albert said the only thing he could say, "Pass."

"I will call in one minute." The line went dead again.

Albert's pulse slowed. He had bought himself some time. A little time. He thought of Ying in her booth staring at the demons in front of her. It was impossible to know how many demons she had. It could be six, it could be eight.

The phone rang again.

Albert chuckled to himself. *Ying must have passed, too.* He picked up the receiver, and, before Lucifer could ask the question, he barked "Pass" and hung up the phone. "I guess we could just sit here and pass all day," he said to himself as he tapped on the walls of the booth.

He stopped. That was it. It wasn't impossible. When he and Ying both passed, they weren't just refusing to guess, they were communicating something. He had an even number of demons, so he knew Ying's number had to be even since the total number was either eighteen or twenty. If Albert had twenty demons in his phone booth when the question was asked, he would have known that there were over eighteen and he would have answered. But because he passed, Ying now knows that Albert has at most eighteen demons in front of him. And Albert knows that Ying just passed, so he knows Ying has at least two demons. And now that Albert has just passed again, Ying knows he must have sixteen demons or less because if he had eighteen, he would have guessed.

The phone rang again. That means Ying passed again. That means she must have four demons or more. Albert answered and passed again. *Now, Ying knows I have fourteen demons or less.* They were doing it. They were communicating. They were close. It rang again. She had six or more. He passed, telling her he had twelve or less.

If the phone rang again, they would have it. He would know that Ying had eight demons and because he had twelve, he would know that the number had to be twenty.

It rang.

Albert answered, breathless.

"How many demons are there?" asked the voice.

"Twenty. There are twenty demons."

There was a pause on the other end.

"You are worthy."

"Thank you, I guess."

"You are now part of The Sword of Eden. In six days you will hear my call."

The line went dead.

Albert stepped out of the phone booth in a daze, half-expecting to be greeted by Lucifer in the center of Hell. But instead, he saw the same broken-down bar with a smiling Ying in its center.

"We did it," she said with a grin, arms raised.

Albert ran over and hugged her. "We did it."

She grabbed his hand and dragged him toward the front door. "Come on. I can't wait to tell the rest of the team what we found."

Chapter 18

This doesn't mean shit," said Mana to Albert as they gathered around the kitchen island of the safe house with Weatherspoon and Ying. Albert and Ying had driven through the night from Boston to tell Moini and Weatherspoon the good news.

"What do you *mean* it doesn't mean shit?" said Albert. "We've infiltrated the Cipher. We're behind the curtain, Mana."

"So, what? What am I supposed to do with that? Go to my superiors and say that Puddles and Ying solved some riddles? Has the Cipher even contacted either of you since you solved the riddle?"

Ying and Albert adopted sheepish expressions and looked down at the countertop. In unison they said, "No."

"Do you know who the Cipher is?"

"No."

"Do you have any information about the Cipher's background, known associates, etc.?"

"No."

"Has the Cipher told you what his plan is?

"No."

"Has the Cipher told you if he even wants to stop Cristina Culebra?"

Ying spoke up. "Well, not in so many words, but that test he gave us sort of implied that he was all about stopping Cristina."

Mana slammed her hand on the table. "You two don't get it, do you? You came to me because we are eight days away from a coup in the United States of America. I drop everything I'm doing, pull agents off their assignments, secure a safe house, put my reputation on the line and the first thing you do is spend two days on a wild goose chase solving riddles. Not only that, but now the Cipher knows who you are. Hell, they probably know *where* you are, right now."

"Easy, now, Mana," said Weatherspoon. "Now, I'll admit this wasn't exactly what I was hoping for, but this is progress. We already know that the Cipher's been sabotaging Culebra's rallies. And from the questions in his little loyalty test, it's pretty obvious he's hoping to take her down. Right now, we need all the friends we can get."

"We don't *know* he's our friend, Spoon. From everything he's done so far, he looks like a whacked-out terrorist to me." She raised her eyebrows. "You know, the kind you follow because everything sounds grand and pretentious, and then you find out he wasn't speaking in metaphors, he's just batshit crazy."

"So... what?" Albert could hear his voice rising. He struggled to control himself, but it seemed as if the entirety of the past years was crashing in on him at once: Turner's death, his arrest, the haze of days in his apartment, the hangovers every morning, the jet lag... "What do you want us to do? You know we can't stop Cristina by ourselves, right? That's obvious even without the Tree. So, what else can we do?"

Mana sighed. "I don't know. I just know that we need some help." She held up a hand and gave them all a glare. "And I know that trusting the wrong person is worse than trusting no one, so don't tell me to trust the Cipher just because we need an ally."

Albert was opening his mouth to disagree when the doorbell rang.

He froze.

So did everyone else.

They all looked to the door. Albert felt as if he were floating. It had happened. RED was here for them. He had come back, and Cristina had sensed the threat of the Book Club once more. His optimistic side, which he had believed until that moment was long dead, argued that this could be the Cipher.

But Moini's words had filled him with doubt on that front, too. What if this *was* the Cipher, and the Cipher was a lunatic? What if the Cipher was just a distraction invented by Cristina? What if–

Moini put one finger to her mouth. She withdrew her revolver and crept across the hardwood floor, toward the door, taking care to avoid the floorboards that squeaked in the aging house.

Weatherspoon gestured to Albert and Ying and pointed straight down, urging them to crouch behind the kitchen island. He put a finger to his lips when they were all hidden and then removed his own gun from its holster.

Albert wasn't sure what he expected, but he didn't expect Moini to meet the threat head-on. He heard Moini open the door from the inside. It gave a little sound of protest as it swung, and then there was silence. Albert prayed he would not hear Moini's body hitting the ground.

Then Moini said drily, "This is a surprise."

There was a murmur that Albert couldn't make out, and then two pairs of footsteps came back toward the kitchen, stopping at the kitchen island. The other woman was wearing heels, but Albert could tell little else. There was the sound of a coat being taken off, and then a voice said,

"Oh, come on, Dilbert, stand up."

"Eva?" Albert stood up so quickly that his vision went spotty. He swayed and put a hand out on the counter to steady himself.

"Hello," Eva said. She gave courteous nods to Weatherspoon, who was still holding his gun, and Ying, who was making no attempt to hide her contempt, and then she looked back at Albert.

"I thought you and your friends might need a hand."

Chapter 19

Ying recovered first. "Thanks, Eva, but I think we're all good, here. We appreciate you stopping by, though. Good luck to you and your mom on trying to take over the world."

Her dismissal was clear, but Eva ignored it. Instead, she looked at Albert...

... who hesitated.

With a mutter to herself, Ying got up from the kitchen island and moved to the sitting room, where she opened the flue of the fireplace and crunched and crumpled old sheets of newspaper to make a fire. Each one of her movements was jerky and overly emphatic, making firewood clatter and newspaper tear.

Albert barely noticed. He was gazing at Eva, who was more stunning than ever. The overhead lighting reflected off the dark silk of her hair. Freckles and other hints of age dotted her face, adding the subtle imperfections that made her beauty real. And her eyes were still starbursts with browns, oranges, and yellows. The scowl was gone, too. She was happy.

For a moment Albert forgot all the pain this woman had caused. How she had killed the security guard at the Bank of Princeton. How she had beaten Ying on that rooftop in Long had eviscerated every semblance of a life he had prior to seeing her again. Their connection was too powerful. Too chemical.

He noticed that both he and Weatherspoon had stood up like they were greeting a guest at a dinner party. The room was silent and thick with tension. He dared not act. Both Weatherspoon and Moini looked at him, waiting for his next move. Moini threw an arched black eyebrow at him, prodding him to say something.

"Would you guys mind giving us a moment?" Albert asked.

He thought they would argue, but both simply nodded and exited the room.

Albert looked over toward the fire. Ying continued to crumple paper and glare at Eva. Each paper crumple was louder than the next.

"Ying?" he asked finally.

"Nah, I'm alright, Albert. I'm going to stick around to see the whopper this girl's about to drop on us."

Albert gave a pained look at Eva, who only shrugged and smiled at him.

"OK, I guess I'll start with the obvious... what are you doing here?"

"Do you mind if we sit?" Eva pointed to the bottle of wine on the table. "And, honestly, I could use some of that."

"By all means."

Albert poured her a glass of wine and sat down at the table across from her. Ying's eye rolls prodded him from the periphery, but he couldn't take his eyes off Eva. A draft of her scent wafted over to him, and he was hooked.

Eva told Albert everything. About the movement. About her mom. About her plans. About the missing journalists.

"She's changed, Albert. When she started this movement, it was all about making people's lives better. But now... she's slipping over the edge of something. It's all about control, about *winning*. The Tree made everyone on earth her marks."

Albert heard a snap as Ying lit a match and started the fire in the fireplace. He glanced over. She just shook her head and mouthed the word "Bullshit".

"So, what now? You want to help us?"

"Yeah. I want to help you."

She slid her hands across the table and placed them on Albert's. He sunk into the feeling.

Ying leaped up from the floor and threw the oversized matchstick in the fire. She stormed over to the table. Her face flushed with too much wine and disbelief.

"I'm sorry, Albert. I can't listen to this, anymore. This is a woman who has done nothing but lie, cheat, steal, and terrorize us since we first met her. And now, we're supposed to believe that she's a sweetheart, and that her mother–we still have no evidence that she has done anything wrong, mind you–is the real villain. Please. What about you, Eva? What about Moloch?"

Eva took a sip of her wine and nodded, never losing a scintilla of composure. She reminded Albert uncomfortably of her mother.

Her words, however, were anything but what Cristina would say. "I admit that I've made mistakes, Ying. I'm sorry for what I did to you, and I...." Her voice broke slightly and she took a moment to steady herself. "I never wanted Professor Turner to be hurt. I believed he would be kept safe, no matter what. And that was before I knew he was my..." Her voice trailed away.

"Wait. You're not telling me that was true?" Ying looked like she was going to laugh. "Come on."

"It is, though." Eva shook her head. "It just is. I don't know how I know, but I do." She straightened her shoulders. "And I can also assure you that Moloch is indeed a terrible guy. At first, I thought he was a bad influence on my mother, but now, I think he really is doing what she wants. She always knew he would do things like this, and that's why she brought him in. He does the dirty work that she can't do. Maybe she thought I would do the same... But I know who I am, now, and what I want."

She paused and flipped a glance at Albert.

"And my mother and the RED movement aren't a part of that picture, anymore."

Ying threw up her hands and returned to prodding the fire.

Albert searched Eva's eyes, hoping he could find her true intentions. They returned his stare, but they weren't searching. Certainty stared back at him.

"Let's say I believe you," he said finally. "And I'm not sure I do. How do you propose we stop Cristina? Do you have a plan?"

Eva let loose a triumphant smile.

"As a matter of fact, I do."

She rubbed her hands.

"Step one is getting your Book Club back together."

Chapter 20

Chaos. Digital chaos.

That was all Cristina could see as she and her entourage stepped out of the Nasdaq Stock Exchange onto the alternating patterned and solid stones of Times Square Plaza. Billboards hocking every item and service imaginable flickered above the many balding heads of the assembled press corps.

Cryptocurrencies.

Disney characters.

High-end fashion.

Comfort fit jeans.

New movie releases.

Anthropomorphized M&Ms candy.

The billboards spoiled a gorgeous day. The sky hovering above the massive buildings shone a bright periwinkle, and a gentle breeze snuck in from the Hudson River. Behind her stood the usual suspects, Moloch, the Mayor of New York, the Head of Nasdaq, her security detail. Reporters huddled four deep in front of her. Cristina looked them up and down. Embarrassing. Schlumpy bodies. Guts hanging over belts. Mis-sized pants and shirts. Beaten down shoes. She could almost smell the coffee breath and body odor. *Have some self-respect.*

"Madame President! Madame President!" shouted the reporters.

Madame President, Cristina thought to herself. *At least they're falling in line.*

She held her hand up like a middle school teacher waiting for children to calm down. The reporters quieted.

"Today is a historic day. I am ecstatic to announce that not only has the RED Network completed an initial public offering on the NASDAQ stock exchange at a record valuation of over $1 trillion, but I have just been informed that people of the great State of Illinois have just voted to join the Republic of Enlightenment and Democracy."

She let the announcement sink in. She smiled as the reporters scrambled to check the news on their phones or text their editors.

"With Illinois joining the Republic, we are now fortunate to represent over half of the population of the United States. I am humbled and honored by the faith these folks have put in me, and I can't wait to share the RED Network with the entire country and someday the world. Now, I'll be happy to answer any questions you have."

She scanned the hands waiving in front of her and sighed to herself. She knew the questions that would be thrown at her. "What do you know about the Cipher?" "What about the missing journalists?" "How does it feel to be so rich?"

She also knew how she would respond. How she would steer them where she wanted them to go. Seeing the future had a certain monotony to it. She longed for the day when journalists would no longer exist.

Soon.

She pointed to the one woman in the assembled throng of men. "Yes."

"Madame President, what is your response to the recent reports that journalists and others critical of your administration have gone missing."

Shocker. Cristina evaluated the reporter. She was different from the rest. Strong and fit, with searing blue eyes.

"That's the first I'm hearing of this... I'm sorry, what's your name? You're new on this beat."

"Erin Ratner."

"Erin, welcome. This is a very troubling question, and we'll have our people investigate it at once."

She nodded to Moloch who returned her nod with forced seriousness.

Erin wasn't put off. "So, for the record, you're saying you know nothing about the disappearances."

Cristina stared more intently at this plucky, young upstart reporter. The eyes held something in them. *Knowledge? Or suspicion?*

She held her own smile. "That's correct, Erin. Our movement is a people's movement. We welcome all voices, including the voices of those who would criticize us. That's why you're all here." She flashed a smile at them.

Laughter.

"No, but seriously Erin, the inclusiveness, and hopefulness of the RED movement is why we've been so popular and why great states like Illinois are voting to join our cause. I can't tell you anything about folks going missing, but safety is our number one priority. As you know, in the Republic states, crime has dropped by over seventy percent. I'll make sure my head of security looks into it first thing. Next question."

Cristina tried to ignore the skyscraping screens of Times Square flashing in her view and pointed to a more traditional, reliable reporter.

"Are you concerned about this person calling themselves the Cipher? He disrupted a campaign event of yours down in Austin, and reports have said there was another appearance at RED Network headquarters earlier this week."

Cristina paused and took in the scene as though she hadn't been asked and answered this question in her mind multiple times. The stars and stripes of the Army Reserve Recruitment Center shined back at her. A new flavored vodka was now available in stores.

"No, Tim, we're not concerned," she said finally. "The Cipher, as he calls himself–or his puzzle–seems to be someone with, how should I say this... too much time on his hands. Right now, he's probably holed up in his parents' basement covered in Cheetos crumbs playing video games. If he's in the Republic, I would guess that our security folks will have him in custody by the end of the week, and we'll find out he was hoping to get more subscribers to his YouTube channel or something. Next."

Another reporter piped in.

"With all due respect, Madame President, this is an accomplished hacker. He has successfully hacked your network twice and now has over fifty million social media followers, not to mention all the groups that have spun off to try to crack the code in his 'SOLVE THE CIPHER, FOLLOW THE CIPHER' message."

"Yeah, well, Pokemon Go had millions of users once, too. And where is it, now? I'm not worried about the Cipher. Next question."

A loud white noise drowned out the next round of questions. Cristina looked up at the electronic billboards over the reporters' shoulders. Static burst from every screen. No more American flags. No more flavored vodka. No more cryptocurrency. Just static.

Then the grinding, Amber Alert sound echoed through the Square.

Cristina dreaded what was coming next.

One by one, the static fell from the billboards. Replaced by the image of an ancient blade spinning on its end. As the screens changed from blinding advertisements to the black-backgrounded message, the light of Times Square dropped like a setting sun. In the darkness, the blade and the one message that stoked fear in Cristina's mind.

"SOLVE THE CIPHER, FOLLOW THE CIPHER."

Realizing the moment, the reporters spun back to Cristina, spraying questions in rapid-fire sequence.

"We're done, here," said Cristina.

Her security detail ushered her into the awaiting car on the corner of 43rd Street.

She glared at Moloch sitting across from her in the limo. "What the fuck was that?"

"I don't know, Madame President," said Moloch.

He was beginning to show his age.

"General, when we started this journey, I told you it wouldn't be straightforward. That someone would come for us and would try to take away everything that the Society has built. And what did you say to me?"

"I said I would take care of it."

"That's right. You said you would take care of it. And have you?"

"No, Madame President."

"No. You are clearly incapable of handling this. We need someone better. We need Eva."

She looked around to the rest of her entourage in the limo.

"Where is Eva?"

Chapter 21

The Wynn casino in Macau was a buffet of sights and sounds. Bright red carpets, red awnings, and red blackjack tables. Busty cocktail waitresses sidestepping their way through the crowds of drinkers and gamblers. The beeps and boops of slot machines hoping to be discovered. Guests dressed in their finest and most form-fitting clothing.

This was Albert's first visit to what tourists termed 'Asian Vegas', and he wasn't sure what to think. He had flown to Macau with Eva and a reluctant Ying in search of Raphael Salazar, who– rumor had it–was having quite the time in the city.

Moini and Weatherspoon felt that their respective bosses might not approve of a weekend getaway to China, regardless of the reason, so they had remained in Virginia. Moini was calling high-ranking officials in the FBI, DOJ, and any other acronym she could think of, while Weatherspoon leaned on his buddies in law enforcement. The reaction from the halls of power had been tepid. No one wanted to take action against a 'peaceful protest'. When Albert and company had left, Moini and Weatherspoon were buried behind four giant bags of coffee beans on the kitchen table in anticipation of several all-nighters.

Albert wished he had stayed with them. Eva and Ying both seemed entirely at ease in their gorgeous dresses, but he felt like a fool in his suit. From his vantage point, the casino floor seemed to run forever. Blackjack tables, craps tables, and tables of games he couldn't pronounce splayed out in front of him. He saw revelers rolling dice and shouting, shoulder to shoulder with grandmothers holding plastic buckets and pulling slots. No Raphael.

Eva tapped him on the shoulder and pointed. In the distance a crowd gathered around a blackjack table next to the circular lobby bar. At the center of the table sat a small, boisterous man in a cowboy hat twirling a toothpick in his mouth and pumping his fists in the air. It was Raphael Salazar–and he was winning.

Albert smiled upon seeing his old friend. He looked at Ying who was smiling, too.

"Some things never change," she said in an undertone.

Salazar sat in the center of the table with multiple stacks of pastel-colored chips stacked several inches high. On his right sat two Chinese men in sport coats who were hoping his luck would rub off on them. To his left were a group of women celebrating a birthday, complete with sashes, tiaras, and other accoutrements. Behind him stood other voyeurs, wanting to experience a taste of this quirky man's success.

"Dealer breaks!" shouted the blackjack dealer in Chinese, as Albert, Ying, and Eva approached.

The crowd let out a roar as the dealer slid another stack of chips in Salazar's direction. There were slaps on the back and the clinking of glasses, and Albert stepped up behind Salazar and joined in with a back slap of his own.

"Get your hands off me, Puddles," growled Salazar, without turning from his seat. He still carried a faint Mexican accent. "You've got some nerve, coming here."

Albert took a quick step back in surprise. He was glad to see that Ying and Eva also looked confused.

Salazar swiveled his chair, his brows drawn together in a scowl. Albert calculated what could have set him off. He noted the other man's tensed shoulders, clenched hands, and offset feet. The people closest to them stepped back, as well, and Albert saw the dealer reaching subtly toward a button on the inside of the table, ready to push it if Albert and Salazar came to blows.

"Raphael." Albert used a slow, liquid voice to deescalate the situation.

Salazar stood rigid, fury rolling off of him in waves... and then the crease of his lips broke, and the round tissue of his cheeks rose to his eyes to reveal the familiar mischievous smile.

"Haaaaa!" He pulled Albert into a rough hug. "I'm just messing with you, man. Got you good, too. I thought you were going to break out the Tree and go into fight mode on me. How are you?" He didn't wait for a response, however, before he pivoted to take Ying's hands and gave her an admiring once over. "And look at this: my little *chiquitita* is here!" He kissed his fingertips. "Ah, you're a sight for sore eyes, *conejita*, and that dress–I hope you made Puddles, here, pay for it."

Ying laughed, charmed despite herself. It was impossible not to be beguiled when Salazar put you in his sights.

Salazar pivoted to look at Eva last. He considered her for a moment and then turned back to the table without acknowledging her. He lifted his drink to the onlookers and the dealer, scattered a few chips to the sound of cheers, and took the rest of his winnings before leading the others away from the crowd.

"What brings you all to Macau?" he asked with a raised eyebrow. "Ah, but why do I wonder? You missed me, of course, you could not live without me in your lives."

"We did miss you," Albert admitted with a smile, as Ying laughed. "But that's not why we're here. We need your–" He broke off as Raphael's eyes locked on something across the room, and then began scanning, looking for something in particular. "Is there a problem?"

Raphael's jaw clenched. "Yes. We need to go. Now."

"What?" Albert restrained the urge to look over his shoulder.

"We need to go, right now. Follow me."

He led them out of the casino and past the lobby bar, walking quickly. Eva was the only one keeping up with him without seeming to be in a hurry, while Albert and Ying found themselves speed walking, the motion incongruous in their formal clothes. As they turned a corner, Albert snuck a glance behind them without being obvious.

Several men in gray suits were following them, their attire not out of place within the casino, but their movements far too purposeful for guests.

Salazar pushed open one of the casino doors and ushered the three of them through brusquely, out of the climate-controlled elegance and onto the crowded walkway. Tourists streamed along the sidewalk, and Frank Sinatra hummed a tune from the hotel speakers. Everyone was in a good mood, unbothered when Salazar cut across their paths to lead his friends up an outdoor escalator.

"Who are we running from?" Eva asked him. Her tone was steady; Albert recognized she was assessing the situation, trying to figure out the scope of the danger.

"Hotel security," Salazar replied tightly.

He crossed the pedestrian bridge and then skipped down the escalator on the opposing side, where there was a man-made canal to evoke the atmosphere of Venice. A gondola sat empty, and Salazar jumped in and grabbed the flat straw hat that an unsuspecting gondolier had left behind. He beckoned to the rest of them.

"Get in!"

Albert, Eva, and Ying jumped in the gondola.

Salazar snapped his fingers at Eva. "Give me your scarf."

Eva complied, looking more amused than anything else. Albert could see that she respected the man's quick thinking.

Salazar tied the red patterned scarf around his neck, grabbed a paddle and shoved the gondola into the canal. With the straw hat and red scarf, pulling the gondola gracefully through the waters, he looked the part of a casino employee.

Albert stole a glance behind them as the gondola slipped under a bridge and glimpsed the security team reaching the bottom of the escalator before they vanished from view. The team wasn't running; they had not yet realized Salazar had escaped.

Salazar, meanwhile, sang like a true Venetian gondolier. "Ayy, yaaay, yaay, Ayy yaaay yaaay." In an undertone, he added, still singsong, "The Italians cannot write love sooooongs, ayyy, yay, yayyyy..."

Albert laughed. It was always an adventure with Salazar. "So, why are people chasing us?"

"Chasing us? Who's chasing us?" Their gondolier gave a wink.

"Raphael. Seriously. What's going on?"

"That was hotel security." Salazar dipped his oar in the water and pulled the boat forward. "I might have been doing a little card counting."

"Unbelievable," Ying muttered.

"What?"

"I'm out there in NYC busting my butt to try to catch the guy who killed Turner—your friend—and you're out here on vacation, counting cards and drinking martinis."

Salazar looked deeply offended. "First, I never drink martinis. Second..." His face softened. "I miss that guy every day, *chiquitita*. But what are we supposed to do about it? Culebra's too powerful. Speak of the devil. What's she doing here, anyway?" Salazar pointed at Eva.

"Trying to help you." Eva kept her tone calm.

"How do I know you're not just here to spy on us?"

Eva raised an eyebrow, and Albert got the sense that playtime was over. "Yes, my grand plan was to fly to Macau to spy on a man who can barely keep himself from being arrested by hotel security."

"Okay, play nice, everyone," said Albert. "Raphael, the truth is that we think we can stop Culebra, but we need your help to do it."

Their gondola now floated along the canal inside the Venetian Shoppes mall, and Raphael steered toward a small dock. He motioned for everyone to climb out and then stepped out himself. There was no security in sight. He removed his Gondolier's hat and handed Eva her scarf. It was clearly a peace offering by his standards, and, whatever she might think of him, Eva accepted it gracefully.

"Okay," Salazar said, with only mild misgiving leaking into his tone. "How can I help?"

Albert cleared his throat. "Well..."

Salazar groaned. "For God's sake, Puddles, what did you get me into? Spit it out."

"Mmm." Albert straightened his cuffs and put on his most winning smile. "Well... first, we need you to help us break Brick and Gabe out of a Chinese prison."

Chapter 22

Eva's private jet hummed as it sliced through the night sky. Ying had drifted away in one of the reclining seats and was mumbling in her sleep, while Eva swiped through documents on a tablet. She held a glass of wine in one hand, but Albert was fairly sure she hadn't taken a single sip. From her swept-back hair to her indifferent half-lean, everything about her was...

... elegant, Albert thought.

And isolated. It wasn't the sort of isolation that was wearing at her, at least as far as he could tell. It had become a part of her, something she had been shaped by. Being a part of her mother's organization had taught Eva to function with purpose, even when others might be relaxing. The wine was an affectation–a gesture she copied, but with none of the sentiment behind it.

He wondered what it must have been like, trying to hide her changing loyalties.

The sound of a cleared throat caught his attention, and he jumped, looking over to see Salazar watching him with a glint in his eye. Albert flushed and sank into his chair. Salazar could be a lot of fun while hustling them out of a casino, but Albert was in no mood for being teased about his interest in Eva.

Right now, the other man took pity on Albert... in a manner of speaking.

"So. You wanna explain why you ran off to Cambridge and we didn't hear from you?" He looked Albert up and down critically, as if every detail of Albert's appearance somehow compounded the disappointment.

"To put it simply...The Tree of Knowledge." Albert looked over at him.

"You're going to have to be more specific than that."

"You can't figure it out?"

"Well, seems to me that Angus came up with it and taught us a few tricks, and then that snake Culebra took it and decided to take over the world." Salazar settled into his chair with a faint smile. "So, no. That's not enough of a clue."

"Fair enough. At first, I went to Cambridge because I needed to get away from Cristina. Even though her real enemy, Turner, was gone, I worried she would come for me if she thought I was a threat. Or that she'd come for Ying, too, if I was in the U.S. I also needed to crack the code to Turner's book, and what better place to do research?"

Salazar nodded his agreement.

"While I couldn't crack the code in Cambridge, I found the real reason I needed to stay."

Salazar scratched at his cheek and considered. "You're talking in riddles again, bro."

Albert sighed. Out of the corner of his vision, he thought he saw Eva look up, but when he raised his eyes, she was still looking at her tablet.

"When we scattered," Albert said finally, "Cristina and Moloch didn't follow us. They knew they outmatched us. They weren't going to risk dead bodies turning up over a bunch of people who couldn't do anything to derail her."

Salazar made a small, contemptuous noise.

"She was right–as were we–that we didn't have enough power to stop her. But, when I was in Cambridge, I realized that our retreat might be the key to this whole thing."

Salazar said nothing. It wasn't clear from his expression whether he thought Albert was onto something, or whether he should be committed.

"If you, me Brick and Gabe had stayed in the country and openly formed a resistance to fight Cristina, then she would have had exactly what she wanted: a known enemy that she could manipulate and control. Like she did with Ariel," he paused as the grief welled in him.

"However, if we were to leave, there would be a vacuum, where a new resistance could develop. One that Cristina couldn't fully see coming, couldn't account for. We needed that resistance to develop, and now, with that, we have a chance." Albert explained. "I think that's why Turner sent Brick and Gabe to China. He wanted us to leave."

Salazar considered this. "But there's no coordinated resistance against Cristina? Those asshole politicians in Washington are just arguing with each other. As usual. None of the states she campaigned in have gone over to her opposition–"

"The Cipher," Albert said. "That's the resistance. He said he would contact us three days from now, and my hope is that he will give us the variable we need to unbalance Cristina's equation."

"Someone hacked a screen, put up some fancy symbols." Salazar waved a hand. "That's not exactly Miguel Hidalgo y Costilla."

"Who's that?"

"Ay, Puddles. He's the priest who led the Mexican independence movement against Spain."

Albert shrugged. "The Cipher's movement might be larger than you think. But it's more than that. You can say it's just some symbols on a screen, but it's gotten under Culebra's skin." Now, when he looked over, Eva *was* watching him. "Am I right?"

She nodded. "Yeah, I've never seen her like this. I think she's been able to see what's coming for so long that she forgot what it was like to be surprised, to feel vulnerable. You can see that she's off balance."

"Huh." Salazar's smile was not exactly friendly. "I hope it eats her up inside, wondering."

Eva smiled and went back to her tablet.

"Is that the sword?" Albert asked, nodding at her screen. "From the Cipher?"

"Yes. There are a lot of people online discussing the meaning of the symbols and working out the puzzle."

"You're not trying to break it yourself?" Albert asked her, amused.

She smiled back. "It's always better to harness the ingenuity of thousands when you can, Dilbert." She lifted one shoulder in a shrug. "Besides... between defecting from my mother and escaping a casino, I've been swamped."

She went back to her research, a smile playing around her lips, and Salazar reached over to tap Albert on the back of the hand.

When Albert frowned in confusion, Salazar leaned close for a moment.

"Be careful with that one."

"I know–"

"Exactly." The other man cut him off. "You know you need to, which means you think you're too smart to get bamboozled. Well, trust me, *jovencito*, that's when you get bamboozled the worst. Someday, I will tell you the story of how I ended up in Macau."

Albert considered this. "We still have a couple of hours left in the flight, why not tell me now?"

Salazar only smiled, reclined his chair, and closed his eyes. "Someday," he said.

Chapter 23

The Hongkou district of Shanghai was a charming, historic neighborhood that had once been known as Shanghai's Little Tokyo. Amidst the steep-roofed houses and apartment buildings, however, and looming over the trees and outdoor produce stands, squatted Tilanqiao prison, the 'Alcatraz of the Orient'.

Albert wondered how the residents felt about such a menacing neighbor, steeped in dark secrets, and housing criminals of all stripes. Very few people spared it a glance, though he could not say if that was a habit born of discomfort or simple apathy.

An imposing brick and concrete gate guarded the main entrance to the prison. Beside the two hulking, green steel doors of the vehicle entrance stood a hobbit-like visitors' entryway, where Albert and Ying were waiting in line behind anxious Chinese families, hoping to spend the thirty minutes allotted each month to see their sons. Ying alone looked calm, though she kept her eyes on the floor so as not to attract attention. Albert tried to suppress the simmering sickness in his gut and focus on the Tree–on what he was about to do.

But his mind kept drifting back to Angus.

When Angus had first told him about The Tree of Knowledge, Albert had leaped at the thought of possessing extraordinary powers. He loved the idea of seeing the future and bending the arc of history in a better direction. Never one to embrace emotion, he had also excitedly assumed that, as his knowledge of the Tree increased, his fear would decrease.

But the opposite was true. The Tree increased the *demands* on him, both in his capabilities and in its unflinching view of all available options. It consistently pushed him out of his comfort zone. Instead of being asked to crack a simple cipher like he had on that fateful day in Princeton, now Albert was being asked to rescue his friends from a Chinese prison. He wondered if it would ever end.

"Xingming!" barked the prison guard at the entrance.

"Albert Puddles he Koh Ying," responded Ying. She handed him their passports and visas.

The guard flipped through the papers on his clipboard, then nodded and stepped aside.

Albert followed Ying through the gate and into a surprisingly peaceful cobblestone courtyard. Ivy vines lined the walls, and birds chirped gently. Only the guards standing atop the walls with automatic weapons showed that the courtyard they had entered was attached to a prison.

It grew much more apparent, however, as they stepped through the second door to the security screening. The security entrance walls displayed nothing but concrete. The smell of must, mold, and unwashed bodies clogged the air. Each visitor emptied their pockets and passed through a metal detector. The guards then executed a perfunctory pat-down.

Albert followed the branching paths of the scenario in his mind. If he passed the search, they would be taken to see Brick and Gabe. If the guards discovered their contraband, they would attempt to detain them. The four guards in this room would be manageable. The guards in the rest of the prison represented an unknown.

Ying stepped through the metal detector.

No alarm.

The guard patted her down.

Nothing.

Albert stepped through the metal detector.

No alarm.

The guard motioned for Albert to put his hands up. He patted down Albert's arms. His chest. His back.

When he reached Albert's lower back and butt, he paused. He shot a look at Albert and said something in Chinese.

A tremor of anxiety rippled through Albert's heart.

"ā yā, *gàn má*!" shouted Ying at the guard.

Albert did not know what that meant, but assumed it meant something like "C'mon!"

The guard turned away from Albert and replied something in Chinese to Ying. The two bandied back and forth for a couple minutes. Finally, another guard stepped in and waved them on their way.

"That was close," whispered Albert. He tried to keep his voice low, as the concrete walls would reflect the sound back easily, and he did not want to find out the hard way that the guards spoke English. Still, he didn't want to look suspicious. "What did you say to him?"

"I told him you had incontinence issues and wore adult diapers." Ying shrugged. "And that this was embarrassing to you, and it would be very humiliating for him to continue patting you down."

"How flattering."

"Hey, it worked, didn't it? As Angus used to say, emotion is the key to persuasion. I played to his emotions, instead."

Albert gave a wry smile. The way things were going he was going to need adult diapers by the end of this visit.

The visiting room resembled an elementary school cafeteria from the seventies. Yellows, oranges, and browns bounced off concrete, windowless walls in a desperate attempt to make prison cheerier for the visitors. Thick plastic, orange circular tables dotted the space. There were only two doors. One door at the rear led into the prison and one at the front led out of the prison. Albert and Ying sat down at the table closest to the prisoners' entrance and waited along with the other families for their guests.

One by one, prisoners entered the room. Families were temporarily reunited. There were exclamations of joy, which quickly settled into the melodic hum of Chinese.

Albert glanced at his watch. Twenty-five minutes.

Brick entered first, and Ying gave a soft exclamation. Albert said nothing, but only through sheer force of will. He barely recognized the man standing in front of him. Brick's ruddy face had grown pale and thin. His hair was grayer than it had been when Albert saw him last, and even the cleft in his chin appeared weaker. Most worrisome were the yellowing bruises that rested beneath the surface of his skin.

Albert was pleased to see that, while Gabe's wiry frame carried less heft, as well, his eyes still gleamed with energy and intelligence. Deep cracks cut through his lips, and his sunken brown eyes carried deep circles, but prison had failed to defeat him.

The two men joined the table, with Brick pulling a chair out so Gabe could roll his wheelchair beside them. Albert and Ying, meanwhile, settled into their seats.

"Boy are you two a sight for sore eyes," said Brick.

"Even me?" said Albert with a grin. The voice was familiar and reassuring, a sign that Brick's spirit was undimmed even if his body had suffered.

"Even you, Puddles." He placed his meaty hands on the table. Despite his diminished state, Brick still brimmed with intimidation.

"Is any of what they're saying true?" said Ying

"It depends on what they're saying."

"The Chinese authorities say that you two are spies."

"Ha!" said Gabe. When he grinned he reminded Albert of a hamster.

Startled by his tone, two guards took a step forward toward their table. Ying motioned Brick and Gabe to be quiet.

Gabe sighed. He ran his hand over his receding hairline. He was more unnerved by the various indignities than he was letting on. "No," he said, "we're not spies. Before he died, Turner said that if we were ever in trouble, we needed to find an old friend of his here in Shanghai. The man's name is Genji Wu."

"Did you ever find him?" asked Albert.

"No. We came here and started making some inquiries–and discreet ones, if I do say so, myself. Next thing you know we're being 'detained' on charges of espionage. No trial, no nothing."

"It's lucky you've got us then, huh?" said Ying.

"I guess so," said Brick. "I guess so." The words came out more slowly the second time, and he looked between the two of them. His question was clear.

Albert gave an infinitesimal nod, and Brick's massive shoulders settled slightly. He gave no obvious sign of relief that would alert the guards, but his energy had changed: he was ready, now, for whatever might happen.

One guard was patrolling the room in a circle and, as he drew close, the group shifted their conversation to more mundane matters.

When the guard was out of earshot, Brick leaned in and whispered. "So, what's the plan to break our asses out of this place? Because, let me tell you, I've been looking, and I haven't seen a good way... but you two seem confident."

Ying tapped a little melody on the table with her hands. "Yep! But first we're going to need to break *into* this place."

Gabe blinked several times and adjusted his frameless glasses. "I... beg your pardon?"

Albert leaned in closer. "She's right. We need to get inside the prison to get you out of the prison."

Brick leaned back in his seat, shaking his head. Some of his confidence had drained away. "Only you, Puddles, would try to break *into* a prison."

"Brick." Albert tried to keep the annoyance out of his voice. Salazar had noticed how he'd changed, but to Brick, Albert would always be a wrong bet on Turner's part. He looked Brick dead in the eyes. "I've mapped this out in my mind a thousand times. Trust me on this."

The other man didn't miss a beat. "I trusted you once when he broke into Culebra's headquarters, Puddles. That ended up with

Turner dead, and Gabe and I in the back of a squad car." There was no joke there, no smile.

And, if Brick didn't play along, this plan was going to fail very quickly.

Albert took a deep breath to calm himself, and immediately regretted it when he got a nose full of the prison air. "I know," he said. "But I won't let you down this time."

When Brick opened his mouth to argue, Gabe put his bony hand on his companion's forearm. "I don't think we have much choice, Brick. Besides, Albert knows what he's doing."

Brick pursed his lips, but he didn't argue. "Alright, Puddles, what's the plan?"

Albert looked at his watch. "In about a minute they're going to give us the signal that visiting hours are over. There are four guards. Two of them are going to take you out that rear door back into the prison, and two are going to take us out the front door. But I need you guys to be the last two out and to hold your door for us."

"What about the two guards on your side?"

Albert looked behind him to make sure no one observed them. He lowered his voice. "We'll take care of our guards. You just make sure that the guards on your side go out ahead of you and hold that door–because, if it closes, it's locked and things get a lot more difficult."

Brick nodded.

A little over a minute later, a deep buzz sounded over the loudspeakers. The families and prisoners all stood up and said their goodbyes, and the inmates headed to the rear exit while the families headed to the front. Albert and his friends said slow, exaggerated goodbyes to ensure that they were the last to leave the room.

When the guards finally started barking at them, the group parted with visible reluctance. Albert followed Ying toward the family exit, checking his watch once more.

Four minutes.

The guards in the rear had exited the room and were standing inside the prison watching the prisoners as they filed through the door. Gabe and Brick joined the back of the line of prisoners exiting. Only two guards remained in the visitors' room.

In the front of the room, Ying and Albert stood at the end of the line of visitors waiting to exit. Ying looked over her shoulder at Albert for the signal and he nodded to her. His heartbeat burst back into high gear. He listened and waited. Dimly, he heard a mechanical clank on the other side of the room, and Gabe's voice raised in annoyance. He was pretending that his wheelchair was stuck to prop the door open for Albert and Ying.

Follow the steps, Albert told himself.

While the two remaining guards turned to watch Gabe, Ying slammed the visitors' exit door closed with all her might. Albert snatched a baton from the closest guard's belt while his back was turned and slid it through the door handle, across the frame. Ying jiggled the handle and confirmed that the visitors' exit door was locked.

Albert pivoted to the two guards behind them, both looking at Ying, dumbfounded by what they were witnessing. The training manual didn't cover guests locking themselves inside a prison.

Albert struck a fighting pose and sized up the guards in front of him, while Ying pressed her ear to the door to see what was being said. He heard faint mumbles from the visitors on the other side of the door, but no alarms. For now, it was just Albert, Ying and the two guards left in the room. The men were young, one sported a mustache, and the other a baby face. He saw fear in their eyes. They did not want to fight. When he, Ying, Salazar, and Eva had sketched out the plan to break into the prison they had hoped the guards would capitulate once they were locked inside, but Albert could see, now, that this wasn't the case. One problem with being a bookish professor was that people weren't often intimidated.

The one guard who still held a baton, the one with the mustache, removed it from his belt and approached Albert. His hand shook, but his eyes showed determination. Albert hated the thought, but he was going to have to put this young man down.

Albert eyed the side of the man's head, looking for the temple. One strike to the temple and he would be out cold, and the other guard would be paralyzed with fear. The mustached guard took a step forward. Albert slid inches to his right to give himself better access to the man's left temple. The guard drew back his baton. Albert cringed. The easiest way for him to get a shot at the guard's temple was to take a blow from the baton. He braced his left side. The guard swung. As he gathered force to bring the baton down on Albert, his head turned and his left temple became exposed.

Albert swung his right fist at the man's temple just as the baton crashed into his shoulder. His arm burst with pain as the knuckles of his right hand slammed into the guard's skull. The man's head swiveled ninety degrees and then snapped back. For a second, Albert wondered if he had missed. Then he saw the guard's eyes roll back and his body go limp. He fell to the ground, and the baton rolled along the linoleum floor toward the baby-faced guard. He looked down at the baton, looked up at Albert, hesitated, and then raised his hands to the ceiling. He wanted no part of whatever this was.

Albert nodded to him. "Good choice."

"We need to move, now," said Ying. "Reinforcements are coming."

First objective completed.

Albert pivoted to the rear entrance into the prison. Gabe was still pretending to be stuck. Albert heard the guards inside the prison shouting in Chinese at Gabe, presumably to hurry up.

"This damn wheelchair," said Gabe.

Seeing that Albert and Ying had dispensed with the other guards, he dislodged his chair and allowed the door to begin closing behind him. Albert and Ying darted across the room just in time to grab the door before it shut. They slipped through the door behind Brick and Gabe, and closed it, leaving the guard in the corner of the visitors' room with his arms still raised in stunned silence.

They stood inside the prison now. *Second objective completed.* The thought helped Albert keep his mind focused on the tasks ahead instead of on his nerves as he looked around and took in the prison.

The prison walls and the cells they contained formed a circle around a main floor like a sad stack of donuts. Albert looked up and could see five floors capped by a concrete ceiling with a circular window in its center. The only natural light in this dreary place. He looked at his watch.

One minute.

Much to Albert's surprise, the guards on the other side still hadn't noticed them. In the preparation in his mind, he had assumed the guards would notice or an alarm would go off, but here he and Ying were, strolling behind the line of prisoners on their way back to their cells like it was just another day. He needed them to stop moving. Now.

Albert stepped into the center of the circular floor and clapped his hands before announcing grandly, "Thank you all *so* much for having us."

Everyone stopped to look. Prisoners and guards alike took in the sight of Albert and Ying, looking like lost American tourists who took a wrong turn at Shanghai Disneyland.

The guards recovered first, likely from the basic assumption that anything that happened unexpectedly in a prison was bad for the people running it. They reached for their radios and began shouting in Chinese. The prisoners scattered toward their cells, leaving Albert, Ying, Brick, and Gabe standing in the middle of the room.

Salazar and Eva, please don't be late, Albert thought.

Albert pushed his blazer out of the way and dug his hands into the rear of his pants, while Ying reached into her bra.

"Please tell me that this is part of the plan, Puddles." Brick was wearing a pained expression.

"Oh, it is." Albert pulled two gas masks out of the back of his pants and handed one to Brick. Ying handed one to Gabe.

"Oh, c'mon," Brick muttered.

"I know, I know. Just put it on." He and Brick put the masks on. Albert checked his watch as he heard the opening of doors and thunder of boots. "Ying, now."

Ying flung two tear gas grenades away in each direction, sending them tumbling end over end. Gas poured out of the cannisters, choking both guards and prisoners alike.

The alarm on Albert's watch went off. "Get back," he shouted.

A shattering sound echoed through the prison, and he shoved Brick out of the way, following just as a concrete block smashed through the roof window to the ground where they had been standing. Amid the dust and smoke, four black fast ropes slithered down from above. The rhythmic thud of a helicopter echoed from overhead.

The four secured themselves to the ropes, grabbed hold and were yanked into the air. Cheers and applause from the prisoners on other floors echoed through the room as the group ascended, Gabe's wheelchair the only item left behind.

Albert tried not to look down as the helicopter's winch pulled them up through the hole in the prison roof towards the floor of the chopper. He looked up and saw Salazar, smiling at the helm of the helicopter with Eva in the co-pilot's seat waving.

Never again, he told himself, but he was already shaking his head. With his luck, he'd have to do even more insane things to take down Cristina Culebra.

The ropes pulled them up the last few feet to the edge of the helicopter, and Albert heaved himself in followed by Brick, Gabe, and Ying.

"What's she doing here?" shouted Brick, pointing at Eva.

"You mean, besides saving your life?" Eva called back. "Salazar, take us up."

"Everybody in?" Salazar shouted.

"We've got contact, get us out of here!"

The sound of prison guards shouting from the rooftop had reached Albert's ears, now. He looked down to see guards piling out onto the roof, and then he jerked back as one opened fire. Bullets clanged against the steel panels.

Salazar shouted something at Eva, and Albert made out her reply: *I got this.*

She leaned out the side of the helicopter and aimed a long-barreled stainless-steel revolver at the guards. Heedless of Ying's scream of protest, she squeezed the trigger once, twice, three times, and the three guards with guns fell to the ground.

The helicopter shuddered and ascended quickly before banking out into the Shanghai sky. Eva screwed the long barrel off the revolver and stowed it, taking in the expressions of the others with a single, sweeping glance. Then she returned to her controls.

No one spoke.

Chapter 24

Later that evening, Eva's Gulfstream Five ripped through the night sky on the return trip back to the States. Albert looked around the cabin and was struck by the hollowness of wealth. The jet was perfect. Fine leather seats in groups of four rested on a rich white carpet. Polished wood paneling framed the cabin walls and trim. Artisan-crafted plates of cheeses and fruits rested on the tables between them. Every member of their group held a glass of champagne.

In a photo it would have looked perfect, but reality told a different truth. The roar of the engine hindered the conversation. The food trays sat uneaten. Brick, Gabe, and Salazar slept and snored in the other section of chairs behind them. Albert was awake, but the combination of champagne and turbulence gave him nausea. Ying sat across from him, seething at Eva, while Eva sat beside him, pretending to ignore her.

So much money spent, Albert thought, on so few people, for so little enjoyment.

"Can I help you?" said Eva, fed up with Ying's stares.

"Umm... yeah. You can help me, Eva. You could start by not killing people. I don't know how you do things where you come from, but our little group doesn't just take shots at people for fun."

Eva squinted her eyes and stared at Ying. Albert could see the flashes of orange and gold reflecting in her irises as she played out the conversation in her mind.

"Ying, you know damned well that I didn't kill those men 'for fun'. They were firing on our helicopter, and if they had hit a propeller or the fuel tank, we'd all be dead. Would you have preferred that?"

"Obviously not, Eva. But the point is those men weren't going to hit us. Those weren't trained assassins. They were undertrained, underpaid prison guards with families who are just trying to do a job. Do you prefer that their kids no longer have fathers?"

"OK, everybody calm down. We're all on the same team, here," said Albert attempting to stifle the conflict.

Ying shot a laser stare at him. "Are we, Albert? Are we on the same team? Because I don't think that's what this team is about. Up until a few days ago this girl was working side-by-side with General Moloch, a man we know is trying to overthrow the United States government. And now, we're standing side-by-side with Eva while she kills people."

"Ying, those guards *were* pointing their guns at us," said Albert. "If we waited too long and let them fire at us any longer it would have been too late. They could have hit a propeller, the fuel tank, or worse yet, you? And Eva's the one who came to us with the details of what Moloch and her mother are planning, remember?"

"So, you're taking her side, now?"

Albert stifled a groan. "I'm not taking anyone's side. I'm just trying to explain that things aren't as black and white as you're making them out to be."

"I'm making them black and white? Albert, you're just assuming that everything she says is true, when everything about her past says that it isn't. She lied to you about killing that security guard back in Princeton. She has worked hand-in-hand with Moloch. She built the RED Army, for God's sake. Everything we know points to the fact that she and Moloch are the problem, *not* Cristina Culebra. Open your eyes!"

"Ying–"

Ying turned her face away from him, looking out the window. In contrast to her strong words, her face was bright pink and tears were flooding her eyes. She slugged her champagne in one quick, angry movement.

Eva leaned forward and touched Ying's leg.

"Ying, let me tell you a story. When I was a kid, my mother used to tell me a Chilean legend about a Spanish explorer named José de Moraleda y Montero. He believed himself to be a sorcerer, and he collected rare books filled with terrible spells. He refrained from performing the worst of them, thinking them monstrous, but he couldn't bear to destroy the books, nor could he stop himself from seeking more and more knowledge.

"On one of his voyages, he discovered Chiloe, which is a small group of islands off the Eastern coast of Chile. There, he met the Huilliche, who had spells they would not share with any others, no matter how they begged. Finally, one day he challenged the Huilliche witch Chillpila to a magic competition. The witch agreed that, if Montero won, he could make a book of all their spells. They worked in... truly horrific ways, and any rational person would have shuddered to hear about those rites, but Montero's curiosity was too strong for him to resist. He would pay any price to learn more."

Ying did not look back. Her body was rigid, pressed against the back of the chair as if she might sink into it and escape the jet.

Eva was undaunted. "Montero lost the competition and attempted to escape, but the witch drove his ship aground. In exchange for his life, he gave them one of his own books of magic, and in it, they found new spells to strengthen their tribe. From this book, the Huilliche formed a secret society of Brujos, warlocks that ran the islands for centuries. To join the cult, an acolyte had to kill a loved one and use their skin as a purse to carry their own book of spells.

"But the true strength of the Brujos, the reason their secrets survived for so long, was because they had learned from Montero's book how to make a fearsome monster that would guard their cave. It was called the Imbunche. It was a child who was abducted, mutilated and raised to adulthood on human flesh. Its head was sewn on backwards and its appendages broken and bent in all directions. An Imbunche cannot speak. It only communicates with cries and grunts, and so it is impossible to say how old one might be, or what powers it possesses. It sees other humans only as meat."

"Good Lord." Albert stared at her in horror and pressed a hand to his stomach; the story had done his nausea no favors. "Your mother told you this story when you were a *child*?"

Eva nodded.

"That's terrible, and explains a lot about why you turned out the way you did." Ying had looked back, now. She was holding herself still with such effort that she was almost vibrating, but her gaze was clear. "But... I don't see the point."

"The point is that the world is vicious and cruel." Eva held her gaze. "And that, if you give an inch like José de Moraleda y Montero, if you fall prey to your own vices, lose a competition, show weakness, let your ship run aground... the monsters will win. Those monsters are everywhere, and every inch you give them they will take.

"I understand I have done nothing to earn your trust, and you don't like my approach to things." Eva's voice strengthened. "But you have to understand that we are not at Princeton anymore. This is war. My mother, General Moloch–they don't care about civil liberties... or honesty, or loyalty. They will lie to you, stab you in the back, even kill you if they have to in order to get what they want.

"So, we can't take chances by letting guards shoot at us or by giving people the benefit of the doubt. We need to assume the worst of everyone and get the smartest, best people working together to stop them. And that's why I'm here. Because I think the people on this plane, working together might have a chance of stopping my mother... if you can stop playing by the rules. Because the Imbunche doesn't play by the rules."

Ying shifted in her seat. Slowly, she leaned forward until she strained almost out of her seat like an attack dog. "Then why should I give *you* the benefit of the doubt?" she asked precisely. "Shouldn't I assume the worst of *you*, as well?"

Eva leaned back in her chair and smiled. She nodded once. "You certainly could, and I wouldn't blame you. You're right to examine the motives of every potential ally, and also to think about the worst that might happen if you trust any of us. But..."

She shook her head, and Albert saw a flicker of kindness in her face.

"What it comes down to," Eva said, "is this: you cannot do this alone, Ying. So, ask yourself, who do you trust? My mother... or me?"

Ying stared at her for a long moment, and Albert tried not to make a single movement that might jolt her out of her thoughts. No one had yet convinced Ying that Cristina Culebra was behind the violence, and he had hoped that the tenuous trust between Ying and Eva might help Ying come to terms with who Cristina Culebra truly was.

He even thought that she might believe Eva's speech. The two women had locked eyes, and there was more there than simple hatred or mistrust. It was almost, Albert thought, as if they were having an entire conversation without speaking.

Then Ying pointedly turned her head away to look out the window again, and Albert's heart sank.

A hand came to rest on his own, and he looked up to see Eva mouth the words, *it will be okay.*

He looked out the window of the plane. They would land soon. He wished he could believe Eva, that everything would be okay, but he couldn't. What he did believe was what she had said to Ying: that the people in this plane might, just might stop Cristina if they worked together.

And, right now, they were not working together.

Chapter 25

From outside, the Virginia safe house looked like the set of a holiday commercial. All that was missing was the car wrapped with a bow in the front driveway. Snowflakes tumbled on the roof. Smoke wafted from the chimney. Warm, yellow light streamed out from the windows to make squares on the fresh snow outside. One expected to find hot cocoa and freshly baked Christmas cookies inside, as well as an exquisitely decorated pine.

Unfortunately, one would find none of those things, but instead, tense silence and mutters, as well as the scents of old coffee and half-eaten food. Tonight, Weatherspoon stood at the kitchen island, washing the dishes and collecting his thoughts, while Mana opened and closed cabinets, putting away the ingredients of the evening's meal.

Albert, Salazar, and Eva had retired to their rooms upstairs, and Ying continued in her role as official fireplace manager, with one hand near the poker and the other holding a sheaf of printed documents that she was scanning as quickly as humanly possible.

Brick and Gabe sat in the great room, each holding a drink, and both looking shell-shocked. Twenty-four hours ago, they had been navigating a Chinese prison, and now, they sat with full bellies in an exquisite FBI safe house. Life was strange.

Both of them, however, knew better than to dwell on the luxury surrounding them.

"Okay, the kids may have gone to bed, but I sense we don't have much time." Brick pitched his voice to carry into the kitchen. He swirled the large ice cube in his whiskey glass. "Let's talk brass tacks, so I can at least sleep on the problem."

"Sure." Mana poked her head into the living room. "What do you want to know?"

"How much time do we have before Culebra takes over this whole damn country?"

"Five days," said Ying. She reached out to toss another log on the fire, and sparks peppered the air.

"Probably longer than that before she runs the entire country," Mana interjected, "but Ying is right that her opening gambit will be in five days." She came out into the living room, holding a glass of red wine.

"Five days?" Brick looked between them. "You said we didn't have much time, but five *days*?"

"That's right." Weatherspoon uncorked the bottle of scotch and poured himself a dram. "January 20th–the Presidential Inauguration Day, yes?"

"There wasn't a presidential election last year," Gabe murmured. He swiped up on his phone while he spoke, attempting to soak up all that he had missed in prison. The research and problem-solving soothed him. Made him feel like he was in control.

"Culebra doesn't need elections, you know that," said Weatherspoon, taking another self-satisfied sip of scotch. "And, trust me, she will not let something so small stand in her way. It'll be January 20th, and she'll make sure we get a new president."

Gabe put his phone down and focused on Weatherspoon. His eyes firing with calculations. "So, she's going to..." Gabe shook his head and raised an eyebrow. "What, march up to the Capitol and host her own inauguration? If I had known it was that easy, I'd have a President Gabe party."

Weatherspoon didn't even waver at the other man's humor. "You got it."

"Shit." Brick rose from the couch and paced. "That's just perfect. This is straight out of the dictator playbook. 'Our dear leader' marches up to the White House with her supporters and declares herself the president. And, let me guess: all of those supporters are going to be armed and trained members of the RED Army, right?"

"You two are good at this," Weatherspoon said.

Brick was not amused. He had seen too many wars. He knew what preceded them. Incredulousness. Jokes. A million small decisions that add up to one overwhelming misery. "What's the cover if she's marching in enough people to make a play for the White House?"

"A protest," Mana said glumly. "The Federal Government refusing to acknowledge the secession of the states, yadda, yadda. They've been really laying it on thick, comparing themselves to the peace marches during the sixties and seventies."

"... Which will mean the feds can't intervene without looking like they're breaking up a peaceful rally," Gabe said. "It's really quite clever. That's probably what I would do." He went back to his phone, pulling at his eyebrow, calculating the best ways to break up a protest.

"Now's not the time for appreciating her tactics," Brick told him bluntly. "First, we figure out how to stop her, because the Feds sure as hell won't have time to deploy forces if they only realize what's going on when she's storming the White House." He turned to Moini. "Is the FBI aware of this?"

She hesitated. "Yes and no. My office is aware of the possibility that Cristina Culebra is planning something, but because of her stature and the complications of the U.S. Government trying to figure out how it's handling all of this... up to this point they've only been willing to dedicate limited resources."

"What does 'limited resources' mean? I need exact numbers."

Moini sighed. "After Eva's little house call the other day, I secured fifteen agents to guard the safe house, which you may have seen on your way in."

Brick nodded.

"They can assist us in any operation we deem necessary."

Again, Brick nodded, waiting for more. His steel chin jutting out in frustration.

"We also got the safe house," said Mana.

"And?"

"And, we got you guys." She sounded waspish now, still waiting for him to get it.

"You mean to tell me," Brick said slowly, "that the FBI believes there is a real possibility of a coup, and their response is to assign you, fifteen agents, and Puddles to the case."

Ying looked up. "What am I, chopped liver?"

Brick rolled his eyes.

"That's correct," said Moini. "And it was an uphill battle even getting that."

While Moini dug into a pouch of Big League Chew and began chewing, Brick stomped over to the bronze bar cart and poured another whiskey. He banged the ice back and forth in the glass while he thought.

Weatherspoon attempted to brighten the mood.

"Look, Brick. We all know this isn't ideal. Heck, I wish the FBI guys would get their heads out of their asses and put some real resources behind this. But, after our last visit, I can assure you that ain't gonna happen. Now, Puddles says that with your 'Book Club', we got all the help we need to at least disrupt this coup. Gabe, you can disrupt their information networks?"

Gabe nodded. He put his phone down, but kept pulling at his eyebrow, thinking. "Yeah, we should be able to block their communications once they head to the White House. We can disable the networks, jam signals. It will take some work, but it's doable."

"Salazar can put together any explosives or poisons we need. Brick, you can draft a battle plan. Eva knows Culebra inside and out. And, hell, Puddles, and Ying can see the future, for God's sake. Now, that's not the way I would draw it up, but we got a shot."

Brick stared up at the vaulted ceiling of the house and clinked his finger on his whiskey glass. He looked back to Weatherspoon and fought a smile.

"That was a pretty good speech."

"Yeah, I almost convinced myself." Weatherspoon gave a chuckle.

"We're not the only ones gunning for Culebra, though," Gabe said. He had been staring at the fire, and now, he looked up at all of them. "There's this... Cipher. Tell me about him."

"No one knows much of anything. He sets puzzles and is making a game of drawing people in, but he hasn't sent out any directives, yet." Mana nodded to Ying. "She and Puddles solved one riddle he set."

Gabe and Brick looked over at Ying.

"It was actually three riddles. It was a long, roundabout journey to get to a quote about the virtuous falling to grief at the hands of less virtuous people," Ying said, with a shrug. "And, while we're on the subject, you're all still missing a huge point, here: we don't know that Cristina Culebra is the one planning a coup."

Weatherspoon and Moini suppressed sighs, while Brick's eyebrows shot up.

"Excuse me?"

"She's making good changes," Ying argued. "Culebra could be in as much danger as anyone else during this march."

"Are you... suggesting that Cristina Culebra is misunderstood and a force for good? Brick suggested.

"Yes," Ying insisted.

"Kid..." He came back to sit down. "I appreciate this. It's good to think outside the box. But you gotta see she's in on it."

Ying's face screwed up in a scowl. "You, too, huh?" She looked over at Gabe. "What about you?"

Gabe wheeled his chair backwards as if to distance himself from Ying's comments. He looked down at his lap for a moment before answering. "The short answer is... I think it's complicated. I think she is doing a lot of good for people in the Republic. And I believe she thinks she can continue to do a lot of good for people if everyone just gets out of her way. But Brick and I have seen many people who wanted power and who were very good at convincing others, and sometimes themselves, that there was a good reason for it. I know because I ended up in this wheelchair fighting one of those people.

"I see those qualities in Cristina Culebra. I can't say for certain that she set out to seize power for some nefarious reason." He shook his head slightly. "But I believe she is absolutely a part of this plan, and that she is aware of just how cruel her organization is becoming. And, Ying... she hasn't stopped it."

Ying stared at all of them. She looked between Brick, uncharacteristically gentle, and Weatherspoon, who refused to meet her gaze. She looked at Moini, whose pity was enough to make Ying want to scream, and then she looked back at Gabe.

She shook her head once, fiercely, her back ramrod straight and her face pinched with frustration. She shoved the papers to the side and stormed from the room.

* * *

Albert heard the faint mumbles of Brick, Gabe, and Weatherspoon from downstairs and smiled to himself. He hated to admit it, but it felt good to have the Book Club together. The warmth of the camaraderie bolstered him. Steadied him.

He looked out the window of his bedroom and enjoyed the sense of peace. The full house felt like family. Thick snowflakes bobbed and weaved down through the moonlight. White pine trees stood guard. The winter chill crept through the walls. Light from the fire flickered against the darkness of the room.

He crouched down by the red brick fireplace. He grabbed the black metal poker and prodded the fire, watching the ashes burst to life. He took three logs and placed them in a teepee formation, something his mom had taught them on their canoeing trips back along the rivers in Minnesota.

As the fire roared back to life, Albert thought of his mom. Of his dad. Of the people he loved. It had been over a year since he had spoken to any of them, and that was intentional. He had run the numbers, and the danger to them was just too high.

The sense of isolation was soul crushing, but it was also irrational... so, Albert had ignored it. He had attempted to distract himself from it with alcohol, another irrational move–though he had certainly told himself that drowning his mind was a perfectly logical response to an illogical situation.

But he had been alone, and afraid. When he withdrew tonight, it was to be here, in his own room but hearing the voices of the others. Something about it was comforting, exactly what he needed.

Albert pulled himself away from the fire and the secrets that it held and threw himself onto the bed. He turned the knob on the bedside table lamp up a click. He adjusted his plaid pajama suit and reached into his bedside drawer. The soft leather of Angus's journal both soothed him and haunted him. The memory of his mentor deformed by Albert's inability to decode his last message.

He opened the book and flipped through the worn, dog-eared pages. The paper carried line after line of numbers, letters, and symbols in no discernible order. Albert thought back to the many code-breaking methods he had tried. Most ciphers were alphabet-based ciphers in which the code could be broken by shifting forward or backward to different letters of the alphabet. Or substituting one letter for the other. But because this cipher used symbols and numbers as well as letters, it had to be treated like learning a new language with a different alphabet. Something that took time...

... time that Albert didn't have.

"It looks like a Pottery Barn catalog in here," said Eva.

Albert gave a full-bodied flinch and put a hand over his chest. He hadn't heard her enter the room.

"Jesus, Eva," he managed after a moment.

To his annoyance, Eva's mouth twitched. She attempted to hold her amusement in, but it got the better of her, and she buckled over, laughing.

Albert sat up, offended. "What's so funny? We're on the run from–"

"I'm sorry, Dilbert." She held up a hand and tried to stop her laughter. "It was just the way you brought your hand to your chest. It looked like a housewife clutching her pearls." Seeing his frown, she placed her hand over her borrowed t-shirt and mimicked his reaction.

Albert broke out in a smile and tilted his head back with a groan. "Okay. Still, I thought I was going to have a heart attack. Can you knock next time?"

Eva suppressed her smile and raised her right hand. "I promise to knock next time."

Albert returned the muffled grin. "What's Pottery Barn, anyway?"

"You don't know what Pottery Barn is?"

"Well, no. I'm not into that stuff, really."

"What 'stuff'? Shopping? Well-known consumer brands?"

"No, pottery, or animals or whatever."

Eva slapped her head with her hand.

"Dilbert, you're killing me. Pottery Barn doesn't actually sell pottery, and it's definitely not a barn. It's a home and furniture store that is known for lovely home layouts and settings on their website and in catalogs. So, you laying there, looking handsome in your plaid pajama suit with the roaring fire was very reminiscent of a page in a Pottery Barn catalog."

Albert only heard one word in that sentence: handsome.

He slipped Turner's journal into the bedside table drawer and slid onto his side, doing his best James Bond impersonation. It was woefully inadequate.

"Watch'ya reading?" said Eva as she hopped onto the bed and lay down on her right side next to Albert. Her rich black hair slid down off her shoulders and around her face, framing it perfectly.

He peered into Eva's eyes. *Was it safe to tell her?*

"Dilbert, it's OK. I'm on your side, now. Besides, I know that's Turner's journal."

"Yeah, sorry. It's just hard to get used to us being on the same side."

Eva slid her feet back and forth together. Her tanned, lotioned legs swayed from side to side. Albert reminded himself to keep his eyes up.

"It's freezing in here," said Eva.

Albert nodded and unfurled the blanket at the bottom of the bed. He draped it over both of them. "Yeah, it's sixteen degrees in this bedroom."

"It's not that cold."

"Oh, I'm sorry, sixteen degrees Celsius. I only use the metric system. English measurements make no sense."

Eva shook her head. "You're an interesting man, Albert Puddles."

She grabbed a piece of Albert's hair that had fallen in his face.

Albert slid closer in the bed. He smelled the subtle coconut scent of her hair. The warmth of her body radiated from under the blanket.

"And you're an interesting woman, Eva Fix."

He leaned in. Closing his eyes. Their lips touched.

He heard the door open, but there was no time to react as Ying said, "Albert, do you have any dental flo–"

There was a silence. Albert pulled away from Eva and opened his eyes to see Ying wearing a rose-pink terry-cloth robe and a barbie pink towel on her head. Her face burned an even brighter pink.

"I... I'm sorry," she managed, finally. "I didn't... I didn't know you..."

"Ying," Albert pleaded.

But Ying took an unsteady step backward. Then she spun on her heel and ran out of the room, slamming the door behind her.

Chapter 26

The snow-filled grooves in the tires of Cristina Culebra's black SUV slowed to a stop thirty yards in front of the driveway of the Virginia safe house. Exhaust poured from the twin pipes in the rear, creating a haze of steam and smoke in the night sky. Two members of her RED Guard security detail exited the vehicle and surveyed the property.

"How quaint," Cristina murmured. She opened the door and placed her black knee-high leather boots on the pavement beneath her. She tightened her coat and raised the fur collar around her neck.

"Madame President." The guardsman ducked his head respectfully. "I request that you stay in the vehicle until we can secure the location."

"Thank you, Corey, but we're here to put on a show." Cristina smiled at him. *And every show needs a leading lady.*

She patted Corey and Leonard on their shoulders and started walking toward the house with the two RED Guardsmen dutifully following behind her. Two FBI agents stood at the entrance to the driveway blocking her path. As she marched toward them, Cristina closed her eyes and pictured how the next five minutes would unfold. She took deep breaths and felt the snowflakes rest on her eyelashes and melt on her face. The cool breeze brought flush to her cheeks, and she could hear the pine trees rustling with snow.

Tonight, she had one objective: recruit. Inside that house were an unusually valuable assembly of talented individuals, all of whom could help her eradicate this so-called Cipher. The best way to recruit someone was to show them they had no other alternative. That resistance was futile.

And to do that... you had to put on a show.

She knew from the start that the safe house would inevitably be guarded by some number of FBI agents. It could be ten, or perhaps twenty; the more, the better. Of course, she could have them taken out with snipers without them even knowing she was there, but what was the fun in that? No, she needed these people, this Book Club, to feel her power.

She pulled out her phone and sent a message to her daughter: *Look outside.*

Simple, elegant. Eva did not respond well to dramatics; she had never understood their true role in something like this.

It didn't matter. Cristina could play to everyone here.

"Ma'am, this is private property," said one of the FBI agents as Cristina came closer. "We're going to have to ask you to turn around."

Cristina kept walking toward him and his partner. Her bright white teeth shone in the streetlight. In her peripheral vision she could see motion in the house. People were coming to the windows.

OF GOOD & EVIL

The show had begun. She smiled brilliantly. "Good evening, gentlemen."

One of the FBI agents started muttering frantically into his walkie-talkie, while the other pulled out his sidearm and readied it. Cristina made sure she was in the brightest part of the streetlight before she paused. She turned her head and glanced at the house at the end of the drive.

Silhouettes in every window. She had their attention, now. Good.

To the agents, she said, "I assume you know who I am."

"Yes, ma'am," said the agent. The revolver was at a forty-five-degree angle and his finger was off the trigger, but he had adrenaline pumping. It wouldn't take much for him to raise the gun to fire. "But I'm still going to ask you to leave."

Cristina shook her head and began walking once more. *Men and their guns. Such a false sense of security.* As she stepped closer, she remembered what Turner had taught her all those years ago: *A gun can't protect you. It can only harm others. If you aren't protecting your vulnerabilities—your sight, your sound, your smell, your senses, then you're never safe.*

"Ma'am, this is your last warning," said the agent. He released the safety.

"That's quite alright," Cristina assured him. She pulled off her leather gloves, one finger at a time. "I won't need another one."

She placed the gloves in her pocket, and then, with the speed of a gunfighter drawing a pistol, she removed a flashlight from her coat and shone a three thousand lumen beam of light directly into the agent's eyes. At thirty times the strength of an ordinary flashlight, it could blind anyone in its path, sunglasses or not, and the agent doubled over, moving his left hand to block the rays.

Pathetically easy. Cristina took one step to the right and out of the gun's path. With her left hand she grabbed the slide of the gun and with her right she jammed her palm against the agent's wrist. In one circular motion, like the hands of a clock, she ripped the gun out of the agent's hands and spun it back in his direction.

She swung the gun three inches left and took one shot at the thigh of the agent behind him. As he fell to the ground, screaming, she slammed the butt of the gun against the temple of the agent she had just disarmed, knocking him unconscious. Finally, she removed the magazine and dropped the gun and bullets in the snow.

With both men on the ground, Cristina resumed her walk down the driveway. The FBI agents would not get up quickly, but by the time they did, they would both be restrained, courtesy of Leonard and Corey. The two men also collected the guns of the downed FBI agents, motioned to one more guard to come and bind the leg wound of the agent that had been shot, and then followed Cristina.

She smiled. She could see her guards were wondering who, exactly, was protecting whom. She eyed the windows of the house. Puddles and Eva watched from a second-floor window, with that nosy girl, Ying Koh, in another.

It was working. They were enthralled.

Cristina kept walking and put on a pair of fur earmuffs that resembled headphones. *First, we start with sight... then, sound...*

"Freeze, Ms. Culebra." Two more agents approached, guns drawn. The time for niceties had ended. "And put down your weapons, or we will fire."

"Of course," said Cristina.

She stopped and put her hands in the air. In each palm she held a black circular object. She subtly pointed her palms at each of the agents. With the slightest flick of the pointer finger on each hand she slid the devices from off to on. Cristina watched as the sonic weapons in her hands vibrated.

Within seconds each agent was on the ground, grabbing their ears and writhing. One agent vomited on the driveway. Cristina kept walking. As she passed, she kicked the agent's guns back to her security detail.

She reached the front door of the house.

"Drop your hands and turn around... slowly," shouted another agent.

Cristina complied–but, as she turned, she let a small canister fall from one hand and kicked it toward them with a swing of her foot. Smoke billowed out from the canister, and the scent of tear gas filled the air. Men scattered as the gas attacked their eyes and lungs.

Now, smell.

"Enjoy the fresh air, gentleman." Cristina pulled two masks from her coat and threw them to her security detail.

"Corey, Leonard, make sure I'm not disturbed."

She kicked open the front door of the house and slammed it shut behind her.

Eva bolted downstairs the second she saw her mother approach the door. As she descended the Persian stair runner, she calculated her mother's ends. She had assumed that at some point Cristina might try to find her when she left. But not this way. This was too dangerous. Too risky.

Cristina Culebra was a woman who wrapped caution and calculation in a façade of boldness and spontaneity... but this was real.

She's getting desperate.

Eva arrived at the main floor just before her mother reached the blue, paneled front door. Puddles, Moini, and the rest of the group followed, and stood behind her. She looked back at them. Such an odd collection of people, all ready to fight for her. Her eyes met Albert's, and he gave her a stiff-chinned nod. It struck her. Eva had been alone so long that she had forgotten what it was like to have someone watching her back.

Bang.

The slam of a boot against the door shook her from her thoughts. Her mother was here.

Bang.

Another slam. Eva could see the lock wobbling and the wood frame splitting. She braced herself.

Bang.

The door flew open revealing a vibrant woman, hair dazzling with snow.

"This is how you greet your mother?" said Cristina, brushing the snow off her black, cashmere coat as she stepped over the threshold. She closed the door behind her.

"That was quite a show you put on, Mama," said Eva. She tilted her head and gazed into the powerful woman's eyes. On the surface Cristina displayed an arrogant composure. But her eyes revealed something different. Fear.

"Show? That was no show. That was just a sampling of what I'm capable of. An amuse-bouche, if you will."

Cristina looked away from Eva and one by one held the eyes of everyone in the room.

"I'm not coming back to RED," said Eva.

"Oh, I'm not here for you, Evalita. I know better than to argue with you once your mind is made up. I'm here for these extraordinary people."

"I beg your pardon?"

Cristina walked toward Eva, heading for the kitchen. Eva stepped aside, as did everyone else. Cristina gazed through the floor-to-ceiling windows out onto the snow-covered lawn rolling down to the lake. She turned to address the group. Eva noticed that everyone instinctively circled around her mother. That was Cristina. She had that type of gravity.

"Let me start by saying I'm not here to harm you," she said as she stripped off her gloves. Old Hollywood glamor practically rolled off her in waves. "I have nothing but respect for the people in this room. Agent Moini, Detective Weatherspoon, from what I can tell you are two of the best that law enforcement has to offer."

Moini and Weatherspoon dutifully nodded.

"Gabe, Brick, Mr. Salazar–my team tells me you are the elite of ex-military personnel."

Salazar smiled, but Gabe and Brick stared straight ahead.

"Albert and Ying, I know from personal experience what you can do."

Eva watched in surprise as her mother winked at Ying and Ying winked back. She attempted to break the connection.

"This is a wonderful compliment buffet, Mama, but I assume you didn't come here to give us a pep talk."

"You're quite right." Cristina smiled. "No, I'm here because I want all of you to join our team."

"You've got to be kidding me," said Eva.

"Why don't we hear her out?" asked Ying.

"Are you serious?"

Most people quailed before Eva's temper, but Ying met her eyes stubbornly. "Yes."

Eva shook her head and walked into the great room. "OK, great. Yes, let's hear her out. Mama, please explain to them why they should 'join your team'."

"Thank you, Eva. I think I will."

Cristina pivoted back to the group.

"It comes down to three reasons."

She held three long fingers in the air. Then dropped two so that only her pointer was showing.

"First, it's the right thing to do. As you know, the Republic states have done more for our citizens in a few years then the United States has done for their citizens in a few centuries. Our streets are safer, our students learn more, and our families are better off financially. But for us to maintain that takes smart people who are committed to making the world a better place. People like you, Ms. Koh, or you, Mr. Salazar. If you join the Republic, I can promise you that you will be at the top of the leadership chain with full freedom to do what you think is necessary to improve our Republic for our citizens. Think of all the good you could do. Detective Weatherspoon, imagine what you could accomplish if you weren't stuck at a desk on the Princeton police force. When you're on your deathbed, don't you want to say that you did everything you could for your fellow man?"

Cristina paused and let it sink in.

"Second, it's better for you personally. Regardless of what you think of the RED movement you must acknowledge that it is the future. We are, quite simply, inevitable. Every day a new state joins the Republic, and soon the United States as you know it will be a memory. Do you want to spend your life fighting a losing battle? Do you even know what you'd be fighting for? Albert, I know you've done the calculations. Agent Moini, you saw what I did to your agents out there. Do you really believe that you have a hope of stopping us? Do you want to spend your days locked in a futile struggle?"

Albert and Moini looked down at the floor.

"I didn't think so. Last, but not least. If the idea of making the world a better place or avoiding a war that you will certainly lose isn't reason enough for you, I have one more: the Cipher. I don't know who he is, and I don't know what he wants, but he is a terrorist who won't stop until he tears our whole country down. And if you don't like RED, you're really going to hate the Cipher. He grows stronger every day that we wait. Join me, and we can at least protect ourselves and our country from this terrorist. If you don't, then you are terrorists yourselves."

Eva observed the reactions in the room. Moini, Brick, and Gabe stared out the window, defiant. Albert, Salazar, and Weatherspoon inspected the floor and shifted back and forth in their stances. *She had rattled them.* And Ying. Ying nodded along with Cristina. The spell was working.

Eva stood up from her seat in the great room and slow-clapped.

"That was wonderful, Mama. Sounds like bliss to me. Of course, I noticed how you skipped some of the downsides of the Republic, like how you killed my father–and their friend–how the Republic won't allow elections or free speech, and how you're bent on world domination. You know, the little details."

"Evalita... always the overactive imagination."

Cristina stepped up to Albert and Ying and put a hand on each of their shoulders. The tremor of helicopter blades approached in the distance.

"Albert... Ying... I apologize for what happened to Angus. I am sick about it. As I told Eva, I loved that man and never wanted to hurt him. General Moloch was trying to protect me, and he made a mistake. If I could turn back the clock and prevent that awful tragedy from happening, I would. I'm very sorry."

Albert and Ying nodded but said nothing.

"Regarding what Eva said about the Republic, that is just not true. We have temporarily suspended elections so that we can accomplish the great work that I just talked to you about without the bureaucracy getting in the way. And you're always free to speak up and disagree with what we're doing. In fact, I encourage it, because that's how we can make a better Republic together."

The sound of the chopper blades grew more immediate. Eva looked out the window to see the presidential helicopter descending onto the white lawn.

"That's my ride," said Cristina. "But please, all of you, consider my proposal. I won't ask again."

She opened the door and stepped onto the porch. The frigid winter air burst into the room, shaking Eva and her companions from their trance. Cristina descended the porch steps to the lawn. Her long black coat fluttering in the wind.

"Wait!" shouted Ying.

Cristina stopped and turned.

"I'm coming with you," said Ying.

"That's my girl!" Cristina smiled and waved her out to the lawn. Ying stepped out onto the porch and started toward the stairs.

"Ying, wait! What are you doing?" said Albert.

Eva could hear the heartache in the timbre of his voice.

"I'm sorry, Albert. You want the world to be how it was. But I never fit into that world. I'd rather be a part of shaping a new one."

"Ying, don't do this!" shouted Weatherspoon in the most fatherly voice he could muster.

"I'm sorry, Michael. But I have to."

And with that, Ying Koh stepped onto the lawn and into the welcoming arms of Eva's mother. Eva could only stare as the two women boarded the crimson helicopter and took off into the forbidding night sky.

Chapter 27

E va lay in bed, barely there.

Her mind rewound and fast-forwarded back and forth like film, playing and replaying what had transpired that evening. Kissing Albert. Her mother's rage. Ying's decision. Her thoughts raced like an engine that couldn't catch. Revving and revving until it overheated.

Her mother had always had a knack of tightening and loosening the chains of manipulation until those closest to her broke. When Eva left, she had known on some level what her mother would do: find a new prodigy to shape. She would choose someone who wouldn't question her, who wouldn't disappoint her.

Who didn't know who she really was.

She had known, Eva told herself. She simply hadn't expected it to hurt as deeply as it did, an emotional ache that was so strong, she could almost feel it in the center of her chest.

Eva tossed over on her side. Her pillow was hot. Her sheets were hot. The comforter was hot. Every sound in the darkness seemed to echo through the room. The cotton felt scratchy. She tossed aside the bedsheet and paced in the darkness.

She looked out her bedroom window at the lake. The stillness of the water was an irritating contrast to her current state. She thought about Albert. Was he in his room thinking of her, right now? What about the kiss? Did he enjoy it as much as she did?

She had surprised herself with that kiss. She both loved and hated herself with Dilbert. She loved how alive she felt. How young she felt. How the world seemed to broaden to something happier, warmer, more kind.

But with that kindness came vulnerability. Weakness. She could sense her mother looking over her shoulder shaking her head. *Oh, Evi, this man will hurt you.*

That was the curse of her mother. She stuck with you, always tweaking and manipulating you, so that even when she was physically gone, she was with you. Evaluating. Steering.

Eva gave herself a couple of gentle slaps in the face. It was time to let go of her mother just as her mother had let go of her, today.

She eased the knob on her bedroom door to the left. The lights in the hallway were out. The hall was silent. Salazar's snoring purred from the room across from her. Albert's room stood silent, one room down to the left.

In her bare feet, she took two steps on the gray wool runner. The floor creaked beneath her. She paused to make sure no one stirred. She took two more delicate steps until she arrived outside Albert's door. She placed her ear to the door and listened. All she heard was the occasional crack of the fire and deep breathing. He was asleep.

She stalled for a moment, wondering if she should go in the room. Part of her couldn't believe she was hesitating. The Eva Fix that her mother raised lived by the motto *never hesitate,* while the Eva standing outside Albert's door froze and wrestled with butterflies.

She took a deep breath and tapped her pointer finger on the door. The modest pat sounded like the pound of a fist in the silence. She listened to see if anyone in the other rooms moved, but Salazar's snoring continued to rumble. She put her ear back to the door to see if Albert stirred.

Nothing.

If she tapped any louder it could wake Weatherspoon, or worse Ying, but she couldn't bear the thought of going back to that stuffy room alone. She decided to take the plunge. She gently turned the knob to Albert's room and slid in through the crack in the door. He slept on the far side of the bed with his back turned to her, hugging a pillow. The last remaining embers of the fire crackled, leaving kaleidoscopic shadows around the room.

Should she wake him? Should she leave? What was she doing?

For once, she turned her mind off and followed her heart. She gently lifted the down comforter off the bed and slid under it. The sheets were soft and the mattress firm. She nestled into the bed, comforted by the warmth emanating from Albert's body. She noticed he was shirtless. Thank God, he'd ditched the pajama suit top.

She placed her arm around him and squeezed.

He grabbed her arm with his soft hands and nuzzled his back against her chest.

She was home.

Then his breathing stopped, and he flinched awake. He turned and looked at her, confusion shining in his eyes.

"Eva?"

Had she made a mistake? Eva slid backwards in the bed.

"Yeah?"

He squinted and smiled.

"This is a pleasant surprise," he whispered, and rubbed the sleep out of his eyes.

"I just thought we could pick up where we left off, earlier," she whispered back.

He grinned.

Eva realized how much she loved this sleepy version of Albert. All the up-tightness and seriousness wiped away until all that was left was this sweet, kind man. She ran her fingers through his floppy hair and stared at him.

She kissed him. This time it was real. Not the hesitant explorative kiss from earlier in the evening, but a passionate make-out. Letting go. Just two people forgetting everything but the moment. The richness of now. The smell of each other's skin, the plushness of each other's lips, their tongues dancing as a prelude to something deeper. She kissed his ear, his neck, the freckles on his shoulders. He grabbed her hair and clutched it in his grasp. She felt the goosebumps perk up on his neck.

His strong hands grabbed her lower back and pulled her closer. Her breasts pressed against the muscles of his chest. His fingers glided along her legs. In that moment all she wanted was to be closer to him.

That night they made love. Not movie star love, but the real, imperfect, joyful love that comes when all pretense is gone and two people are their most authentic selves, wrapped in each other. Oddly, it didn't feel like their first time. It was more intimate. More comfortable.

When it was over Albert rolled onto his back and pulled Eva into his arms. She placed her head on his chest. It fit perfectly right beneath his collarbone. She wrapped her left leg over him and enveloped him. She inhaled his beautifully unique scent and nuzzled closer. It was as if she had spent her whole life looking for this one place, and now, she had found it. Looking into his eyes she could see he had found it, too.

***

Later that night Eva awoke to the flickering of the fire and the sharp snap of burning firewood. She ran her hand back and forth across the cold sheet, searching for Albert. He was gone. She shot up in the bed and squinted through the fog. She was relieved to see Albert sitting in the bedroom's rocking chair staring at the fire, sipping on hot chocolate.

"Is everything alright?" she said in a soft voice.

He stopped rocking and turned toward her. His eyes carried a warmth that Eva could feel in her chest. His brow an unknown weight.

"Yeah, I'm fine. Just thinking."

"About what?"

"About how this all plays out."

How this all plays out? Did he mean how their relationship plays out? Or how this whole mess with her mother and RED and everything else plays out? She hated that she couldn't tell. Hated that she cared.

"You mean how we're going to stop my mother and RED?"

"I love how you say it with such confidence."

Eva slid out of the bed and pulled the comforter off. She wrapped herself in the comforter and sat down in the rocking chair opposite Albert. The dance of the fire entranced them both.

"I am confident. You're not the only one who can see the future, Albert."

"Clearly, we're not looking at the same future, because the one I see doesn't end well for us. Hot cocoa?"

He handed a Christmas tree mug to her.

She took a sip and smiled. The rich chocolate soothed her. "That's because you have 'imperfect information' as we used to call it in the Society," she told him.

"Is that right?"

"Yes, it is. In the Society we used to have these rules about how to think. The rules were premised on the idea that perfect logic makes perfect choices."

"That's true. It does. I taught that in my classes to the two students that actually listened to me."

"Yes, but those choices are only perfect if you have perfect information. The weaker your information, the more likely you are to err. That's what happened to me with that security guard back in Princeton. I was sloppy. I didn't do my research on him and didn't know he had a heart condition, and he died. Or, I guess. I killed him."

The two of them sat silent for a moment, picturing the body of Wally McCutcheon splayed out in the Bank of Princeton. The original sin.

"I'll grant you, I don't have perfect information," said Albert. "Are you saying that you do?"

Eva smiled, still staring at the fire. "No, of course not. But I know a lot more than you, no offense. I know my mother. Her strengths, her weaknesses. I know the people in the RED leadership. I know their plan. I know the false assumptions that it's built on."

"Like what?"

"Like who they're fighting. They think they're fighting the United States Government. That if they take over the U.S. Government that they've won. But they're not fighting the United States Government. They're fighting the people of the United States. The United States Government is dead. You can see it happening every day with these states voting to join RED. That's probably what you see when you map out the future."

"Yes, that's exactly what I see. The states are joining RED one by one. The politicians in Washington aren't popular. So, when she marches on the White House there won't be enough support for the government to stop her. And the whole edifice collapses."

"But that's your problem, Albert. You're stuck in the past trying to hang on to how things used to be. Ying was right. The U.S. Government, as we know it, will not survive this. You can forget about the Declaration of Independence and the Constitution. They're going to burn."

"And be replaced by what?" Albert demanded.

He stood up from his chair and walked over to the window. Eva could see his mind's synapses firing as he took in the landscape.

"By us," said Eva.

Albert laughed as he turned to her, but the smile faded when he observed her face.

"You're serious?"

"Albert, think about it. Everybody knows our government is a mess. That's why my mother has garnered the support that she has. The only problem is that she thinks she is the answer, and that anything and everything justifies that. Lie to the public? No problem. Kill journalists? Not an issue.

"If we were in charge, we could do so much better. We could bring the smartest people together to solve the toughest problems and do it in a way that values ordinary people. But if we're ever going to be in charge, we can't do it by following all the old rules. By getting warrants. By gathering evidence. By having trials. That's what she's counting on. What you're counting on. And that's why the only thing both of you can see is her winning."

Albert sat back down in his rocking chair and pivoted it toward Eva.

"Eva, I don't want to be in charge. I just want things to go back to how they were. I happen to believe in the Constitution and Declaration of Independence. And warrants and trials."

Eva slid her rocking chair closer to Albert and grabbed his hand.

"I know that, Albert. But whether you like it or not, those days are over. We are about to be in the war of our lifetime. To win that war we can't fight with two hands behind our back. We need to do whatever it takes to stop her. When she's defeated, then we can go about building something better."

Albert pulled his hands away and spun his rocking chair back to the fire. He crossed his arms and clenched his jaw.

"Eva, I care about you. And I will help you stop your mother. But I won't do anything unethical. Because if we do, we're just as bad as her."

Eva admired Albert's profile as the fire lit and shadowed his face. The big nose and small stubborn chin. The soft hazel eyes. She wished he would just agree with her but loved the fact that he didn't. That his moral compass was too strong. She scooched her rocking chair next to him and hugged him.

"It's OK, Albert. We can agree to disagree. We're in this together 'til the end."

He leaned his head against hers and nodded. She resumed her rocking.

All was good.

What he didn't know wouldn't hurt him.

Part 3
Destiny

Then the Lord saw that the wickedness of mankind was great on the earth, and that every intent of the thoughts of their hearts was only evil continually. So the Lord was sorry that He had made mankind on the earth, and He was grieved in His heart.

–Genesis: 6:5

Chapter 28

Ying awoke to the sound of boots stomping on soft ground. She peered out the window of her bedroom. Young RED Army cadets marched in single file lines across the grounds chanting songs with funny rhymes. *Was she dreaming?* Last night she had been with Albert and the Book Club. Now, she was waking up in the lion's den, at one of the RED Army's schools.

A knock on the log cabin door startled her.

"Ms. Koh?" said a young woman's voice from the other side.

"Yes?"

"President Culebra has asked to see you at the main house in fifteen minutes."

"OK. I'll be there."

Ying took a cold shower. Apparently, the RED Army didn't believe in heat. She toweled off and stepped out of the bathroom. On her bed next to her dirty clothes was a pair of clean underwear and a RED Army dress uniform, like one might see on an army officer. She looked back and forth between the dirty clothes and the clean uniform and went with the uniform. She put her hair in a bun and stepped out of her cabin. Outside the door stood a freckle-faced cadet with a long red braid waiting to escort her.

"Ma'am," said the Cadet.

"You don't need to call me 'Ma'am'. My name is Ying."

"Yes, Ma'am," said the cadet. Ying thought the girl looked familiar but couldn't place her.

The two marched through the grounds, which looked more like a campground than a school. Ying marveled at the perfection of it all. Idyllic log cabins rested here and there, gentle curls of smoke billowing out of the chimneys of some of them. Winding footpaths covered in cedar woodchips connected the cabins to each other in a familiar patchwork. The smell of campfire hung crisp in the air. Strong, red-cheeked, red-uniformed cadets marched and jogged in different directions, powered by an unseen, but seemingly limitless fuel. Ying absorbed the stunning contrast of the sun's rays colliding with the droplets of melting snow on the trees and felt something she hadn't felt in a while: hope.

After a short walk, the cadet brought her up to a large lodge perched in the center of the camp. A rich cherry porch wrapped the lodge from front to back. Cristina Culebra sat out front with a cup of coffee on the porch swing surveying her cadets. Two members of her security detail stood on each side of the swing, eyeing Ying wearily.

"Ahh, there she is. My new recruit."

Ying stepped onto the porch, her feet making loud thunks against the dense wood.

"Yes, Madame President," said Ying.

"The uniform suits you," said Cristina.

"Thanks," said Ying. "I never pictured myself as a solider."

"Well, you are, now. Let's take a walk."

Cristina snapped her fingers, and seconds later a waiter came outside and handed Ying a cup of coffee and a blueberry muffin. Ying inhaled the delightful coffee aroma decorated with sweet blueberry scent. She jogged to keep up with Cristina who had begun power walking off the porch.

"Thank you, Madame President," said Ying as she caught up to her.

The two stepped along the cedar chip paths through the center of the campground. Ying took a measured sip of coffee and savored the perfect blend of rich and bitter. It was surreal to be walking next to this great woman. She had been so many things to Ying: idol, enemy, inspiration, savior.

"What do you think of our little school here, Ying?"

"It's spectacular. Did this used to be a camp?"

"Good eye."

Cristina patted Ying's back. It felt good to have approval from an older woman.

"Yes, previously this was an old Baptist summer camp and leadership center. We bought it five years ago as a training ground for our most elite cadets."

She walked her into a large cafeteria building. Row after row of cadets sat at long picnic tables eating their breakfast. Ying noticed a series of pills on each cadet's tray.

"What are those?" asked Ying

"I wish I could tell you they were super pills, but those are just the cadet's daily supplements. Got to keep them strong."

Cristina showed Ying the rest of the cafeteria and then led them toward a small horse ring on the east side of the grounds where cadets were training. Steam issued from their snouts like the horses she had seen at Brick's farm.

"How are they selected?"

"We use our military schools as feeder systems. Instructors are asked to identify high-potential kids. Kids with strong mathematical and logical abilities. Mental calculators. You know, kids like you."

Cristina smiled at Ying and gave her a wink.

"All these kids are mental calculators?"

"No, of course, not. Only a small percentage of them are, but we find that the mental calculators elevate the kids who have less natural mathematical skill, but more physical skill, to nearly their level. Look here."

The two of them walked up to the warped wooden fence lining the horse ring. Two teenage boys in red sweatsuits stood in the middle of a circle of other teenagers, arms raised and legs flexed in fighting position. Their hands and knuckles hung purple and raw from the cold. An instructor moved back and forth between the two, adjusting their arm positions, straightening their backs, while the cadets in the circle devoured the scene. Ying noticed one cadet was the girl who had knocked on her door this morning.

The instructor barked something to the two boys and then stepped back. The boys began to fight. But this was unlike any fight Ying had ever seen before. It was more akin to the scripting of a fight. Fists and legs flew with incredible speed and fury in both directions. Yet every punch and kick was blocked and countered, as though the two boys could see every punch before it was thrown.

"The Tree. They're using it," said Ying.

"That's right," said Cristina.

"I... I've just never seen two people so evenly matched. It's like a chess game between two perfectly equal players."

"Well, in many ways it is, Ying. It's very similar to how you would teach someone math. You don't start with calculus. You start with addition. Then subtraction. Then multiplication, et cetera. Both young men are at the same stage of learning, so they don't have the tools to bring more creative solutions to a problem. Fortunately, for us they don't have to, because anyone they would likely fight will be so far behind them, it won't matter. Now, see this young lady over here?"

Cristina pointed to the red head with the long braid. The one who had escorted Ying to the main lodge.

"This is Cynthia. She's a mental calculator like you. One of our star pupils."

Ying looked at Cynthia again. *Where had she seen her before?* Then it hit her. The girl. It was the same girl from Moloch's house. The one who had taken down a grown man in less than thirty seconds.

Cristina brought two fingers to her mouth and whistled. Everyone in the horse ring stopped and looked at her.

"Cynthia, why don't you show our guest here the RED Army way."

Cynthia nodded and stepped into the ring. She pulled her braid behind her shoulder and assumed a fighting stance. Both boys shook their heads and backtracked to leave the ring, but the instructor pushed them back in. Cynthia closed her eyes. Ying could see her doing the calculations. Which boy would strike first? Where would they strike? To Ying's surprise Cynthia never opened her eyes.

While the girl's eyes were closed, the first boy swept at her knees with his leg. She jumped in the air as his leg swung under her feet. She snatched the left shoulder of his red sweatshirt and spun him toward her. She jammed her right bicep into his trachea and began choking him. The second boy swung at her head with his right, then left fist. She snapped her left forearm back and forth jackhammering away the blows. Then with her left foot she kicked the boy in the groin, bringing him to his knees. While the other boy lay on the ground Cynthia tightened her chokehold on the first boy until he passed out. She dropped him to the dirt like a bag of grain and then reared back to finish off the second boy.

"That's enough," shouted the instructor.

Cynthia hesitated. Her fist poised in the air, a thoroughbred waiting to leave the gates. A maniacal look in her eye.

"That's enough, Cynthia."

She put her fist to her side and looked at the two boys in disgust.

Ying observed this with a combination of admiration and trepidation.

"Let's keep walking," said Cristina. She led them along a footpath that ran along the border of the camp. "I know what you're thinking," said Cristina.

"You do?"

"Absolutely. You're thinking 'isn't it wrong to teach kids this violence?'."

"Yes, that's exactly what I was thinking."

"You're right. It is wrong to teach kids violence. But let me pose another question to you... What made you decide to come with me last night?"

"I've been asking myself the same question," said Ying.

They both laughed.

"No, seriously, though. From the first moment I saw you on that old television at Angus's house I've believed in you. America is such an incredible country. And I'm so happy I came here. But we have some enormous problems, whether it's homelessness, or poor education or crime. And what kills me is that in Singapore, where I'm from, we've mitigated most of these problems. So, I know it's possible to fix them. But I feel like Angus, before he died, and Albert and the others are all so focused on protecting the world as it is that they forgot about what it could be. You reminded me of what it could be with your speeches when you were running for governor. And you've backed it up with all the amazing things you've done in the Republic. I guess I just wanted to be a part of that."

"Yes. That's what I hoped you'd say."

Cristina put her arm around Ying as they walked.

"And I want you to be a part of this. But let me tell you a short story. When I was a little girl in Chile, my family and I lived on a farm. We had a few old farm horses. My horse was named Descarada, which basically means Sassy. We called her that because for some reason she gave my Dad and my brother the hardest time when they tried to ride her. Bucking, snorting, neighing. But whenever I rode her, she was a perfect lady. I loved that horse. Well, one day I was riding Descarada around the farm, and her leg just gave out. She didn't hit anything. I didn't do anything different. She just collapsed. I ran to get my Dad, and he told me she broke her leg.

"I asked him how we fixed it. He said we couldn't, and he handed me his gun. I told him we didn't need to shoot the horse. That I would take care of it. He told me that would be cruel. I asked him why. He said 'you would rather have this horse suffer for the rest of her life, then send her to a better place. That is the coward's way, and you're not a coward, Cristina'."

Emotion pooled in her voice. She paused and then looked at Ying.

"I shot Descarada that day. I was ten. It was one of the hardest things I've ever had to do. But it was the right thing to do."

Ying swallowed. The image of a ten-year-old girl shooting her favorite horse struck something deep within her.

"That is how I see our choice, today, Ying. We have the choice of letting millions of our countrymen, children, mothers, seniors, continue to suffer in poverty, violence, in despair, or we can make the hard short-term choices to bring this country to a better place. But you must understand that if we're going to achieve that world, we have to upend the status quo. And to do that we need an army. And the only army capable of posing a counterweight to the United States Army is the RED Army."

"So, Albert was right. You are planning a coup?"

"A coup? No. A coup is when someone overthrows a government. Thirty states have joined RED. And those that have are so much better off than the ones that remain in the old United States. You said that yourself. We are the legitimately elected government. And we will stake our claim to that on January 20th when we march into Washington D.C. But in the meantime. I need your help. Will you help me?"

Ying took a sip of her coffee and tried to absorb the surrounding majesty. She was scared, but she believed that one woman might just be able to make a difference.

"I will."

Cristina hugged her.

"I'm so happy to hear that."

She grabbed Ying's shoulders.

"Now, I've got a special project for you."

"My turn to guess. You want me to find the Cipher."

"Impressive. How did you know?"

"The way I see it is that you already know that the Book Club can't stop you. Albert, himself, doesn't even believe they can stop you. You're planning to march on the White House on January 20th. This camp can't be more than five miles from the capitol, and I'm guessing there are lot more troops than what I see here. So, the only thing that you're probably worried about is the Cipher. This would normally be something Eva would tackle, but I guess you're stuck with me."

"Ha! My new daughter. You got it. So, how do you propose to do that? Moloch and the rest of his team have fallen woefully short, and I unfortunately don't have time for this nonsense."

"I've thought about this a bit, and the easiest way would be to wait for the Cipher's next contact. I assume your team solved the flaming sword cipher?"

Cristina grimaced.

"We did, but we took too long to get started. The cipher had been solved before our team could dig into it. And once the first cipher is solved, the trail dead-ends for anyone who solves it after. By the time our codebreaking team cracked it the screen just showed a message with the seven deadly sins."

"Why the seven deadly sins?"

"Sloth was underlined."

"I see. Then I guess we're going to have to do it the hard way."

"The hard way? What are you envisioning?"

"We'll set a trap."

Chapter 29

Gabe sat alone at the kitchen table of the safe house reading one article after another about the Cipher. Searching for something, anything that could lead them to him. The more he read, the more fascinated he became. The mission, the vision, what people had written. He had seen too much war in his lifetime. He knew the pain and destruction it caused. The Cipher made him feel that at least they might be able to win it That they had another ally in this fight against Cristina. It made him feel alive. Like there was hope.

A phone on the table started buzzing. Gabe reached to answer, but then realized it wasn't his. It was Albert's. He scratched his nascent beard, he had been so engrossed with the Cipher, he'd forgotten to shave. *Should he answer Albert's phone? What the hell?* He tapped the screen. A blue text preview showed a simple message:

"THE CIPHER SPEAKS IN TWO MINUTES.
https://www.cipherjkdloylarnnppj923wayyknm624pbulaa.onion/"

"Albert, get in here... Now!"

Albert jogged down the stairs into the kitchen, confused. "What's up?"

Gabe held up his phone. "A message from the Cipher. He's speaking." Albert dove toward the table. Gabe typed in the URL the Cipher had included in his message.

The screen showed the familiar white flaming sword against a black backdrop. A countdown clock ticked beneath it. 20... 19... 18.

"I'm actually kind of excited," said Gabe. "Clearly, I've been cooped up in this house too long."

Albert nodded his agreement. "I know, I'm putting way too much faith in this guy, right now."

The clock counted down. 5... 4... 3... 2... 1...

A video feed started. On the screen stood a figure dressed in a black military jacket in front of a black backdrop with the white flaming sword behind him and two torches on either side. A black mask made of a composite material covered his face. A cipher consisting of numbers, letters, and symbols in white decorated the mask.

The Cipher spoke. When he spoke, he used a voice modulator that gave his voice a metallic timbre. But behind that timbre lay a self-assurance and authority built on total conviction.

"Greetings my brothers and sisters. I am the Cipher. And you... you are the chosen. The worthy. From this day forward you are not alone. You are a part of us. The Sword of Eden."

Gabe grabbed Albert's shoulder and smiled. *They were a part of something. There was hope.*

"You are here from all corners of the globe because you have all shown a special blend of intelligence, creativity and daring. Something the world is badly in need of, right now. I will need every ounce of those skills for what I am about to ask of you. But first, I must tell you the story of what brought us to this day.

"Several years ago, a single mother in California was driving home from a meeting in downtown Los Angeles, and she took a wrong turn. The wrong turn took her through Skid Row, a neighborhood in L.A. known for having a large homeless population. As she drove through the streets, she saw our society's failings splayed out in stark relief. Thousands of people sleeping in tents or sidewalks. Drug addicts stumbling through the street. Prostitutes. Rapists. A child in the alley, filthy and alone, screaming for her mother.

"In one of the richest cities, in one of the most beautiful regions in one of the richest countries in the world, our government's indifference had created hell out of heaven. She resolved that day that she would do something. That she would not allow her daughter to grow up in a world that showed such disdain for humanity.

"Being the tough businesswoman that she was, she reached out to political and civic leaders to lobby them to do something. They nodded and expressed concern and sympathy, but nothing was done. The bureaucracy was too thick, too tangled. For every solution she brought them the politicians and bureaucrats had five reasons why it couldn't be done. 'You have to go through this committee. You have to get this permit, they said.

"So, she said, 'If you won't do anything about this, I will. And she started a new organization. She called it the 'Society for Reason, Enlightenment, and Democracy' or: RED. She and her organization provided aid to people in crisis. They cleaned streets, built shelters, and fed the poor. But she quickly realized that it wasn't enough. That they were just working around the edges.

That she couldn't really make the changes she wanted until she took over the government.

"So, she started a political party. And she ran for Governor of California. But as she ran for Governor, she realized she could not do everything she wanted with the legislature in the way. So, she abolished the legislature. Now she was Governor of California, and she had the power to change things. And she did change things. She cleaned up Skid Row and improved the schools.

"But then, she realized California was just a part of the problem. That if she was really going to change things, she needed to change the United States.

"I'm sure, by now, you know that this woman I'm talking about is Cristina Culebra. And I'm also sure that you now know where this story is headed. Soon, if left unchecked, Cristina Culebra will control the United States Government. And it won't be long before she realizes that what she really needs: To control all the governments in the world. And once she controls all the governments in the world, she will realize that she needs to control every person in the world.

"That is why you are here, my brothers and sisters. Cristina Culebra wants to smash down the gates of Eden. We are the flaming sword standing over the gates protecting Eden. We are the smartest, boldest, baddest people on the planet. And if we work together, we can form a 'global mind' that can defeat any challenge we face. The RED tide is coming, my brothers and sisters, and we are the bulwark.

"But RED is just one of the many tyrants on this planet who seek to bind us. The Sword of Eden seeks to bring all the world's tyrants to their knees, so that people across the world can be free. We must start with RED because that is the most vicious of the tyrants, but we will not rest until we have destroyed every last one of them.

"What is your role in all of this, you ask?

"My brothers and sisters, you are the soldiers of the Sword of Eden. Not soldiers of the battlefield, but soldiers of the mind. On January 20th, Cristina Culebra and the RED Army will storm the White House seeking to claim her tyrant's throne. I need you to work together and use your intelligence, your creativity, your daring, your global mind to stop them. I have messaged each of you a link to a virtual workspace where you can connect with your brethren. You have three days. On the 20th we will meet in person in our nation's capital. Be there, and I will message you where to meet.

"Welcome to The Sword of Eden, brothers and sisters."

The screen went black.

Chapter 30

Ying bit her fingernails as Cristina Culebra's black motorcade roared into the grounds of Battery Park. It was almost midnight, but a raucous mob in red still pushed and shoved to steal a glimpse of the candidate's motorcade entering the grounds for tonight's rally. The black, icy waters of the East River splashed against the banks. The Statue of Liberty stood like a sentinel in the distance.

Ying and RED's top hacker had spent the last twenty-four hours preparing for this moment. It was her first, and probably only chance, to prove her loyalty to Cristina.

Cristina's security detail exited the vehicle and evaluated the scene. They barked orders at each other and glared at the onlookers before finally opening the door for the President. Cristina stepped out of the vehicle. Her eyes connected with Ying's. Gone was the warm, motherly woman that she had bonded with at the campground. This was Cristina the conqueror. The woman who vanquished everything in her path.

"Hello, Madame President," said Ying, her voice quavering.

"Who's this?" said Cristina, pointing to the hacker.

Ying looked at him. He was just a skinny man in a red hoodie. And he was terrified.

"This is Nithin. He's the best hacker we've got."

"OK, what do you two have for me? Impress me," shouted Cristina over the din of the crowd.

"Well, Madame President. We've set up what is called a honeypot."

"Alright. What is it?"

"It's a false entry point into the network that enables us to gather information on the hacker."

"I know what a honeypot is, Ying. I meant, what are you using as the honeypot? What's the bait?"

While she interrogated Ying, Cristina put on her paper white smile and waved to the adoring crowd.

"You see that big screen behind the stage, Madame President, that says, 'President Cristina Culebra'?"

"Yes."

"We know the Cipher loves to make a splash, so it's our hope that he will hack in and place his flaming sword calling card on that screen behind you right as you're making your speech."

Cristina's face was cold. "This plan needs to get a lot better quickly."

"This is where it gets good," Ying assured her. "The Cipher hasn't just been spearfishing into our networks, he's been downloading a slow trickle of files from the RED network. Once he starts downloading tonight, we will have visibility into his location. That will enable us to see the Cipher's location. What do you think?"

"I think it's garbage," said Cristina. She started walking toward the stage.

"What? Why?"

Cristina turned back to Ying. "Ying, you don't think we've thought of this before? Whoever the Cipher is, he's smart enough to hide his location. He's not going to use a personal internet connection or anything that reveals his identity."

"No, Cristina... I mean, Madame President. Wait. I didn't tell you the best part. We found a way around that. Once he starts that download, we can send a data burst. Essentially pushing a mountain of data through a limited network, which will allow us to control the 'shape' of the traffic in order to inject a signature that can reveal the downloader as it permeates through the Tor network. Once that data hits Tor's exit nodes we can then mine IPs to see what IP received the burst at that moment. Then we've got 'em."

Cristina paused her march to the stage. Her lips slowly grew into a knowing smirk. "That's my girl! OK. Do it."

She waived two members of her security team over. One of them wore red aviators.

"Corey, Leonard. This is Ying and Nithin. It's a long shot, but these two might be able to find us a lead on the Cipher. I want you to have a team ready, so that if they give you the signal, we can get moving and find this bastard. I don't care if you have to fly to Russia."

"Yes, Ma'am."

"Good. This ends tonight."

While Cristina took the stage, Nithin, Ying, and red aviators jumped into an unmarked van. Ying slid the van door closed behind her, but left it open a crack.

"What happens now?" said the agent.

"Now, we listen and wait."

Ying leaned her body toward the door so she could hear Cristina's speech live. It was a speech she had heard before, but it still moved her. Cristina spoke of her childhood in Chile. Of being sent away from her family to America. Of the American dream and how it was being squandered. Of what we could do to recover it if we all worked together. The speech echoed with the sentiments of politicians who had come and gone, but behind it was a unique passion. A sincerity. The experience of making those words a reality.

The crowd knew it, too. Ying heard the applause. The chants of "Cristina, Cristina, Cristina". The outbursts of "That's right" or "You tell 'em!". But these weren't the exclamations of an angry crowd, bitter about the opposition or some unspoken grievance. These were exclamations of joy, of belief.

And in a moment, it was broken.

A loud static sound filled the air. Cristina stopped her speech. The crowd groaned and booed. Ying peaked her head out the van door. The flaming sword spun on the screen behind the President. Ying turned to Nithin.

"Alright, Nithin. This is it. This is where you make your money."

The skinny hacker with sunken eyes pivoted towards his keyboard. His gaze bounced up and down the computer screen. Unlike the hacking scenes in the movies where dazzling graphics and giant buttons covered five different giant screens, Nithin looked at a couple of monitors showing data passing through various networks.

"What's happening?" asked red aviators.

"The Cipher has hacked into our network, and now Nithin is trying to track his location."

"A few terabytes of data headed to the Cipher," said Nithin. He leaned back in his seat and pulled on his spiky black hair. His foot tremored against the floor with anticipation.

The van door flew open. It was Cristina.

"Did you get him?"

"We're about to find out," Ying called back.

Ying glanced at Nithin's screen. It showed a series of data patterns of information rolling through different IP addresses, none of which matched the pattern in the data they had sent out to the Cipher.

"Here it is!" shouted Nithin.

Ying leaned over his shoulder and looked at the screen. One IP address showed that distinct pattern.

32.213.36.67

"Holy shit!" said Nithin.

"What?"

"It looks like this is one of the IP addresses used by RED Social."

Chapter 31

Three black SUVS growled down the West Side Highway, red, and blue lights flashing from their interiors. Ying watched from the rear seat of the middle SUV as the cars in front of them scattered like pigeons on a sidewalk. Her fingers twitched slightly in her lap; she could not seem to settle them since she left the safe house. Purpose ran through her in every moment. The world would be different after this. She was part of something now, and she would not fail.

She almost leaped out of her skin when her cell phone rang. She answered the call.

"Madame President. What may I do for you?"

"You've done well, my Ying-lita." Cristina's voice was warm, full of pride. In this moment, Ying could almost believe that no one else in the world existed except the two of them, so glaring was Cristina's regard.

"Thank you, Madame President."

"I don't think even Eva could have come up with this."

"Thank you, Madame President."

"Now, go bring me this traitor," Cristina instructed, and the line went dead.

Ying's lips twitched in a half-smile. It had been so long since she'd been appreciated. Her parents loved her, but they had been very traditional, always telling her what she was doing wrong. Her brothers treated her like an invalid, a burden to be cared for because she was family. Albert teased her. Weatherspoon held her back. The Book Club ignored her, unwilling to see that there might be more to the world than they could understand from one viewpoint.

And now, here she was, sitting in the middle of a motorcade, her motorcade, being praised by the most powerful woman in the world. She hadn't felt so seen since...

Since Professor Turner.

And he was gone.

What would Turner say? What would he think of her, now? Would he think she was a traitor for leaving with Cristina, or would he understand? Would he get that she just saw the world differently than he did? What would he think of the Cipher? A terrorist or a freedom fighter? When Ying thought of Turner, she couldn't help feeling that everything was more complicated than she wanted it to be.

Her dad would tell her, "*Kewajipan*", *Duty*. The thought calmed her.

The SUVs came to a quick, but silent, halt in front of the RED Social building in Chelsea, and Ying's door opened a moment later to reveal Cristina's own security detail.

"Ma'am, we need to secure the building before you can go inside," Corey said. "Please remain here while we apprehend the Cipher."

His respect made Ying feel like royalty. Was Cristina truly used to this, or did she not see it, anymore? She wasn't sure, but it gave her the confidence to raise her chin in an imitation of Cristina's posture. "Corey, I'm coming with you."

"Ma'am, please–"

"President's orders, Corey." Technically, those orders were to use all tools at her disposal to apprehend the Cipher, which could easily include using Corey, but he didn't need to know that.

He nodded in acquiescence and stepped back, holding out a hand to help Ying out of the car. She looked up at the historic building as she climbed down. Only three office lights were on: one on the third floor, one on the tenth floor, and one on the floor second from the top. The rest of the building slept in darkness.

Here we go, Ying, she told herself silently. *You can do this.* She didn't need to think about what was going to happen to whoever she found in here. She just needed to do her part.

She put on her best Cristina-Culebra-badass face and swept past Corey. As he had done for Cristina, he stayed at her shoulder until she reached the door, which he opened for her.

You can do this.

The security guard in the lobby nearly fell over upon seeing the President's entourage. "Can I... I help you?"

"Yes," Ying said, and she was glad to hear the word come out crisply. "My name is Ying Koh, and I'm here on the personal instruction of President Culebra. There has been a security breach."

The man looked around himself, terrified. "Ma'am, I–"

"What is your name?" Ying interrupted him coolly.

"Joe. Joseph. O'Neill."

Ying swept a hand out to indicate the rest of the security detail she had brought with her. "Mr. O'Neill, I need you and these gentlemen to lock this lobby down. Nobody gets in or out without my personal say-so... *in person.* Understand?"

The security guard's throat bobbed as he gulped and nodded. They weren't blaming him for the breach, and his relief was palpable.

No weakness, Ying told herself. She gave Corey a nod. "Let's do this."

Corey used his personal badge to open the security gate, and Ying smiled to herself as she walked through it. Her memory of the guard's fear was already fading into the much more pleasant memory of him staring at her, wide-eyed, as she walked into the building with Cristina Culebra's personal guard at her side.

I could get used to this.

"There were three office lights on," Ying said as they reached the elevators. "As we walked in. One on the third floor, one on the tenth, and one second from the top. Our 'Cipher-'," she used finger quotes and a contemptuous expression, "–is likely in one of those offices. I say we check them one at a time."

"Yes, ma'am. Please stay behind me."

Ying gave a silent nod. Corey didn't know about her skills, so she played along. At least, he realized she wasn't going to remain behind while he did this alone.

The two stepped into the elevator and Corey pressed the button for floor three. A few moments later, the door opened into a waiting room with a laminate reception desk and glass walled conference room behind it. The conference room was empty, and everything was dark except for a faint light from down the hallway to the right.

Corey had drawn his gun in the elevator. Now he motioned for Ying to stay back while he checked the corridor in both directions, and then beckoned her after him as they moved down the hallway together.

Ying listened for the clicking of keys on a keyboard, but she heard nothing. With each step, new possibilities flashed through her mind: a familiar face, perhaps, or a mocking message written on the whiteboard. Perhaps this was even a trap; that thought sent a shiver down her spine.

When they reached the lit office, Ying drew against the wall while Corey advanced. His gun came halfway up and he swung around to face into the office before lowering the weapon.

Empty, he mouthed at her.

Ying tried to mask her disappointment, but her heart hadn't stopped going double-time–if anything, she was more aware of it, now. In contrast to her elegant entrance in the lobby, she followed Corey's cues, for now.

In the elevator, Ying sighed.

Corey looked over at her briefly, then away, as if remembering his job.

Ying swallowed and linked her hands behind her back. "This is stressful," she admitted.

To her surprise, Corey gave a chuckle. "Welcome to my world."

Her lip curled. The elevator dinged, and the doors to the tenth floor opened. This floor was different. The floor-plan was open. Row after row of long stand-up desks ran across a rectangular floor. Each desk held five computer monitors and keyboards, but no people. Everyone had gone home for the night.

Except for one.

A long glass office stood on the other side. Ying's breath caught. From a distance, Ying saw a man frantically typing on his computer. His face was inches from the screen. Doubt worked in Ying's stomach, but there was no time to wonder what was going on. The man didn't seem to have noticed them, yet, so she and Corey crouched down and crept through the office corridor, using the stand-up desks as cover.

As she approached, Ying stole a glance. The man was not wearing headphones, but he was not looking up. He must be deeply focused not to have noticed the sound of the elevator.

He had no idea what was about to hit him.

She could see that the man was wearing glasses. Not only that, they showed the reflection of the screen in the lenses, and it was absolutely unmistakable: a flaming white sword against a black background.

Ying reached out to touch Corey's arm. She motioned in the man's direction, indicated glasses and waited for Corey to look. He gave her a tight nod and then burst out of cover with his gun drawn.

"Freeze!"

The man jumped and then froze entirely. His keyboard had been knocked askew in his movement, and his face showed naked fear. He had deep brown skin and close-cropped, curly black hair. Slowly, he raised his hands in the air.

"What... what's going on?" he asked. His voice trembled.

"Stand up," Corey told him. "Keep your hands above your head."

"I don't understa–"

"Secret Service." Corey's voice was a snarl. "Get out from behind the desk."

"But–"

What would Cristina do? Ying walked to the door and looked in. "You are speaking to a member of President Culebra's security detail," she said coolly. "I suggest following his instructions."

The man looked at Corey and his face took on a grayish tinge. "I... yes, I recognize you. But I don't understand."

"You can drop the act," Ying told him. "We know you're the Cipher, and you've been working to bring down President Culebra. You're under arrest."

"What?" The man took a step forward, hands out. "No. No, you don't understand. I'm Chibuike Abdullah. I'm the lead developer at RED."

"And if I were to turn your monitor, would it not show the Cipher's symbol?" Ying raised an eyebrow. "You don't need to answer. We both saw it reflected in your glasses."

"That? Uh, I don't... I don't know why that's there. I was working at my computer and that just showed up. I was trying to figure out how when you busted in and pointed a gun at me."

Corey scoffed. He gave a look at Ying, who smiled.

"Mr. Abdullah, we just caught you red handed. We know you hacked the rally tonight. We know that you're the Cipher." She tilted her head. "This will be much simpler if you just tell us the truth."

"I am telling you the truth. You have access to these computers and this network. Check the logs. You'll see this was–"

"I've heard about enough," Corey said. "Mr. Abdullah, you're coming with us." With his gun still pointed at the man, he jerked his head to direct him. Into his radio, he said, "Backup needed on ten. Yes. We have apprehended the Cipher. Yes, do a sweep of twenty-four to be sure. We will be down, shortly."

Chibuike made a noise, something that could have been words, but wasn't. He seemed to be in a trance as Corey handcuffed him and directed him out of the room.

"Ma'am, would you please retrieve the laptop?"

"Certainly." She sounded like Cristina. Ying smiled and took the laptop. "We should inform the President of the good news."

Chapter 32

The Book Club had been holed up in the safe house for forty-eight hours mapping out scenarios to stop Cristina and the RED Army, and they still had little to show for it. The shock of Ying's departure permeated the house, but there was little choice other than to focus on the work. Mana, Weatherspoon, and Eva had set up shop in the kitchen and had been working their connections at the White House, while Albert, Brick, Gabe, and Salazar whiteboarded alternative strategies in the living room.

Mana was stuck on a call, pacing back and forth in front of the kitchen island, while Weatherspoon and Eva watched.

"I understand that, Bob. Bob, yes. I know but. But this is just a precautionary measure. For the President's safety. Yes. Yes. Yes."

She rolled her eyes heavenwards as if praying for patience.

"Yes, I know. Bob. I do know. Because I'll explain it to you in plain English, that's how you'll know. He can't call in the National Guard every time there's a protest because it's a waste of resources and it sets a bad precedent. It's not great optics. I know."

She took a deep breath before continuing.

"But this isn't a run-of-the-mill protest. Yes, you do know that. No. It isn't. What it is, is the army of a woman who is literally taking over the United fucking States one state at a time. Bob? Hello?" She hung up the phone with a snarl. "Fucking fuckers. Spineless, lazy bureaucratic fucks!"

Weatherspoon cleared his throat. "I take it your call with the White House didn't go so well."

"No shit. I told those fuckers everything. I told them, Cristina Culebra and the RED Army are going to march right up to your front door on January 20th. They know that. I told them, you have a military that is not loyal to the United States marching through the streets of Washington, D.C. They know that, too."

"... But?" Weatherspoon asked.

"But," Eva said when Mana looked more ready to explode with rage than answer the question, "My guess is that they said something about taking this tip under advisement and being unable to comment on current matters of national security. Am I right?"

"They wouldn't even agree to increase the security detail," Mana said. "It's fucking unbelievable. I'm telling them that an army of ten thousand soldiers is going to storm the White House, and they can't be bothered to get over themselves and–"

She dug into her pouch of Big League Chew and began gnawing.

"He doesn't want to look weak," Albert called from the living room, having overheard the discussion. He looked at the whiteboard and finally said the words that had been circling in his brain for hours. "Our only option is to disable the RED Army when they get into the city."

There was a resounding silence from both rooms.

Brick recovered first. "No way," he said flatly. "I will not be part of any operation where we're taking out innocent soldiers who are simply marching."

"Brick." Gabe put his marker down and rolled his wheelchair over to his friend. "These aren't innocent civilians staging a peaceful protest. This is a full-blown army marching on the White House with the goal of intimidating people into capitulating. We have to do something, or they could seize the White House."

Brick said nothing. He looked away, his jaw clenched, and Albert saw a muscle twitch in the man's jaw.

Gabe continued, "But regardless, I've been chatting online with some of the Cipher's followers, and I think there are some alternative approaches that could work."

"You mean the riddle solvers sewing circle? Didn't Culebra's people catch the Cipher last night?" Brick's voice was heavy with contempt.

"Well, that's what the RED Network's reporting, but I'm not sure I believe that."

"Regardless, I'm sure they've got some interesting ideas on the Cipher's little chat group, but let's be realistic, we can't stop an army that big on our own without doing some pretty nasty stuff. And I'm just not willing to bomb, shoot, gas, or otherwise incapacitate a group of people whose only crime is marching. A lot of these people who are going to be marching are kids, Gabe. Are you really willing to take out a bunch of kids?"

Gabe hesitated. He turned the dry erase marker over and over in his hands before, at last, shaking his head. "But, I'm not sure we have to—"

"I didn't think so. No, the only way we can stop these guys without getting ugly is to meet bodies with bodies. Cristina Culebra does not actually want a fight. She wants us to roll over."

Brick turned his chair toward the kitchen.

"Eva, you're a big muckety muck. Isn't there someone you know who can get us access to the President Brooks, so we can explain the gravity of the situation."

Eva shook her head. "Normally, yes, but I've been making calls, and anything I say they just think is being planted by my mother."

Gabe started flipping his blue expo marker in the air, a habit he used when he was thinking. "Fine. How about this? We could cut their lines of communication. We could fire off an EMP and disable their cell phones. Put some type of jam on any radio signals. That would at least slow them down."

Albert set his own marker down on the steel shelf of the whiteboard and walked toward the window overlooking the lake.

"That's not bad," he said, after thinking for a bit.

"But?" Gabe guessed the caveat.

Albert looked over his shoulder with a rueful smile. "But. Yes. But you know as well as I do, we need more to tip the scales. They'll still be able to keep marching even if it's a little confused. Look, guys, I promise you, I've mapped this out every which way there is, and we've been going back and forth on this for twenty-four hours, and we're still stuck with two options to stop the attack on the 20th. We either hit the Red Army first, with some type of non-traditional weapon–"

Weatherspoon interrupted. "I'm with Brick. We can't do that, Puddles. Even though I agree that they're probably up to no good, we can't just attack a group of men and women who have done nothing wrong, yet. Then we're just as bad as them."

"They're right," said Mana. "The Bureau can't be a part of anything like that."

Albert sat down on the sofa. "Well, we may not be able to do it, but maybe the Cipher can... if he isn't in jail. He's allegedly going to do something big tomorrow. Mana and Gabe, why don't you two go into D.C. and bird-dog the Cipher just in case the RED Network's blowing smoke about catching him. All he's produced up to this point is a bunch of riddles, but maybe we'll get lucky.

"Now, that's what I'm talking about," said Gabe. He gave his wheelchair a one-hundred-eighty-degree spin on the back wheels.

"Then, the rest of us can work on convincing the President to call in the National Guard and anybody else he can get to defend the White House on short notice. The only problem is, as you've so eloquently shown Mana, we can't get an audience with him."

Salazar, who had been sitting silently chomping on microwave popcorn stood up, walked into the kitchen and tossed the oily bag into the garbage can. Half-eaten kernels covered his t-shirt. He wiped his hands on his faded jeans and put on his cowboy hat.

"So, when are we going to do this?"

"Do what?" said Albert.

"Go to the White House and talk to the President."

"What are you talking about? Have you been listening at all to what we've been saying?"

Salazar gave him a look. "You just said we needed to talk to the President and tell him to call in the National Guard."

"Yeah?"

"So, we got to go do that, right?" Salazar gestured expansively.

Mana laughed and touched his shoulder. "Salazar... we can't just walk into the White House and talk to the President."

He pinned her with a stare. "Why not?" There was no hint of a smile on his face.

"Umm... I don't know. Security? Gates? Secret Service?... Guns?"

He relaxed at last. "Ahhh. That's easy, *chiquitita*. You and Gabe will go check out the Cipher. Weatherspoon and Eva, you hang back in case we get a message from the Cipher, and tell us Cristina's movements. You book us a White House tour, you know, the ones the tourists take. I'll do some distraction. Albert and Brick kick some butt. Next thing you know we're in the Oval Office. Puddles convinces the President. Bing, bang, boom. Problem solved."

"We don't even know if the President will be there," Albert said helplessly.

Mana cleared her throat. "Uh... yes, we do. I checked that much before I called, and they confirmed it." She looked around at them. "Not that I'm saying this is a good idea, mind you."

"It's not." Eva rose from the kitchen chair and kissed Salazar on the cheek "It's a great idea. Finally. I love this guy."

Salazar patted her hand fondly and threw a toothpick in his mouth.

Everyone looked at Albert, waiting for him to list all the reasons Salazar was wrong. Albert put his hands in his pockets. He opened his mouth and then stopped himself. He opened it again and then paused again. He started a final time.

"I can't believe I'm saying this, but... he's right. I think we're going to have to break into the White House."

Chapter 33

The next morning, while Albert and company prepared for their White House tour, Mana, and Gabe started the hunt for the Cipher in front of the United States Capitol building. The pair stood outside the shining dome and marveled at the iconic blend of Roman and Greek architecture. Steam rippled out through the building's vents into the crisp, dry air. Staffers in rumpled suits carrying bags full of papers scampered up the steps. School tour groups full of sleepy kids ambled past them. The smell of pretzels from the early bird food carts wafted through the air. Small bands of protesters for this cause and that trickled by with muted enthusiasm.

In his mind, Gabe had pictured an incredible spectacle. Everything he had read and seen about the Cipher had been so well thought out, so performative. But now that he was here, he was struck by what a typical Washington D. C. morning it was. No sign of the Cipher. No RED Army. *Maybe it was true. Maybe the Cipher had been apprehended.* He wondered if all of this had been nothing more than one big prank. He looked at Mana and pulled at his eyebrow, which was growing thin.

"This doesn't exactly look like the beginning of a revolution does it, Mana?"

She squinted at him.

"Don't be such a fucking downer. You know what they say, 'Every revolution seems impossible at the beginning, and after it happens, it was inevitable'."

"Well, I'm thinking that it's inevitable that we're going to freeze if we stay out here in this cold. What do you think we should do?"

"I think we should stop by this little vendor here and pick up some coffee while we wait to hear from the Cipher. If he's still alive."

Mana strolled over to a small green kiosk. She ordered two cups of coffee. The smell of Arabica beans filled the air. The barista handed her two cups, and Gabe looked on in amusement as Mana poured out half the cup of coffee to make room for a gargantuan helping of cream.

"I'm sorry that coffee is getting in the way of your cream."

"And I'm sorry you've had to go through your life not knowing the proper way to make coffee. Should we survey the grounds?"

The two moved around the North side of the Capitol and down the steps toward the Capitol Mall. Gabe had been to Washington, D.C. many times but still found the scene awe-inspiring. The long rectangular mall splayed out before him. The Washington Monument jutted skyward, while the Lincoln Memorial observed in the background. Joggers ripped by them seemingly oblivious to the architectural marvels in their midst. They kept walking along the lawn's sidewalks toward the Washington Monument as if drawn by an invisible force. Two RED Army soldiers walked past them. The Mall seemed calm, but Gabe sensed an unrealized energy, a coiled spring waiting to release.

Mana's phone dinged. A text from Weatherspoon read, "Cristina's coming. The march has started."

Gabe perked up. "A message from the Cipher?"

"No, Cristina's apparently started her march." She put her phone back in her pocket and took a sip of her coffee. "So, what do you think is actually going to happen today?"

"I think it's going to go down exactly like the Cipher said. I don't believe that the guy they caught is the Cipher. He's too smart for that. I think the RED Army is going to come marching into Washington, D. C., and we're going to stop them."

"You really believe that? How are we going to stop them?"

"With intelligence."

"Seriously? You really think the Cipher and some nerds throwing out ideas online is going to stop the RED Army? Do you think it could actually work? I mean how would the Cipher even execute that?"

"I know it can work. I've been watching the Cipher's group online, and the people in that group are smart. And, think about it. Full-blown revolutions in other countries have been started and succeeded just with Facebook groups. I'm not sure exactly how the Cipher will execute it. But look at what he's pulled off, so far. He's hacked into Cristina Culebra's campaign. He's recruited a bunch of really smart people to the cause. He got us to come down here, today. At this point, nothing would surprise me."

Mana's phone dinged again. Another text from Weatherspoon. "It's a message from the Cipher! You were right. He's still free.

They must have caught the wrong guy." They stared at each other bug-eyed.

"Now, the shit hits the fan," said Mana.

Gabe grimaced, afraid she was right.

She read aloud. "He drove the man out; and at the east of the Garden of Eden He stationed the cherubim and the flaming sword which turned every direction to guard the way to the tree of life."

"That's it?" said Gabe.

"Yep."

"What are we supposed to do with that?"

"I'm guessing it's the final clue. One last test for us to figure out where we should go."

"Ugh. This Cipher is a real ball buster. Haven't we done enough?"

"Apparently not. What do you make of it?"

They huddled around her phone searching for an underlying meaning.

"It's a Bible quote, right?" said Mana.

Gabe laughed and slapped her on the shoulder. "Yes, it's a Bible quote. It's from Genesis when Adam and Eve get booted from the Garden of Eden."

"Sorry. I'm not Christian. I don't know what fancy tales you all tell yourselves. Do you know any quotes from the Quran?"

"No."

"I didn't think so. Anyway, maybe the Bible verse is telling us the time to meet?"

Gabe tapped on his phone to look up the quotation.

"Genesis 3:24? It can't be the time. The Cipher said to be in D.C. in the morning, and the RED Army will be here long before then."

"What about 'gardens'? Garden of Eden? Maybe there's some type of garden," said Gabe.

He searched on his phone.

"There's a nightclub called the Garden of Eden? Do you think the Cipher wants us to start the revolution there?"

"Probably not."

"Regardless, we should definitely go. Just probably not today."

Mana grabbed his shoulder. "This might be a possibility. The U.S. Botanical Garden. They're right here on the Mall."

"Yes. Let's go."

Gabe wheeled south across the Mall toward the Botanical Garden, with Mana not far behind. His anxiety and fear subsided at the thought of finally meeting this mysterious man. He looked for any sign of the Cipher, or–failing that–anyone like him dressed in black with the same confused look on their face. Nothing. Just a sign that said, "closed for the winter".

"Damn." said Mana. "I was really hoping that was going to be it. It seemed a little off, though."

Mana looked around, thinking. "What about Adam and Eve? Maybe there's something there? Some statue or museum."

"I think I'd remember that, but I'll check."

Gabe searched on his phone. After a few seconds he started laughing.

"What?"

"Adam and Eve adult entertainment store. We could make a night of it. Start at Adam and Eve Adult Entertainment and then close out the evening at Garden of Eden nightclub."

"Love it. But probably for another time."

Mana and Gabe continued to make their way along the mall and pondered.

"Read it to me again," said Gabe.

"He drove the man out and at the east of the Garden of Eden he stationed the cherubim and the flaming sword which turned every direction to guard the way to the tree of life."

"That's it!"

"What's it?"

"The flaming sword. It must be something to do with the flaming sword. The Cipher calls his movement The Sword of Eden. Look it up."

Mana Googled 'Flaming Sword Washington'. "Holy Shit."

"What?" said Gabe.

"There is a Flaming Sword statue at the 2nd Division Memorial."

"No way."

"Yep. And guess what major monument it's by?"

"The White House?"

"Exactly."

"That's just a few blocks away, isn't it?"

"It sure is."

"Let's roll."

Mana and Gabe hustled north across the National Mall and headed west along Constitution Avenue. They weaved past the tour groups and hot dog vendors toward the White House. As they approached, two other young women in all black outfits began jogging along beside them with the same eager looks on their faces. Then, an old man in all black shuffled past them. Then, an Asian couple. They smiled and pointed.

Gabe looked up and saw a hulking gold flaming sword statue gleaming in the distance. In front of them was a sea of black. Other folks of all backgrounds, ages, races, and sexes, just like him and

Mana, who had solved the Cipher and traveled from all over the world to see him. To follow him. To stop the RED Army. To stop all the tyrants. It was intoxicating.

Breathless, they arrived at the Memorial. The monument itself was simple. A large rectangular marble pedestal stood between two American flags and hosted a golden statue of a hand gripping a flaming sword. Three small steps lead up to the statue, which sat on an open lawn now dusted in snow. A crowd of five hundred people all dressed head to toe in black encircled the sword.

The Sword of Eden.

Gabe's heart swelled. He looked at Mana and realized she felt the same. They had secretly resigned themselves to the fact that Cristina would win. But now it seemed possible that she wouldn't. That there was promise.

Chants broke out from the crowd.

"We want the Cipher. We want the Cipher."

Gabe and Mana joined the chant.

"We want the Cipher. We want the Cipher."

Chapter 34

Albert stood in his bedroom in the safe house. He sipped on a black coffee and stared at the lake, enjoying the moment's peace. The sky was a striking, cold blue. The lake water sat motionless, considering whether to turn to ice. It reminded him of walks with his dad in Northfield. The calm of the lake juxtaposed against the harsh cold of the winter wind. Albert's eyes took in the peaceful scene, but his mind reverberated with scenarios for what they were about to do.

Breaking into the Oval Office to convince the President that Cristina was coming for him. On its face it seemed so implausible. The gates. The secret service. The snipers. But like so many things, when Albert applied what he knew of the Tree of Knowledge, the implausible became not only plausible, but inevitable.

Moini had scheduled this morning's first White House tour for them. 7:30 AM. This would put them in the East Wing of the White House. The President operated out of the West Wing, twenty meters from the West side of the East Wing. The challenge was how to make it through the most secure twenty meters in the world. But as Albert's mind ran through the Tree, calculating and recalculating, envisioning every scenario, adjusting when it failed, doubling down when it succeeded, he found that the easy part was getting to the President. The hard part would be convincing him. Every hypothetical conversation that Albert played out in his head resulted in him being dismissed and detained. And who could blame the President? A mad man bursts into the White House, and you're supposed to take his council?

His thoughts were interrupted by Weatherspoon shouting from downstairs. "Puddles, turn on your TV." He put down his coffee and switched on the bedroom TV.

Thunderous music burst from the TV accompanied by an angry red chevron. The over-made-up anchor adopted his most important sounding voice.

"We have breaking news this morning out of Virginia. President of the new Republic of Enlightenment and Democracy, Cristina Culebra, and her followers have taken to the streets."

The screen cut to an aerial image of thousands of red-clad marchers tromping down a winding country road.

"I'm being told Culebra and the RED Army are marching down Canal Road toward Washington D. C. There looks to be at least ten thousand troops, and they are blocking traffic on the road."

Albert stepped toward the TV and squinted. It was worse than he had expected. The sea of red uniforms bled across the entire screen. The cars pulled over on the side of the road seemed like miniatures against the size of the army, marching in perfect unison. A hive mind.

"You don't have to do this, you know," said Eva as she slid into the room.

Albert turned from the television and looked at Eva. Her face carried a steady confidence, almost joy.

"What's the alternative?" asked Albert.

Eva walked up to him and put her hands around him. She kissed him and gave his butt a squeeze.

"Let's just take out the RED Army and be done with this."

"Eva, we can't just 'take out' the RED Army. A lot of those soldiers are just kids and are marching because they were told to march. Are you suggesting we kill a bunch of people marching peacefully just because we think something bad might happen?"

"Albert, you know as well as I do that there is nothing peaceful about this march. This is all about intimidation. Have you forgotten who we're dealing with? My mother doesn't care about your ethics. She doesn't care about 'innocent until proven guilty'. In fact, she's exploiting it. She knows people like you aren't willing to violate your 'principles', so she can march her way right up to the White House, and no one will stop her."

Albert turned off the TV and threw the remote on the bed.

"And what about you, Eva? What are your principles? Gun anybody down who might be a threat, someday? What if you're wrong? Are you willing to live with that?"

"I'm not wrong, Albert. And I didn't say we need to gun down the RED Army. I just said we need to stop them. You're banking on the fact that the President is going to listen to you. What if he doesn't? What if the Secret Service stops you? By then, it will be too late."

"So, what are you saying? You're not going to help us?"

"Of course, I'm going to help you. I'll hang back here with Weatherspoon and monitor Cristina and the Cipher while you,

Salazar and Brick go to work. I just wanted to give it one last try to bring you over to my side."

Albert leaned in and kissed her. He loved the contrast of danger and softness, though he wondered if it could last.

"I am on your side. We will stop Cristina. I promise. I won't let you down. I will get to the President and get him to call in the National Guard."

She kissed him on the forehead.

"I believe you."

Weatherspoon popped his head in the room. "These will make it a little easier."

He handed Albert three bright blue staff passes with the White House logo on them.

Albert smiled. "I guess there's no turning back, now."

Weatherspoon slapped him on the back. "Nope."

Brick and Salazar burst into the room wearing suits and adding to the interruption. "You ready Puddles?" said Brick. Salazar looked like he'd been stuffed into the suit by a taxidermist.

Albert looked at Eva and smiled.

"Yep."

"Good. We've got a meeting with the President."

Chapter 35

W elcome to the White House," said a chirpy woman in a navy-blue blazer. "My name is Diane, and I will be your tour guide today. Are you all enjoying your visit to Washington, D. C., so far?"

Cold sweat rose from Albert's palms. He, Brick and Salazar stood in the lobby of the White House's East Wing waiting to begin their tour. The previous evening, they had mapped this out to the last detail. The White House was secure, but not as secure as it might seem. While the Commander-in-Chief resided here. And the Secret Service guarded the building, the White House was at its most elemental, an office building, populated by staffers and visitors who needed to go about their day-to-day business.

Each of them wore suits and ties to impersonate those very staffers, a marked contrast to the rest of the sweater clad group on the tour. Albert took a deep breath and looked around to calm himself. The room carried the smell of history. Wood panels covered the long, rectangular space, decorated with Christmas wreaths. A portrait of Franklin Roosevelt in a long gray overcoat with papers in hand looked down on Albert and his companions in judgment. Albert counted nine other people in the tour group. All with no idea of what was about to happen. The Book Club was going to break into the West Wing.

If they failed, there was no plan B.

Diane led the group from the lobby to the Garden Room, keeping up a lively stream of chatter as she did so. Salazar, true to form, was enjoying the tour. He absorbed the history of the White House and murmured along with the other members of the tour at all the correct moments. Anyone looking at him would think the man did not have a care in the world.

All Albert could think about was their mission. When they passed a Secret Service agent, his eyes scanned the group out of habit, and Albert tried to keep his expression clear; he could be giving off a hundred signals that he was suspicious, and he would not know. *Did he recognize me? Did he see the sweat on my brow?* He stole a glance at Brick, who gave a gentle nod, as if to say, *be calm, it's going to be fine.* Albert longed for the good old days when the President used to take evening strolls by himself.

A Christmas tree held court in the center of the Garden Room, flanked by two giant nutcrackers. Another secret service agent stood against the wall, jarringly out of place with the charming holiday atmosphere. When he bent his head to say something into the microphone on his lapel, Albert's pulse leaped again. *Are they on to us? How could they know?*

No. Replace the thought. He took a deep breath and closed his eyes. He placed himself back in that old barn in Vermont and repeated the advice Angus had given him: *Fear is the enemy of logic. Just follow the Tree.* He felt his breathing slow and saw the path of actions that would lead him to the President, each step illuminated in his mind.

Just a few more steps, and it would begin.

Diane led the group down the narrow East Colonnade connecting the East Wing of the White House to the residence. They were getting closer. Albert was holding onto his composure by a thin thread. When Diane stopped dead in the middle of opening the door to the residence, her hand going to her ear, Albert saw even Salazar shift from jovial engagement to a ready stance.

"I'm sorry," Diane said, "but I'm afraid we have a problem, and we're going to have to redirect the tour." As the group looked around at one another in alarm, Diane said, "I don't want you to be worried. We'll go right this way."

Albert stiffened and held his breath. He glanced at Salazar and Brick who were both frozen.

"It's just that I forgot to show y'all the President's movie theater." Diane said, holding up her hands dramatically.

The group laughed, and Diane took a few steps back to show them the small family theater. Albert pretended to be interested by the luxury of it all, while Diane went through the favorite movies and TV shows of various Presidents and First Ladies, after which, she finally ushered the group into the residence.

Albert, Salazar, and Brick all knew the layout of the residence by heart. On the right side of the first floor was the library, some tradesmen's offices, and the Secret Service office, as well as the entrance to the West Wing, the location of the Oval Office. That door stood at the end of a hallway, guarded by one Secret Service agent. On the left were the Vermeil Room, the Diplomatic Room, and the China Room.

The China Room held the keys to the castle. Albert just had to wait for his moment.

It was here that Diana split her focus, allowing the guests to wander around the different rooms as she told the story of the British burning down the White House in 1817. One family peeked into the Diplomatic Room. Brick, Salazar, and Albert separately drifted into the China Room, on the far side of which was a bathroom.

As soon as they were alone, the trio slid into the bathroom and Albert locked the door. All of them were moving with purpose now, and for Albert, the relief was indescribable. Brick removed the three White House West Wing staff badges and handed them out. They placed the badges around their necks and gave each other once-overs. Unlike the rest of the tour group, the three of them were dressed as if they could be employees, and the badges completed the look–as long as no one looked too closely.

Salazar reached into his pocket and pulled out his key chain. A yellow rubber duck with wheels hung from its base, which he detached from the chain and placed on the floor. Brick had been listening at the door, and at his nod, Salazar opened the bathroom door a crack and switched the power button on the duck's side from off to on. The wheels began spinning and the duck spat out a repetitive quack.

Salazar looked at Albert and gave a delighted grin.

Albert shook his head. He couldn't help but chuckle, but his heart was still pounding. "I can't believe we're doing this.

"Yeah, this is pretty badass," Salazar said. "Even for me."

He placed the duck on the ground, and Albert watched as it trundled along the antique wood floor of the China Room, across the Center Hall, and into the Library, quacking away. Albert had the vivid memory of the cacophony that had filled the safe house as the group assessed a whole set of toys. Some hadn't gone quite straight over long distances, while others tipped over on their sides; even now, there were two backup key chain ducks in Albert and Brick's pockets.

Salazar eased the bathroom door shut, but Albert could hear Diane say, "what was that?" followed by the sound of a Secret Service agent jogging down the hall.

Albert waited five beats and then emerged from the bathroom. He looked across the hall to confirm that everyone was focused on the duck, then he stepped through the China Room and into the adjoining Diplomatic Room with Brick and Salazar close behind. There was no time to waste; the duck distraction wouldn't last long.

They moved from the Diplomatic Room to the Map Room, and Albert peeked his head out of the Map Room door. To the left, the entrance to the West Wing just a few feet away. To the right was the tour group and a very perplexed Secret Service agent trying to assess the threat level of a mysterious quacking mechanical duck.

Albert stood up straight and adopted his most serious business posture. They had to believe that he worked here. It was just another day at the office. He took one last glance down the hall and waited until every member of the tour group was looking the other way. When the coast was clear, he beckoned behind him with two fingers and made his way toward the door.

The shout came just as his palm closed around the brass doorknob to the West Wing.

"Don't touch that!"

Keep up the act, but show caution. Albert spread his hands wide in the universal gesture that said *I am not a threat,* and slowly pivoted.

The agent was not running toward Albert, however, but into the China Room, where a little girl had grabbed one of the pieces of the President's china.

Albert exhaled. *No time to waste.* He opened the door and entered the West Wing, Brick, and Salazar on his heels.

A single agent stood in The Palm Room. He looked to their badges, saw the blue staff color, and gave a perfunctory nod as they passed. Brick pointed to a single door that led to the West Colonnade, the long outdoor walkway leading to the President's office. Albert looked out at the Rose Garden and pictured the iconic photos of Kennedy or Reagan strolling along the tan tiles toward the oval office. It didn't seem real that he might walk the same path as some of the most powerful men in history.

Salazar whispered and grabbed Albert's shoulder: "You ready?"

Albert nodded.

"Okay," Brick murmured. He removed a blue plastic glove and pulled it over his left hand. "Let's do this."

The trio strode out onto the West Colonnade doing their best impressions of harried staffers on their way to a meeting. The Colonnade was a narrow walkway lined by white columns and overlooking the South Lawn to the left. Directly ahead, a secret service agent stood outside the entrance to the Oval Office. Twenty feet away, two agents strolled the lawn, patrolling the perimeter of the office.

Brick took the lead and spoke to the agent at the door to the Oval Office.

"Hey, chief. Help settle a bet for us. Was it Kennedy or Roosevelt who has the famous picture walking down the Colonnade?"

"It was Kennedy." The agent smiled and pointed toward the Rose Garden.

"Good man." said Brick, reaching out his hand to shake the agent's hand.

The agent obliged.

With his right hand, Brick clutched the agent's wrist and twisted it, deploying one of the combat moves he had taught Albert long ago. The agent winced in pain. "What are you–"

With his left, gloved hand, Brick grabbed a transdermal patch from his suit pocket and slapped it on the veins atop the agent's hand. The agent squirmed.

"Not a word. Or I break your arm."

Albert assessed the agent. He was weighing his options. This was the moment, the pivot point. If the agent screamed, it was over. They would lose their chance. If he hesitated, they might make it. The agent's eyes widened, and Albert thought for sure that he would scream. But then the eyes softened. The Fentanyl that Salazar had loaded into the patch was already seeping into his system, calming him.

Brick maintained his vice grip with his right hand, but placed a calming left hand on the agent's shoulder. "Just hang tight with me buddy, a few more seconds, and you're going to be fine."

The agent blinked his eyes and swayed on his feet. "I... no..." He bent over and clutched his knees. Brick continued to hold the patch to the agent's wrist while he pretended to check on him. A few seconds later, the agent collapsed to the ground.

Salazar called out to the other agents on the lawn. "Hey, guys can you give us a hand here? I think this guy fainted."

To Albert he ordered with false concern, "Go get a doctor."

While Salazar and Brick distracted the other two agents, Albert opened the glass-paneled door to the Oval Office, as though he were calling for help. He studied the scene before him.

The President sat at the Resolute desk, signing papers. He was leaning close to the desk, but his shoulders and back stood straight. He was giving his attention to his work, oblivious to the commotion outside.

Albert had to hurry. "Mr. President," he said, speaking with the tone of quiet authority that Ariel had taught him long ago. "I need to speak with you."

Chapter 36

The President looked up and stared at Albert for a moment before setting down his pen.

"I'm sorry. Who are you?" His was not a kind face. It was a face lined with the scars of many political battles.

"You don't know me, sir. I'm Dr. Albert Puddles. I'm here to tell you that there is a plot to take over the White House, today."

"Oh?" The President inclined his head and locked his eyes on Albert's, but–almost unseen, one hand slid down toward the bottom of his desk.

Almost. But Albert had been looking for that exact gesture.

"Mr. President. I beg you. Don't call security, yet. I understand that this doesn't look good, and believe me, if I thought there was any other way to get the message to you in time I would have done so, but Cristina Culebra and ten thousand RED Army troops are marching toward the White House, right now, and if you don't call in the National Guard immediately, you're going to have a big problem on your hands."

The President's assistant walked in the room. "Mr. President, your eight o'clock is here." Her eyes flicked to Albert, confused, and then over to the president, who did not appear to be in danger, or panicked.

Albert grabbed her by the shoulders and gently turned her out of the room, closing the door behind her. He grabbed a chair and wedged it under the doorknob. He turned and saw the President tapping the button under his desk.

"Mr. President, I really wish you hadn't done that." Albert whistled a few notes, and Brick and Salazar entered.

The President stood up from his desk. His face was red with fury. "Look, I don't know who you are, Puddles, but—what are your cronies doing?"

At Albert's gesture, Brick, and Salazar had taken the other desk chairs and wedged them under the doorknobs of the other doors in the Oval Office, then retreated to stand guard.

"They're giving me the chance to speak," Albert said. He had rehearsed the next line countless times, but he still took a beat before speaking to go over the intonations in his mind once more. "Specifically, they are giving me the chance to tell you that you are not crazy, and you are not overreacting to think that Cristina Culebra is a threat. I am here to tell you she is counting specifically on you not wanting to appear threatened… and, thus, not dealing with her march as decisively as you need to."

The President's face darkened further. "I want you and these thugs out of this office, immediately."

Secret Service agents pounded on the doors. Brick and Salazar leaned their weight against them.

"Puddles," Brick called—a warning in a single word.

Fear is the enemy of logic, Albert recited to himself. He could not let the urgency of the situation send him off course. *Do not let the fear of defeat create defeat.* "Mr. President, please, just turn on your television. Look at what's coming your way."

"Damn you." The president slammed his palm down on the desk.

"Mr. President!" an agent called, and a door shuddered strongly enough to send Salazar reeling backwards.

"Albert!" Brick roared.

But Albert and the President were locked in their own battle of wills. To Albert all the sounds seemed to come from far away, and he got the sense that the President was in the same headspace. Even as the agents shouted from outside, the President held eye contact.

"You think I don't know that Culebra's marching today? She's made it the top news in the world. I know. They've got permits, for God's sake."

"Puddles, we don't have a lot more time," called Brick.

Albert saw the paths of the conversation branching and chose silence. He took a slow breath as he looked at the President and allowed the other man's suspicions to circle in his mind. *Don't give into the temptation to hurry this.*

The President gave a grimace and looked away. He hardly seemed aware of the sounds outside.

"I'm not going to call in the National Guard every time somebody has a protest march," he said.

Albert had to end this, and he had to do it now. Thousands of possibilities spun through his mind until one blazed into his consciousness.

"Mr. President, a man doesn't get to where you're standing without being extremely astute," Albert said. "You understand Culebra has maneuvered you into a very difficult position from a PR perspective, and you've been briefed by intelligence staff that she is a smart woman who would not attempt a direct coup with ten thousand soldiers because that would be an insane plan. Yes?"

Behind him, one door splintered and Brick gave a yell of pain. *Stay on target,* Albert told himself.

"Please, Mr. President. You must understand that these ten thousand soldiers are trained in a very specific way that will make your defenses inadequate." He pivoted slowly with his hands up. "Salazar, please let the agents in, so that they can confirm the President is unharmed."

"Are you sure?" Salazar said, as Brick made a noise that might have been either a yell not to do that, or a simple shout of agony.

"Yes." Albert closed his eyes and pictured everything that was about to happen. There were eight agents. Two of them would go to guide the President out of the Oval Office, while the rest would try to apprehend Albert and his friends. Importantly, if they were inside the room, they wouldn't shoot until the President was gone. "It's the only way," Albert said.

Salazar stepped back, and agents streamed into the room.

"Puddles," Salazar called. "This is crazy, man. I don't think–"

"It's the only way." Albert repeated the phrase and held the gaze of the Secret Service agents. He did not move a muscle. Assessing the minutiae of their body language, he made a guess as to which one was the lead agent and stared directly into that man's eyes.

The first agent moved toward the President and said, "Mr. President, we have to get you out of here."

Albert swept his legs out from under him, sending him toppling to the floor. The lead agent used Albert's distraction to make his move and reached for Albert's shoulder. Albert spun on the ball of his left foot, grabbed the gun out of the agent's hand and threw him to the floor. He pulled back the slide and removed the cartridge from the gun and placed the empty Beretta on the President's desk.

He looked at the other agents. None of them wavered, and none of them had anything on their faces except resolve, and some naked dislike. Their training really was very good. It was a pity it wouldn't be enough to stop Cristina Culebra... or Albert. Two down, and Albert knew they realized that–if he had wanted to–he could easily have grabbed either gun and shot toward the president, by now.

It was truly remarkable how fully the Tree had become a part of him. He remembered the glasses he had once used to predict an opponent's moves. He had no need of them, now.

Hope blossomed in Albert's chest. The president had not gone with the agents immediately. He was thinking. He was considering what Albert had said.

Another agent made a move for the President. Albert encircled his neck and began choking him. The agent clawed at Albert's hand, gasping for air.

"Mr. President. Are you starting to see, now?" said Albert. He hated that it had come to this.

"Release him!"

"Yes or no. Do you see that the threat is real?"

The five other agents pointed their guns at Albert. The President held up his hand.

"OK, Yes. I see. Release the man."

Albert let go, and the agent fell to the floor. He put his hands up in the air. The Secret Service agents all stood still. Guns trained on Albert, Brick, and Salazar.

"You've seen what I can do, Mr. President. Imagine an army of ten thousand of me marching on the White House in a few hours."

The President sighed and sat down at his desk. He rubbed his hands through his thinning gray hair and looked down for a few long moments. Then, deciding, he nodded to himself and looked up, pointing at one agent.

"Tom."

"Yes, sir."

"I want you to detain these three in the basement until we can figure out what to do with them."

The agent nodded. "Yes, sir."

Albert's heart sank. All the breath seemed to be gone from his lungs. *No. No, no, no, no—It was over.*

Then the President added, "And, Pete, I want you to call in the National Guard. If this Puddles is telling the truth, and it sure looks like he is, it looks like we're going to need a hand, today."

Chapter 37

Cristina liked to believe herself above the emotional indulgences of most people. Still, her heart throbbed in her chest as she strode down Pennsylvania Avenue toward the White House. Red surrounded her, seeming to pulse in time with her heart. The deep crimson of the soldiers' uniforms moved in unison. Pounding drums echoed off the buildings. Blood red flags with the iconic black three-pronged tree danced up and down above them. The street tremored for blocks from the power of the movement.

Her movement. The rhythmic tramp of boots behind her made her feel as if she were floating, borne forward not only by her own grit and determination, but by the power of forces far greater than most politicians could ever hope to harness. Most could not see these forces, let alone have a hope of capturing them, but Cristina had harnessed them like wind in the sails of an exquisite ship.

She allowed herself this moment of indulgence, then: it was not simply that she was the only one who had the wisdom of the Tree, it was that she was the only one who could wield it fully and truly.

OF GOOD & EVIL

Whether from a lack of intelligence or will, no one else could do what she had done. At her side, there was a new protégé, one of incredible potential... and one with whom Cristina would not make the same mistakes she had made with Eva.

Betrayal curdled in her chest, and she suppressed a snarl. Today was not a day to think of vengeance. She would not allow a mother's weakness to be her undoing.

Instead, she smiled, deliberately settling into the emotions the expression evoked. Thousands marched behind her. Immediately to her rear, the governors of the thirty states that had joined the Republic. All of them glowed with a false sense of newfound power and importance. Behind them marched Moloch and the RED Army he had steered. While Moloch's eyes were blazing with righteousness, the soldiers were proud and ready.

Obedient. Trained to think... within parameters. Cristina would never fully release the strings.

She pretended to ignore the news helicopters hovering in the icy blue sky. They were doing their part, broadcasting her message without even being aware of it; she knew they would continue to do so, keeping the world riveted, drawing new converts to her in a steady stream.

The helicopters had been following since earlier this morning when Cristina and the RED Army had marched from their campgrounds outside D.C. She was sure that their panning shots now captured the crowds of onlookers standing outside the low-rise office buildings of the Capitol. Some cheered and waved Republic flags while others shouted and brandished American flags in defiance.

She spotted an older gentleman standing with his grandchildren, his arms around both of them. His eyes met hers. He was afraid.

Cristina smiled a heavy smile. It was unfolding exactly how she had imagined. All the years of planning. The hard work. The sleepless nights. The scheming, manipulating, and glad-handing. The sacrifices. Friends, family, loved ones, gone. All for this day. The day when the United States would finally be saved.

By her.

The street ahead of her sat eerily empty. Token police officers stood in the streets monitoring the situation but quickly stepped aside as she approached. In the distance, Cristina could make out a car barricade protecting the pedestrian zone in front of the White House. Beside it, trees lining the Eisenhower Executive Office Building adjacent to the West Wing.

They were close, and still she had seen no resistance.

Where are you, Puddles? She would be almost disappointed if he did not manage something for her to overcome. Now that she had captured the Cipher, he was all that remained.

Then she heard boots stomping. But this sound came from ahead of her, not behind her, and the cadence was different. Faster. Cristina knew was that it was not the RED Army.

She looked ahead and watched as Humvees rolled up to Pennsylvania Avenue, blotting out her view of the White House. Thousands of National Guard soldiers in tan camouflage and tan boots jogged into place. Each carried an M-16 over their shoulder and a steely look in their eyes. The RED Army wouldn't just stroll into the White House, after all.

Her smile grew.

Well played, Puddles, she thought. *Well played.*

***

Albert, Brick, and Salazar huddled around a small table in the cramped White House cafeteria. Albert was surprised at his surroundings. He expected the White House cafeteria to be a glamorous modern corporate-style eating area. Instead, it resembled an old Italian restaurant kitchen. Oversized subway tiles lined the walls, and a TV sat atop a dated refrigerator in the corner. The red and white checked tablecloth, meanwhile, was a jarring reminder to Albert of picnics with his mother, out of place within the unfolding nightmare scenario.

Two stone-faced Secret Service agents stood nearby, a quiet presence one could almost forget... until one took in their unblinking attention to their charges. They did not flaunt their weapons; they knew that Albert and his companions were aware of their capabilities.

The 24-hour news channel playing on the TV featured alternating aerial and man-on-the-street footage of what had been dubbed the 'March of the RED Army'. The commentators said little; the awe-inspiring scene spoke for itself.

"Do you think it's going to be enough?" Albert asked. He looked over his shoulder at the Secret Service agents, but neither of them had moved at the sound of his voice.

Brick shrugged. "I think it is, but it's going to be close."

Salazar pointed at the TV. "Look. Our boys are rolling up already. Damn, we're good." He was smiling, as irrepressible now as he ever was.

The news showed a striking overhead shot of tan-clad national guard troops hurrying into place at the intersection of 19th Street and Pennsylvania, just blocks from the White House. Humvees wheeled into Edward R. Murrow Park from all directions. Troops carrying barricades scurried into place. From above, it resembled ants descending upon a drop of honey, though–up close–it did not seem so well-oiled as the machine of the RED Army.

And they were still marching, barely a hundred yards away, now, a tide moving inexorably toward its goal. People in the street, police officers, protesters–all parted as the crimson force swept through.

The camera zoomed in from overhead. At the front of the red horde marched Cristina Culebra, draped in a rich red trench coat. The two forces a clash of color, red versus tan. Though she was facing down the National Guard, there was an assured grin on her face.

Albert's stomach twisted. He knew better than to think that Cristina wore her heart on her sleeve. She would not admit readily that she had been outflanked...

But the smile still worried him. What did she know? Why was there not a trace of fear on that iconic face?

Cristina halted, every movement crisp. She raised a single hand high into the air. The RED Army stopped behind her with dizzying speed. *Not a force of nature, at all, just individuals marching in time.* Still, Albert shuddered to see one woman stop thousands in their tracks with the wave of a hand.

Salazar slapped the cafeteria table with a big grin. "I told you it would work, man. This chica doesn't want to go toe to toe with the US of A. She was just hoping she might sneak through the front door." He high-fived Brick and reached over to Albert.

Albert returned Salazar's high five, but his eyes never left the screen. The news shifted to a ground-level shot of Cristina. She stared straight ahead, the smile still there, and observing, not assessing, as though the problem had already been solved.

Something's coming. He was certain now.

Albert looked at the clock on the wall. It was eight fifty-nine in the morning. The long, thin second hand on the round analog clock ticked away. His eyes darted back and forth between the clock and the screen. Cristina just stood: watching, waiting. She made no move to explain the halt to her followers, nor did anyone so much as fidget.

Except–Albert's heart seized. At Cristina's right shoulder stood a black-haired figure.

Ying. He could hardly breathe. She was in the middle of this, and–traitor or not–she was his friend. Cristina would never hesitate to sacrifice someone for shock value, and Albert found himself gripped by the fear that a young, round-faced woman would make a perfect martyr for the RED Army.

Whether or not that young woman knew it.

The clock struck nine, and a call echoed across the street. The National Guard troops, already at attention, stood up a little straighter as a middle-aged officer in national guard fatigues walked into the street. From the stars on his shoulder, this was a general, and he walked toward Cristina without fear. Albert had seen him give a few nods to the troops as he passed by.

This man was respected. He knew the troops who served under him.

Albert allowed himself to hope.

"That's Sicario," said Brick quietly. "He's head of the National Guard."

Cristina advanced as well. Both left their backup behind, two figures approaching each other on an empty street.

"What is he doing?" asked Salazar.

"It's standard practice." Brick wasn't worried. "Before engaging with the enemy, you want to give them a chance to surrender."

Albert rubbed his chin. If it was standard practice, then Cristina would know it as well–and, if anyone would dare to tell the U.S. military to surrender, it was Cristina Culebra. From the UK, he had watched Cristina's movement advance across the map, and he had only seen her surprised once, at that rally.

There was no surprise, now.

Cristina and the General spoke for a few moments. They both nodded and shook hands, and one camera caught the faint sound of Cristina's laughter.

"Oh, no," Albert whispered.

The general turned and motioned to his troops. He said something into a walkie-talkie.

Silence. Nothing moved.

Sicario spoke again, and even from a distance, it was clear that his gesture this time was more impatient. He had turned his back on Culebra; he did not fear her, but this–*Oh, please.* Albert leaned forward. His heart hammered in his chest. Brick leaned forward, as well, his face as hopeful as Albert's. These soldiers had sworn oaths not to their commander, but to their flag.

A single figure emerged from the ranks and walked toward Sicario, who hurried back. The other figure, a sergeant, saluted, and the two men exchanged words, heads close together. Sicario did not like what he was hearing, but the sergeant pressed on. He gestured expressively.

Whatever Sicario said to the entreaty, it was both harsh and final. The sergeant's shoulders slumped, and Brick swore viciously.

Albert closed his eyes against tears. He was too overwhelmed to be ashamed of his own fear. He did not need to watch to understand the sounds he was hearing: the National Guard troops parting to allow a clear path to the White House.

"*Malparido*," Salazar spat.

Brick stood.

"Sir, sit down." The Secret Service were not watching the TV, at all.

"You gotta let us out of here," Brick said. "We have to secure the President."

"Sir, I assure you, the President is well guarded."

"As well guarded as the White House?" Brick swept an arm out to point at the TV. "Look buddy. We're only here because we want to be here. Now, why don't you step out of our way."

"Sir—"

"No, don't you *sir* me—"

"It's over, Brick," said Albert softly.

"What are you talking about?" Brick rounded on him. "We've come this far. We are *in* the White House, and that devil isn't, yet. We can't quit now."

"Brick." Albert looked up at him and shook his head. "It's over."

He had thought that his despair was complete, but when Brick dropped back into his chair, eyes closed and defeat in every line of his body, Albert knew that this was not only the darkest moment of his life... he also saw the years stretching away from him, endless, holding darkness beyond his worst nightmares.

It was over. Cristina had won.

Chapter 38

W"e want the Cipher! We want the Cipher!"
Women and men, young and old: people of all sizes, shapes, and colors were chanting in unison. The energy of the crowd was electric. Black-clad shapes bounced on the balls of their feet and pumped their fists in the sky, the group rippling as if they were part of one organism.

Gabe couldn't keep himself from joining in the chant, and Mana was swept away, as well. He could hardly see from his wheelchair, but he knew the second the Cipher emerged into the crowd, because the chant changed, and the volume rose to a deafening roar:

"CI-PHER! CI-PHER! CI-PHER!"

Without any fanfare, a single figure stepped through the crowd, moving toward the elevated base of the flaming sword monument. A microphone stood on the platform, a detail that grabbed Gabe's attention at once: this person not only knew how to hack, they knew how to set the stage and play to a crowd.

He also knew how to obscure any identifying features; despite his years of training, Gabe could make out very few details. The Cipher wore black military cargo pants, a black jacket, and a black

Kevlar vest. A black helmet covered in white symbols hid his face. He was a wiry figure, about five foot ten, and the way he stood projected solidity and confidence.

American? Not? Gabe had expected someone from one of the more storied dictatorships: Cambodia, North Korea, the Dominican Republic, Nigeria, someone who would be more aware than most Americans of the dangers posed by Cristina Culebra.

"Ballsy move," Mana murmured from beside him. "No intro. No music. No smoke. No lights. Just walks on stage, grabs the mic and says 'let's go'."

Gabe tried to respond, but the crowd's roar silenced him. He didn't mind. He shared in their tension and excitement. They had all solved riddle after riddle to get here. They had all committed to something they didn't quite understand. Now they would find out whether what they had imagined would become a reality.

His phone vibrated with a text from Weatherspoon. "Cristina just a few blocks from the White House. The National Guard backed down. You better hurry."

The Cipher had reached the stage. He raised both hands now, and the crowd fell silent. He put a hand to his ear as if to encourage the crowd to listen, and in the distance, Gabe heard the whistles and stomps of the RED Army marching on the White House.

Then the Cipher spoke. From the auto-tuned warble of his voice, it seemed that the mask served two purposes. Even the digital sound editor, however, could not disguise the fact that he knew how to speak to a crowd.

"Do you hear that, my brothers and sisters?" The cadence was perfect, the volume rising along the trajectory of the words.

Gabe *had* always appreciated craftsmanship.

The crowd responded with a single voice: "YES!"

"That is the sound of the devil and her RED Army."

"YES!"

"The devil plans to walk through the gates of Eden and take the throne of the righteous," the Cipher called.

Boos echoed through the crowd.

The Cipher held up a hand, and the booing stopped. He leaned in, and although he was speaking into a microphone, he projected the air of someone whispering a secret. "But *we* know something the devil doesn't know..."

The crowd held its breath.

The Cipher pivoted to the shining golden sword behind him: "There is a flaming sword guarding the gates of Eden. Brothers and sisters, we are that sword. We will not let her in."

In amongst the screams and cheers of the crowd, Gabe heard Mana yell, "You tell her!"

When he looked over at her in amusement, she shrugged. "Sorry, got carried away. He's right, though. Somebody's got to take down Culebra. Why not us?"

The Cipher continued. "The devil doesn't know about the Sword of Eden. The devil doesn't know about us." He looked around at the crowd, his presentation still exquisite. "The devil doesn't know the Sword of Eden is made of the smartest people in the world. She believes no one can stand against her. She doesn't know that we've been dreaming, we've been plotting, we've been scheming–and we've found the perfect way to bring that RED Army to its knees."

Another roar from the gathered masses.

The Cipher raised his arms once more, and the crowd quieted.

"Follow me, brothers and sisters." His voice grew louder with every word. "For today, we thrust the Sword of Eden into the belly of the beast."

Amidst the guttural roar of the crowd, the Cipher placed the mic back in its stand, stepped off the platform and began walking toward 17th Street, the road to the White House. His arms swept through the air to urge the crowd into motion, and they flowed behind him without hesitation.

The Cipher marched with total conviction, not even bothering to look back to see if anyone was following, and Gabe had the thought that, if only one or two people had arrived, there would have been no sense of disappointment. The speech would have been the same. The conviction and the confidence would have been the same.

This man, whoever he was, measured odds differently than most of the world, and that was as interesting as the rest of it.

The crowd turned right onto 17th Street and headed north beside the South Lawn of the White House. They passed the Eisenhower Executive Office Building to the West of the White House and reached Pennsylvania avenue, where the Cipher pivoted to his left and stopped.

Gabe had maneuvered forward through the crowd as it moved, and now he saw a sight that made his breath freeze. Marching right through the middle of the United States National Guard was the RED Army with Cristina Culebra at the front.

Gabe had assumed something like this moment was coming, but in the abstract, it seemed much less frightening, much smaller. He wasn't prepared for the sheer scale of the RED Army, filling a full street from sidewalk to sidewalk for as far as he could see. At the monument, the Sword of Eden had seemed an organic, powerful mass, composed of instinct and reactivity, but–in the face of the polished discipline of the RED Army–the group now seemed nothing more than a few nerdy riddle solvers dressed in black.

Not a few, Gabe reminded himself, *a thousand.*

But it wasn't enough. Not against an army of trained soldiers.

"We're so fucked," said Mana.

What it was about that, Gabe wasn't sure, but something in the sentiment made him glance at the Cipher.

Their leader stood ready. Not surprised, not fidgety. Ready. Gabe followed the man's gaze to Cristina Culebra–and felt a spark of hope. Her face showed utter shock. She had counted the Cipher out. Gabe did not know exactly what she had believed, whether she thought the Cipher to be dead, or in jail. But her face was, for the first time Gabe had ever seen, completely without its composed mask.

She stared at the Cipher as if it were a corpse brought back to life.

"Don't count us out, yet," Gabe said to Mana.

Cristina's panic shifted into fury. She motioned in the air and began marching toward them. The RED Army followed.

The crowd around Gabe and Mana shuffled and murmured. They were the only thing standing in between Cristina Culebra and the breach of the Capitol, and they knew it.

The Cipher, however, looked at his watch, pushed a single button on it, and pointed a finger to the sky. Before Gabe even had the time to worry about a bomb going off, he heard the strains of music begin somewhere in the crowd, and he blinked when he recognized the tune: Hail to the Chief.

The Cipher motioned for the members of the Sword of Eden to stay where they were, and then strolled toward Culebra and her advancing soldiers. The man looked like he didn't have a single worry, and he was gesturing as if he were conducting a symphony.

"Oh, for crying out loud," said Mana. "We've been following a lunatic."

"Hang on," Gabe murmured back. "I think I know what he's doing."

A hundred yards away, Cristina kept coming down Pennsylvania Avenue, an angry sneer on her face. The RED Army followed, and Gabe was struck by the contrast of a single man against a thundering red tsunami.

The Cipher pressed forward, arms swinging with the music, the remote like a baton in a conductor's hand. Cristina walked faster toward him, her fury clearly building as the music mocked her. This was exactly the sort of moment she might have engineered for herself, but the Cipher had stolen it, warped it. He was making her look like an imposter, and even if she someday held the office of President...

She would always remember this moment.

"He knows how to twist the knife, I'll give him that," Gabe said in grudging respect. As far as he was concerned, the Cipher was pretty likely to be dead in a ditch shortly, but his timing for satire and presentation was impeccable.

Seventy-five yards, and Culebra was still advancing, her progress matched by the easy, almost dance-like stride of the Cipher.

Fifty yards.

Twenty-five yards.

The music reached its crescendo, trumpets blasting, and the Cipher stopped. On the last rattle of the drums, he dramatically waved his arms in the air and pressed a single button on the remote.

Again, Gabe braced himself for something dramatic, but nothing happened–Cristina and the RED Army kept coming. Closer and closer.

The noise wasn't an explosion or the rumble of heavy weapons, but a human sound of misery. It seemed to come from everywhere at once, and then, in a moment, resolved into a mass of groans, echoing from within the ranks of the RED Army.

Soldiers fell to the ground, grabbing their stomachs. It was only one or two at first, but within moments, row after row of soldiers stopped in their tracks, overcome with an unknown illness. The members of the RED Army leaned on one another or thudded to the ground.

"What the..." Mana's voice was wondering.

Blinded by her own rage, at first Cristina failed to notice the crisis behind her, but as the groans grew louder, she turned to see the ruin. Soldiers lying on the streets, wailing, vomiting, bent over in pain. An army reduced to rubble in a matter of moments.

The Cipher strolled up to Cristina as Gabe, Mana, and a crowd of thousands looked on in amazement.

And then, to Gabe's shock, the Cipher removed her helmet to reveal a full head of long black hair and a familiar face.

"Hello, Mama," said Eva Fix.

Chapter 39

"Eva." Cristina breathed the word. Her head was swimming, and there was a ringing in her ears.

Dully, she traced over the familiar thought: *Newton's Law.* From the beginning, she had known someone would come for her. For every action, there was an equal and opposite reaction. Someone would be spurred to action by her rise. Someone would oppose her. In that one, furious moment when she threw herself over the bomb at the rally, she had faced the fact that she might lose...

Even so, it was nothing to this.

She never dreamed that her opponent would be her own daughter. Her little Evalita, the girl of such potential... Evalita, who had never matched her mother's expectations.

"How could you?" Cristina asked, before she could stop herself. She hated those words and the weakness they conveyed. *I am hurt, which means I am weak. I am surprised, which means I am foolish.* She pressed her lips together, but it was too late: the words were already out.

"How could you, Mama?" Eva was shaking her head. She looked almost as hurt as Cristina. "How could you take our movement, the one we built together, and defile it like this?"

Cristina looked around her. Behind her thousands of troops lay on the ground grabbing their stomachs, writhing in agony. Ying, the perfect successor to Eva, had the discipline to lie still, but even she was curled into the fetal position.

Hundreds of National Guard Troops stood on the sides of the street, unsure of what to do next, and the sight of their confusion and pity galvanized Cristina into action. She had to regain control of the situation.

"I don't know how you did this," Cristina said, "but you should have known enough to see that it won't end well for you."

Her daughter smiled back at her, and though their features had always been similar, for Cristina, it was the first time she had looked at her daughter and felt the sense of gazing into a mirror. Instead of the Eva she had grown accustomed to seeing, she saw her own smugness.

She saw the same self-control she had always thought of as hers.

"That's the difference, Mom." Eva spoke to her as if she were a child. *You asked the wrong question, Evalita.* How many times had Cristina said that? Eva's smile said she remembered each one. "Unlike you, I don't think I have all the answers. I don't think everything flows from me—or that it should. That's why I recruited all these people to be a part of my movement."

She gestured to the hundreds of black-clad followers behind her in the street.

"And I asked them: how would you stop the RED Army?" Eva looked back at her followers, and then at her mother. "*A couple of physicians* came up with the idea: remote-controlled poison. The pill sits in your system until we send a signal. Simple. Elegant. All your troops were stationed at the camp, so all we had to do was replace the vitamins you served to your troops this morning with a little pill of our own. Then with the push of this button the pill releases and *voila*: the vaunted RED Army goes 'poof'."

"Bullshit. That camp was secure." Cristina knew the security protocols. She had written the security protocols. "There's no way anyone could have gotten in who wasn't part of the RED Army."

"No?" Eva looked infuriatingly smug, now. "Then perhaps the problem was who you let into the RED Army."

Cristina turned behind her to see Ying Koh standing upright, smiling.

"And 'scene'," said Ying, bowing.

Rage boiled up inside Cristina. She clenched her fists. *Arrogant little bitches.* For a moment she considered cold-cocking each of them, but she restrained herself. She had lost the battle, today, because she had violated two of her own rules: never underestimate your opponent, and never miss the opportunity to destroy your opponent entirely. It was her own fault.

She regathered her composure and inclined her head to her daughter.

"I tip my hat to you, Evalita. Today, you got me. But tomorrow, you won't find it so easy. Now, I know it's you, and I will come for you. I will not stay my hand because you are my daughter. I feel bad for you, to be honest."

She watched Eva. Deep in the eyes, beneath the arrogance and self-congratulations, she found what she was looking for: fear.

"Of course, Mom." Eva pretended to dismiss her. She raised her chin and put on one of Cristina's smiles. Only a mother would see the fear behind it. "I wish you the best of luck. Now, while I'd love to stay chatting with you, Ying and I must greet our fans."

•

Eva grabbed Ying by the hand and marched back toward the White House, to the sounds of clapping and cheering from the Swords of Eden. Soon, the National Guard members and protesters joined in the applause.

Seething, Cristina watched and memorized every moment: the way the crowd cheered; the way the National Guard troops smiled despite having done nothing but step aside; the goofy grins on Eva's motley followers; the way her army had to be helped off the ground by guardsman and paramedics. The way Eva turned her back on her mother after everything she'd done for her; the way that traitor, Ying, skipped along beside her, so proud of herself.

"Enjoy your fifteen minutes of fame, my Evalita," Cristina murmured. "They'll be over, soon."

Chapter 40

Albert sat in the White House cafeteria, watching the world turn upside down.

Eva had done everything he was too scared to do. She had broken every rule. She had lied and connived and played everyone against each other... and it had worked.

He, meanwhile, had played by all the rules, played within the system. He had worked with the government, not against it. And here he was, sitting in a basement watching the events unfold on television. He wondered what Turner would think of him.

A third Secret Service agent stepped into the cafeteria and walked over to touch Albert lightly on the shoulder, waiting for them all to turn.

"You're free to go," he said. There was no acknowledgement of what they had done or their captivity here for the past hour.

Albert stood, numb.

"What are your next steps?" said Brick to the agent as he threw his suit coat over his shoulder.

"You are free to go," the agent repeated. "The President thanks you for your service."

"Message received," Brick said. "Shall we, gentlemen?"

The Secret Service agents escorted them out of the Navy mess toward the exit.

"Your girl is one badass *chiquitita,* Albert," said Salazar as he slapped Albert on the back. "She saved our bacon, huh?"

Albert nodded. He was exhausted. He had been so focused on how to get into the White House that he had forgotten about Eva. And now she had almost single handedly taken down the RED Army. He couldn't wait to see her, to talk to her.

To hold her.

To ask how, in God's name, she and Ying had done it.

They exited the West Wing into the burst of winter sunlight. Albert looked past the north lawn of the White House and saw a sea of people chanting, brown and peach skin shining against black pants, black hoodies, black masks. Fists were waving in the air, and chants of "Cipher, Cipher, Cipher" floated on the wind.

"Where to now, boss?" asked Salazar.

Albert straightened his tie and scanned the crowd.

"Now, we find Eva," he said.

"Got it." Brick gestured grandly to the center of the crowd. "Lead the way."

In the distance, Eva stood atop a maintenance truck with a megaphone in her hand. Albert couldn't make out the words she was saying, but the audience was lapping it up.

He tried to walk, but quickly broke into a jog–and then a run. Out the driveway of the White House, then past the security gates and onto Pennsylvania Avenue, where paramedics were loading sickened RED Army troops onto gurneys.

He saw none of it; his gaze was locked on her. It was impossible to look away. He had known Eva in many guises: the ingenue, the prodigy, the heartbroken girl, the cold-blooded killer... the turncoat. This, with her in her baggy, black clothes, hair straggling free, was something he could never have imagined, she was a revolutionary, and it fit her to a tee. He pushed and shoved his way through the revelers, hoping she would somehow pick him out of the crowd.

Now, he could hear her words. She was speaking about the Sword of Eden: what they had accomplished and what they could accomplish together. Her eyes met his, and she smiled the most glorious smile that Albert had ever seen. She waved to him, beckoning urgently until he came to the base of the truck. The smile was still on her face—one of the most carefree smiles he had ever seen from her.

"Ladies and gentleman," she called out over the crowd. "I would like you to say 'hello' to the man behind the woman, the man who finally got his cute butt out here to celebrate with us: my man, Albert Puddles."

The chant in the crowd shifted: "Albert! Albert! Albert!"

Albert offered a sheepish grin and slipped through the crowd and up to the truck. Hands were reaching out to clap him on the shoulder and shake his hand. He felt like a fan being serenaded by a rock star.

He stopped in his tracks, however, when he saw who was standing beside the truck.

Ying looked at him and smiled, tears running down her face. "I'm so sorry. I wanted to tell all of you, but I couldn't risk it."

"You're incredible." Albert hugged her fiercely, then drew back. "Was all of it a ploy? You joining Cristina?"

She nodded, laughing now through her happy tears.

Albert laughed, as well. "Well done. I never saw it coming, and... I thought I could see everything coming."

"Thanks. We couldn't have done it without you, though." She leaned around him and slapped him on the rear. "Now, up you go."

From the bed of the truck, Eva reached down to pull him up, then grabbed him by the shoulders and kissed him while the crowd cheered.

Eva leaned her head close to Albert's ear. "We can run this world together, Albert, you and me."

"What?" Albert pulled away to look at her.

"The world is ours, now, Albert." She pulled him back in. "This is just the beginning. The old United States is dead. My mother saw that and seized the chance to replace it with herself... but we can replace it with whatever we wish. The revolution has just begun."

She kissed him again, hard, and when he relaxed into the kiss, she bit his bottom lip. He heard her throaty laugh when his eyes flew open. She was warm against him, her eyes bright. Her mother's raw brilliance ran through her, and her own brand of cool calculation.

He laughed again, and he held her close. He would never be able to predict her. She would be a surprise every day. She would remake the world in ways he had never imagined.

"Yes," she told him, as if she knew exactly what he had been thinking. "And you, too, Albert."

Then she grabbed his hand and raised it to the sky.

The crowd exploded into cheers, the chant rising once more into the blue: "Cipher, Cipher, Cipher!"

Epilogue

The following morning, The Book Club gathered around the sun-soaked kitchen table for one last breakfast at the safe house. The media had followed Eva and the rest of the group home the previous evening, so there wasn't much safety to the safe house, anymore. Mana had ordered her agents to secure the property, but the Bureau wouldn't fund their protection forever. It was time to go.

As a 'thank you' to the group, Albert had forgone his usual regimen of nutrition bars and made breakfast for everyone. The pancakes were doughy and the bacon was burned, but the group appreciated the effort. Albert and Eva sat together on one side of the table with Salazar. Across from them sat Brick, Gabe and Ying. Mana and Weatherspoon held court at each end of the table like proud parents.

"I'd like to propose a toast," said Mana, raising her orange juice glass in the air. "To the Book Club. Spoon, when you and Ying came into my office and told me about this so-called Tree of Knowledge, I thought it was the most ridiculous fucking thing I had ever heard. Then I saw what this lady could do and thought 'hmm... maybe this isn't so ridiculous after all'. And I'm glad I did, because being with you assholes has been one hell of a ride, and I wouldn't trade it for anything."

While she spoke, Albert observed everyone at the table. It was all smiles, and an overwhelming sense of pride.

"I have to admit, twenty-four hours ago I didn't think we stood a chance against Cristina Culebra. But now having seen what this group can do together, I really believe anything is possible. To the Book Club."

The group clinked glasses with each other and shouted, "To the Book Club."

Salazar grabbed some more burned bacon and pointed a piece at Ying. "I gotta tell you, lady, when you walked out of here with Cristina, I didn't think you were ever coming back. You pulled the wool right over my eyes."

"I think she pulled the wool over all of our eyes," said Weatherspoon with a chuckle.

"What about Eva over here?" said Brick. "She was the damn Cipher, for crying out loud. Eva, you should have seen me, Puddles and Salazar. We're sitting in the White House feeling sorry for ourselves just waiting for Cristina to come marching in the front door, and then this crazy guy comes out into the middle of the street and drops the whole RED Army, and it's you. Unbelievable! Puddles, you were sleeping with the Cipher. How did you miss that?"

The group laughed and then fell silent for a moment. Gabe cleared his throat and looked at Eva. "So, what do we do now, Madame Cipher? Do you have any more riddles for us to solve?" Albert noticed the glint of hope in his eyes.

Eva offered a short laugh and a pinched smile. "No Gabe. I'm afraid there are no more riddles. Just a war. We won the battle yesterday against my mother, but she'll be back. And next time it will be tenfold. We'll have to strike fast before she even knows what hit her."

Albert listened as the malevolence grew in Eva's voice. Her face carried an unnerving anger. He wondered how many demons would have to be exercised before the anger faded.

"And it won't just be my mother. We will have to strike at the other tyrants, as well. We will have to show the world that the Sword of Eden is the only way, that the days of tyranny are over."

Weatherspoon raised an eyebrow and gathered a few empty plates. Moini rose, as well, and joined him in clearing the table. The room was silent save the clinking of dishes.

Albert shifted in his seat and tried to ignore the flutter of disquiet in his stomach. He knew Eva wanted nothing but the best for everyone, but her zeal disconcerted him. "I think what Eva means to say is that we–"

The ring of his phone interrupted him.

He put his finger up to signal that he'd be back and walked out of the kitchen and into the entryway.

"Hello?" he answered.

A voice with a thick Chinese accent spoke on the other end. "Hello, is this Albert Puddles?"

A tremor of fear ran up Albert's spine. "Yes, this is Albert."

"You don't know me, but my name is Genji Wu. I was a friend of Angus Turner's."

Albert stopped, and his stomach dropped to the floor. The phone shook in his hand. He paused and tried to regain his composure.

"Hello? Albert, are you there?"

"Yes, how can I help you, Genji?"

"I think I may have what you have been looking for?"

"And what is that?"

"The key... to the Tree of Knowledge."

Albert trembled. Sweat streamed down his face. *Could it be? The key to The Tree of Knowledge?* Albert realized that until this minute some part of him had given up hope. He had given in to the despair that Turner's final gift would forever elude him.

This changed everything.

Maybe now, he could realize the full power of the Tree, not just the branches that Angus has taught them in their short time together. *The question was, where would it lead? Down Eva's path? Down his own?*

He looked back to the kitchen to see if anyone had noticed his shock. But they continued to bicker over Eva's plans. He lowered his voice.

"Genji, How? How did you get this?" asked Albert.

"It's best not to discuss this on the telephone," said Genji.

"OK. How can I meet you?"

"I will find you. Be ready." The line went dead.

Albert removed the phone from his ear and stared at it to make sure he wasn't dreaming. Genji Wu. Turner's confidant. Alive and out from hiding. With the key to a code he had spent years trying to crack. He wanted to run into the kitchen and share the good news, but he couldn't. No one could know. Turner had wanted it that way.

He took deep breaths and wiped his forehead with his napkin from breakfast. He tried to pull the flush from his face as he turned back to the kitchen.

Ying was doing the dishes, while the rest of the group argued at the kitchen table.

"What was that all about?" asked Ying. Albert could see she sensed something.

"Nothing. Just an old friend calling to check in and see if I was OK after all this chaos."

"Oh. Is everything alright?"

He leaned over and gave Ying one of their traditional shoulder bumps and then put an arm around her shoulder. He gazed at The Book Club, so filled with passion and hope.

But fissures lay beneath the surface.

There would be time for that later. Right now, Ying needed a victory. He offered a warm smile to calm her.

"Yeah, everything's going to be just fine."

Thank You

Thank you so much for reading *Of Good & Evil.* I hope you enjoyed reading it as much as I enjoyed writing it. You can find out what happens next to Albert and the Book Club by downloading *The Tree of Life,* Book 3 in T*he Tree of Knowledge* Series. You can also sign up for my newsletter and get updates on upcoming novels and deals at danielmillerbooks.com.

If you enjoyed the book, I also encourage you to leave a review on my Goodreads page and Amazon page. Reviews from readers like you are the fuel that keeps authors like me going, so even a one sentence review can make all the difference. Thank you so much for your support!

Acknowledgments

To my publishing team—Philippa Werner and Susie Helme—for bringing discipline and depth to my crazy ideas.

To Justin Grevich for giving me advice on how the Cipher could execute such technological wizardry. Any mistakes are mine and not his.

To the people of Ukraine and others battling tyranny around the world.

To all the readers who have taken risks on authors like me.

To my family, for always supporting my dreams, no matter how far-fetched they may seem.

To my friends, for cheering me along the way on this writing adventure.

And finally, to Lexi, my perfect match. Your patience and willingness to bring a hard-nosed perspective to my writing has been invaluable. I couldn't do it without you.

About the Author

Daniel G. Miller is an entrepreneur and former business consultant with a master's degree in public policy and economics. In his work in economics and consulting he witnessed the power of complex decision trees and mathematical models in predicting real-world events. The experience with prediction in business inspired the question, "what if we could use math to predict everything in our lives." From there, Albert Puddles was born. He currently lives in Florida with his wife Lexi.

Made in the USA
Las Vegas, NV
25 May 2023